THE REQUIEM

FOR THE LOVE OF MONEY

K. Rosen

Some of the geographical locations including cities, towns and countryside locations
do exist, but all characters and story are fiction only, anything similar to all person(s)
whether living or deceased are totally coincidental and not an intended thing by the
author.

ISBN: 0692277390
ISBN 13: 9780692277393
Library of Congress Control Number: 2014914795
The Rose Publishing Group, Sears, MI

DEDICATION

To my family and friends, I love you all.

ACKNOWLEDGEMENTS

I am grateful and want to thank Glen Kelley for his editing abilities and for giving me the courage to believe in this book. I also want to thank Jamie M. for her listening to my rants and the encouragement she continuously gave me to finish this book and for the generous amount of time that she helped me bring the book together with her computer knowledge.

TABLE OF CONTENTS

PART THREE

PART ONE

FOR THE LOVE OF SEX

1

St. Louis, Mo. Loren is standing just inside the back door of his warehouse talking to Frank his boss and Joe who is Frank's bodyguard. Frank is not happy and says to Loren, "Damn it Loren, this is not the time to have your bimbo friend come down from Chicago to visit you. Business is too good, she's going to slow you down- this is not the time to slow down- we're busting our butts on our end to market the drugs and it is paying off. Another thing you need to do is have a talk with Susie, she is getting way out of line and I've heard pretty good rumor she's talking to someone that could blow our business wide open."

Loren responds by saying, "I'll talk to Susie, I don't think she's talking to anyone, I think someone is trying to get to you, you know, get you scared for their own purpose. Probably someone who is trying to take control of what we've got going. I'll talk to her soon though- just to get it straight. As far as my friend coming down, it's a done deal she's coming, but only for a few days. I need to see her, if you know what I mean, but she will be gone by Monday, I can assure you of that.

Frank is impatient as usual and starts walking to his vehicle with his body guard, Joe, when he turns around to Loren and says gruffly, " O.k.- just don't let this friend of yours involve herself in anything we are doing and have her out of here by the first of next week. Susie - on the other hand, talk to her, if she doesn't come around, I'll have someone else deal with her." At that Frank drove away.

The Dream

In slumber, a misty curtain lifts revealing a long, curving and dimly-lit tunnel- which is slanting in both upward and downward directions resembling an auto parking ramp. Next to the tunnel the sight and sounds of a fast-moving river are perceptible. A sophisticated, intelligent-looking man, of medium height and sporting a goatee is being handcuffed by two policemen while staring intently at a tall woman. The man's expression reveals his belief that she is the cause of his predicament with the police. The tall woman, who is standing only a few feet to the side of the policemen, is still, silent, her head steady and is focusing solely on the bearded man. The two cops show no interest in the woman even though she is totally nude except for the rope that is noosed around her neck and dragging behind her on the ground. The woman pays no attention to the policemen; her eyes are riveted on the bearded man. As the police take him away handcuffed, the woman walks in a daze up the curved tunnel to its end where there is a large dingy room with many stalls. As the woman walks into one of the stalls she notices a large rock is tied to the end of the rope that holds her and then she sees the rapidly flowing water below...the dream ends...

Kate Roarke awakens, just at sunrise as usual. She usually loves mornings and hardly ever lounges in bed, but the dream she had awakened to was a little disturbing so it took her a little longer to sit up and swing her long legs over the side of the bed, establishing in her mind it was just a dream, and to get over it. After a cup of coffee, she stands and stretches, a whole body stretch, these stretches always feel good and help her keep her body limber. Kate is fairly tall and a little larger boned than average, but still slender with lots of soft curves and lusciously luminous skin. She is a knock-out to some people, but sadly those people- always men- seemed to want her for mostly one reason- Sex with a capital "S". Kate is interested in having friendships with men but has absolutely no interest in one-night stands and is repelled by the unwanted sexual advances that routinely come her way. Lately she's had no desire to spend time with any man except Loren Goodson, the love of her life. Kate's natural earthy appeal is something she thinks that Loren genuinely appreciates, and is one the reasons he is so intensely attracted to her.

Kate still cannot get last night's dream out of her mind. Does it have a profound meaning that she needs to decipher? She thinks it may be the case because she has been having quite a few bizarre dreams recently. The images in the dream remain vexing to her but her thoughts begin to drift to a more amusing notion of incorporating some of her dreams into a novel or pilots to a novel. However, this thought quickly brings sadness rather than amusement as she knows she has a tendency to procrastinate the start of a new venture--and writing a novel seems light years away to her at present. This also makes her think of Loren who always seems to have pending ventures that he has developed plans for but never seems to pursue. She is perturbed with herself because sometimes it seems Loren has such a hold on her that she is actually picking up some of his habits even though they don't really fit her personality at all.

This morning Katie quickly does a few yoga stretches but won't have time for her usual morning run because she is planning to leave for St. Louis in about an hour. She has put off packing because lately she has been feeling less excitement about visiting Loren, as he rarely visits her at her house in the suburbs of Chicago, always using the same excuse that "he needs to stick close to the shop because of his work". She realizes what he says may be true but it still bothers her. After her short yoga routine and a quick shower, she feels a little more refreshed and positive about the trip. After drying herself from the shower, she quickly runs her fingers through her wet, relatively short, wavy auburn hair and then proceeds to pick out the clothes she is taking with her for her two or three day stay. Once packed and dressed in jeans and a tank top& jacket she put her bags into her jeep and starts out for St. Louis, only stopping for gas a few miles from home before really starting her trek.

With a quick check of her cell phone, she sees she is starting her trip at 8:35 a.m. It usually takes anywhere from 4 1/2 hours to 5 hours to make the trip depending on traffic and how many bathroom stops she has to make. Once Kate has filled the gas tank in her jeep, she leaves for St Louis. The traffic on the freeway heading south from Chicago is light today and she only has to make two "p-stops" altogether, so she is able to make the trip to St. Louis in just under 4-1/2 hours. She arrives at Loren's warehouse in St Louis just before 1:00 in the afternoon.

She parks the jeep and walks to the front of the 2-story brick warehouse to ring the doorbell. She can hear the very shrill & loud bell ring just inside the front door. She has a feeling of great anticipation as she always does at moments like this after not seeing Loren for a while--a mix of excitement and anxiety are welling up inside of her because she never knows what visiting Loren will bring. When Kate is with Loren, she finds that life is mostly interesting, exciting and certainly unpredictable.   Events and emotions that surround her when she is with Loren are just never the same as when she is anywhere else. After the third long ring, the dust-encrusted board covering the small window in the door swings to the side and she sees Loren's face peeking out at her, which is not an unusual greeting arrangement considering where he lives--a rusty rundown brick warehouse-residential community in St Louis, Missouri, where illegal activities such as drug sales, prostitution, and petty theft are rampant at night and are almost as common during the daytime.

The appearance of the warehouse front door and small window causes Katie to recall an incident that Loren recounted to her that happened one sunny afternoon when he came home just in time to see two men hoisting a tall ladder against his backyard fence, with the intent of scaling the 8-foot barbed wire-topped barrier, to find and steal anything of value to try to sell for drugs. As he approached the intruders they jumped in their old beat-up truck, leaving the ladder behind in their hurried get-away....

At that moment, Loren opens the door while holding his dog, Rex, so he won't lunge into the street. Rex, like his master, has a longing for wild & restless activities and loves to wander. Katie walks inside the faintly-lit warehouse. Whenever Kate and Loren get together after being apart for period of time, there always seems to be a moment when their eyes meet and their passion is almost magically re-established between them—and the moment this time seems to occur after Loren closes the front door of the warehouse. First, he releases his grip on Rex's collar- only for Rex to immediately jump up on Katie- wanting her attention as well as Loren's. After receiving a hug from her, Rex settles down. Kate then put her arms around Loren's neck and warmly hugs him, her passions are so strong that her aura of love almost overwhelms him but he loves every moment of it. Their embrace is long and passionate but Loren is unable to give full expression of love to Kate in return. Loren's passion is given but is somewhat reserved, but he loves the passion that he receives from Kate. Loren is a loner who never urgently wants, nor seems to need too much human contact, but Katie's dynamic personality can sometimes open him up enough for him to share true and passionate love. He does love her--but tries hard not to fully show it.

After their long embrace, Loren picks up Katie's bags and, without a word, they start walking up the stairway of the 1-½ story building to Loren's living quarters on the second level with Loren leading the way.

Katie says to Loren, who is having somewhat labored breathing from carrying the weight of both of her bags up the long stairway, "I made it in record time from Chicago, it only took me 4 hours and 20 minutes to get here."

As he is climbing the stairs Loren stops and looks back at her, his breathing has gotten heavier from climbing with the heavy bags in hands but he still says, "Damn it Katie, I've asked you to slow down, and not only do you not care for yourself, but you're also endangering everyone else on the road. Straighten- up will you? I know you need excitement, but why bring other people into it?" At the top of the stairs they enter the warehouse room where Loren stores his inventory of large columns, tables, huge garden urns and all sorts of wonderful fragments of ancient times.

They then walk to the end of the warehouse area into his one-room living quarters, which is always very cluttered and sometimes downright dirty. "It's funny", Kate is thinking to herself for the umpteenth time, "how this wonderful man can more often than not have a clean workshop and storage area, but his living quarters are so unkempt." She just knows, without even seeing it firsthand, that the bathroom will be disgusting and she will have to give it a good cleaning before she'll use it. Katie isn't exactly a kempt person herself and she keeps her own living area a little disorganized, which she thinks makes it comfortably lived-in, and she is certainly not a stickler for keeping things spotless. But the dirtiness in Loren's living area is at an entirely different level and she realizes it will be on her to do the cleaning or it just won't get done.

Loren plops both of Katie's bags on the floor in the center of the room in everybody's way, then sits down at his chair next to his computer. Automatically, without any thought and just from habit, Loren pushes the key to bring his computer screen to life and starts to play solitaire. He says nothing at all and totally zones out on Katie immediately.

This has always bothered Katie-but then she remembers why she even comes down to see him- all 300 miles. Katie gingerly walks over to Loren and kisses his forehead, a light sweet kiss but with a lot of emotion delivered with it. She looks into his eyes with much softness and desire wanting him to return some kind of mental or emotional stimulation. Loren does so- but just ever so slightly. For the rest of the afternoon they just sit in his room, with Katie making small talk once in a while with Loren barely commenting back.

For a while Katie is flipping through some of the many books Loren possesses, then she starts looking around the room before it dawns on her that it looks exactly like it did when she was here about three months ago. Like nothing has been moved, his clothes are in the same pile, the cluttered tables still have the same clutter, and the drawing of the fireplace that he had been designing is still on the drafting table, with nothing added nor changed to the drawing. She has wondered before if Loren might possibly have a second life somewhere. She'd heard of this happening before a few times with other people and had once even asked Loren if he has another home. In response, he became very serious and using a sincere tone of voice said, "Kate, this is my only home. This is where I live and the only place that I live." Loren stressed the words, "only place", then continues, "Your mind is wandering right now and that thought is just delusional." Because Kate wants to trust him so much and he is the only man she has ever truly fallen in love with, she reluctantly accepts his explanation without comment.

As dusk approaches Loren walks over to the ice chest, which replaced the refrigerator that broke down a few months ago and still stands in the corner waiting to be removed. He gets out two cans of beer, one for each of them, then he goes back to his chair. He feels around on his cluttered computer table for a small plastic bag with a small amount of pot inside. Very adroitly and with the skill of someone who has been doing this for a long time, he pushes a little bit of pot into a glass tube, which had been made into a smoking device for inhaling small amounts of pot. He lights up and takes a hit, adds a little more to the tube and passes it and a lighter on to Katie, who takes both items and lights the additional pot in the tube, then pulls the smoke into her mouth and lungs and holds it as long as she can. It is obvious that she is not a regular user, as she coughs to varying degrees after each hit. The pot that Loren has access to is always very potent, so between a few sips of beer and a couple of tokes of pot, Katie is feeling a sky high buzz. She doesn't smoke pot with anyone except Loren, because she can become paranoid- sometimes panicky- and Loren knows this, much to his advantage at times.

They are both feeling the effects of the pot and beer, and before very long Loren opens himself up to Kate as they converse about music, art, her work, and other pleasures they both enjoy. Then after a few minutes, he says with a deep voice, "I'm glad you've come to visit me, it's about time, I've wanted to see you for a couple weeks now- I miss you and I miss using you", he says the last words with a slight mischievous smile. Katie is getting aroused by his words and goes over by his chair, then kneeling down next to him she starts to caress his upper thighs and groin area through his jeans. She can feel he is very hard, and she begins brushing the raised area in his jeans with her lips and she softly blows long puffs of warm breath- knowing that the warmth is penetrating through the fabric to his hard flesh. Loren takes his hands and holds her face close to his groin area, not letting her head up, as if to silently say, "You're here for me and you're going to do exactly as I command". Katie knows just what he is thinking- and she is willing to do exactly what he wants. Katie loves this man like no other and is convinced that she wants her relationship with him to never end. She has become addicted to Loren and the way he treats her and the excitement he brings to her mundane routine. In fact, she has almost forgotten her own existence, except doing what it takes to please him. Their sex that night ended prematurely- but Kate still enjoyed the sexual pleasure as much as he did. Plus, after having sex, Loren becomes much more talkative and intimate.

The next morning, as is her usual routine, Katie is as happy like she frequently is upon waking and she gets out of bed right away to start a fresh pot of coffee. Loren likes her sunny mood in the morning and he usually enjoys a little banter with her, saying things like, "do you really know how to make coffee?" Knowing full well she can not only make coffee but she is a good cook also. But this particular morning Loren casually requests a favor, "Kate, could you run a few small errands for me at the hardware store and famer's market? I need to start finishing the cupboards and if I leave the shop to do these errands myself it will put me behind." Katie, who is just learning the streets of St. Louis, is a little hesitant at first but agrees to do his favor as he requested. She likes to be of help to him when she can and she is OK with a little adventure today. If she should get lost running the errands, a cell phone call to Loren should enable her to get back on track without much of a problem.

After coffee and eating a crisp apple from the cooler, Kate gets dressed, washes her face, brushes her teeth, then gets the directions and list of things needed from the hardware store and the farmer's market from Loren. As Loren gives Katie the money she needs for purchasing the items on the shopping list, he says to her, "Take your time and call if you get lost." Katie walks down the long stairway to the first floor, which is a large one-room workshop that Loren has and Kate admires. She loves workshops and tools and uses some of these tools herself in her own work as a freelance artist & woodworker. She is mostly self-taught in regard to the use of tools and woodworking, which is a great accomplishment by any standard and she is very proud to have been able to develop these skills without much assistance from anyone. "It just makes me stronger, that's all", thinks Katie to herself as she glances around the shop and, as she does so, it becomes very noticeable to her that Loren has accomplished almost nothing in the building since she was here three months ago. "Maybe he had jobs at other locations that took preference over this one", she thinks to herself. Then she opens the front door, locks it behind her and leaves to run the errands for Loren. She drives her jeep first to the hardware store about 3 miles away, where she picks up the small items that Loren had on the list, including fine sandpaper, wood stain & colored wood filler. She pays for the items at the checkout and then heads for the farmer's market that is located in the other direction, another 5 miles away.

Katie finds the market quite easily using Loren's directions, but once there, she finds it difficult to locate a parking spot because the farmer's market is always very busy on Saturday mornings. In fact, it takes her longer to park the jeep at the farmer's market than it had taken her to drive to both the hardware store and to the farmer's market combined.

The farmer's market is bustling this morning with a big crowd of people. The market building itself is shaped like the letter H, with the vendors on the vertical lines of the H selling mostly fresh fruits & vegetables. The horizontal line of the H is where 3 or 4 shops sell famous meats and bakery items and are always jam packed with consumers. It takes a lot of patience trying to walk through and around the hordes of people filling the isles, who are crowding as close as they can get trying to see the freshness of the food items and the prices being offered. It seems to Katie that some of the food Loren wants is just not available at the market or is only being sold by 1 or 2 vendors, but the small yellow bite-size tomatoes are simply not to be found at any stand. She walks through each isle at least twice, weaving through large crowds of people, in a search for those small yellow tomatoes, but never finds them. Finally, she ends up purchasing the closest alternative, small red cherry tomatoes. Later she will find out this won't make Loren happy. As a special treat, she bought him some nice spinach pastries, which she knows he likes a lot. She stays at the market for quite a long time, but Loren said for her to "Take your time." So time hasn't been critical.

When she finishes shopping she returns to her jeep then drives back to Loren's place. She parks the jeep in front of the warehouse building, then fills her arms with all the sacks of hardware and groceries that she had purchased and struggles and juggles with the numerous bags all the way to the front door to be buzzed in. As she is at the door waiting for Loren to open it, a seedy looking man dressed in many layers of clothing and acting strangely passes by her starring at her like she doesn't belong there. This makes Katie a little nervous at first, but she realizes that it is daylight and that she is reasonably safe where she's standing. Katie continues to stand on the sidewalk by the door, but is barely able to ring the doorbell as the sacks filled with products for Loren are weighing her arms so heavily that she is about to lose her grip on everything. The shrill ring is so loud she swears it can be heard a block away. It takes many rings- 6 or more- with intervals between before the small board covering the window moves enough for Loren to see who is at the door. This long wait makes Katie angry because, in her mind, she thought that Loren would have been anticipating her return to the warehouse. Why did it take him so long to answer the door when he knows she will have a full load in her arms?

Once she is inside the warehouse, Loren looks at her and asks, "What took you so long? I was thinking of calling you if you didn't show up pretty soon. Did you get everything on the list?"

Katie responds, "Yes, except no one had the little yellow tomatoes, and why did it take you so long to answer the door anyway, my arms are killing me." By the tone of her voice in responding to Loren, he can tell she is irritated. Kate tells him, "I don't have a problem going the extra mile for you Loren, but this waiting at the door so long is uncalled for". Loren then retrieves most of the bags from Katie's arms, which starts Rex jumping up and down next to her as they all go upstairs to put the purchases away.

Loren seems a little edgy to Kate- maybe it is due to the fact that she is irritated with him for being so slow to get to the door. Kate doesn't really know nor care if Loren doesn't like the fact that she is upset, as she knows she asks for little from him and he could at least give her some kind of recognition when she needs it. Katie has to clear some space on the table, including where the microwave had been sitting, in order to have a place for the vegetables and fruit that don't need to be put in the cooler. Loren has the bag of small red tomatoes in his hand and reaches in the bag to pull a few out. He stares at them like they are foreign to him and looks directly at Katie as if she had committed a major offense.

Katie says defensively, "Look no-one, I mean not one single vendor, had the small yellow tomatoes. That's what took me so long, I kept going back and forth- over and over each section of the market to try to find them, Loren- no one had them!" Katie then takes a red tomato out of the paper bag and puts it in her mouth saying, "These are pretty good though, just try one, Loren." He just tosses the ones in his hand back into the bag and walks downstairs without saying a word to her. Kate says in a low frustrated tone, "Wow, what a welcome- I hope it gets better or I won't be here too long."

2

THE VISITORS

By the time Kate changes into work clothes and goes downstairs to help Loren, he has moved way back to the far end of the workshop and is talking on his cell phone. He is sounding very irritated and, when he sees her coming, he turns his back to Kate and then walks out to the back storage yard to finish his conversation in privacy. This doesn't bother Katie because she's used to it by now, from the beginning Loren has generally handled his phone calls this way. She looks around for something to do while he is talking on his cell phone. As she walks through the warehouse, she mutters to herself, "I'd swear that he has hardly done anything on any of these cupboards since I was last here." Kate sees the large shop broom nearby and picks it up and starts sweeping the sawdust from one end of the building to the other. The sawdust is tainted with lots of other dirt and footprints that have been on the floor for quite a long time. The lack of fresh sawdust immediately catches Kate's eye, as it confirms that it has been a good while since Loren has worked in the shop.

Loren finishes his phone call and steps back inside. He looks like his thoughts are a long way off and there is a look of concern on his face. He growls to Katie, "Did you buy ice?"

Katie gives him a look that conveys her thought, "what the hell is going on anyway?" Then replies to Loren, "You didn't tell me you needed ice, which was not on your list—by the way--or did you think I'd buy the wrong kind, like the tomatoes for instance?" She's hot now-and Loren is sensing this because there is a hard edge in her voice and the glare in her eyes could light a match. Kate continues, "I think that maybe this trip down here was a mistake. You have been a jerk, almost since I got here." Loren's face softens, he looks at her saying " I'm sorry Kate, I didn't mean to growl at you like that, I've just got other things on my mind right now that have nothing to do with you. I'm sorry, for taking my problems out on you."

That's pretty much all it took for Katie and she melts quickly at almost any kind words he says to her, then she walks over to Loren and gives him a warm hug- his body softens into the hug and as they embrace Katie is thinking to herself, "Everything will be fine now".

Loren then asks her, "I forgot to put ice on the list earlier but we really need some, there is some beer left and the food that needs to be refrigerated, it will get warm and spoil if we don't have ice. Could you please go and get a couple bags of ice, it will only take you a minute? "He takes a key off of his key chain and hands it to her saying, "I might have to go someplace for a little while, if so, this is for you to get into the building. If I do have to leave, I'll be back very shortly-- O.K.?"

When Katie closes the front door as she is leaving she can hear Loren talking on his cell phone again. She is only gone for a few minutes to get the ice and, when she returns, Loren's black truck is still parked in front of the warehouse, which obviously means that he hadn't left as planned. She unlocks the front door and carries the ice in with one hand. As she enters the building she is thinking that Rex will greet her with one of his famous jumps into the mid-section, but Rex is nowhere around, then she realizes that Loren put him on the chain in the back storage yard.

Katie goes upstairs, puts the ice into the cooler then comes back down to the workshop and is surprised she hasn't seen Loren in the work area. She then walks to the back of the shop and, as she gets close to the large opened back door, she sees Loren on the outside of the chain link fence in a private conversation with two men who she does not recognize. She can tell from how they are dressed and, based on the type of car they are driving, they are probably not from this neighborhood either. Both men are dressed casually but in very expensive clothing and are driving a Black late-model Lincoln Town Car.

She can tell that whatever it is that they are talking about must be fairly important business because none of them even notice her until she trips on a metal pipe lying on the cement driveway just inside the fence. She doesn't fall- but the pipe makes a huge racket. All three men turn and seem startled that she is standing there, the two guests look at each other as Loren turns toward her and says, "Hey Katie, I'll be upstairs in a few minutes, why don't you go up and get us something ready to eat?"

In other words, Katie thinks to herself, "Get lost Katie", that's what Loren really means. On the way upstairs Katie says quietly to herself, "I hope these men are potential clients for Loren, he could really use the money."

Kate prepares tuna sandwiches and quarters two apples for their lunch while Loren is still in deep conversation with the men next to the storage yard for at least another half hour before he walks up the stairs. He looks very tired when he enters the room. They both eat lunch mostly in silence and then, after lunch, Loren lays down on his bed for a quick nap.

Katie walks back downstairs and picks up on the sweeping where she left off before getting the ice. She can't stay in Loren's room during the day for long periods of time because it is so dark and gloomy as he keeps the blinds pulled at all times and, secondly it is just one small room, which makes Katie feel uncomfortably confined. Being in a small place for a very long period has always made her feel mildly claustro-phobic for as long as she can remember--her preference is always to be in large open spaces during daylight hours. It is o.k. at night for her to be in Loren's room because it is naturally dark outside and is fine for sleeping. But during the daytime Kate needs as much space and sun-shine as she can absorb.

While she is finishing up sweeping the shop floor, she bends over and picks up small pieces of debris that are in the way of sweeping the fine sawdust. Mixed in with the debris is a piece of paper, just slightly wadded, lying on the floor next to a trash can. As she starts to throw the paper into the trash can, she notices it's a receipt. As Loren can sometimes be absent minded, Kate is thinking she could be about to throw away a receipt that he may need for a tax deduction. Kate then opens up the receipt to flatten it out and put with the other receipts she has piled on the worktable. Scribbled on the back of the receipt she sees an address and the words "she needs convincing", that's all that is scribbled. There is something in the pit of Kate's stomach that tells her that this scribbling is just not a good thing. But all she can think to do is to flatten the paper out and put it with the other stack of papers that Loren absent-mindedly always leaves lying around, which he may need for tax or other purpose at some point. Although Kate would like to ask him about the scribbling and what it means, she won't do it because she knows that he would either just totally ignore the question or get mad at her for even asking. On occasion, including this very instant, her heart tells her that this relationship is way too one-sided and that she shouldn't even be here with Loren. But her love for him is very strong and has only grown stronger over the years that they've known each other. Then Kate reminisces about the first time she and Loren made love and how it changed their lives.

FIRST NIGHT SEPTEMBER 2003

It all started about 7 years prior—the quick transformation of her business relationship into a lovers' relationship.

They had met during a trade show that Kate was participating in primarily as a seller and Loren had traveled to it from Dallas with his primary interest being in buying. He had discovered Kate's booth and was intrigued by her knowledge and the discerning eye that she had for design. Loren already had a good reputation by that time for being a natural craftsman with expertise in wood working, furniture design and architecture. After that first meeting they talked by phone regularly and stayed in touch from their home bases in Chicago and Dallas-- Loren would call her about every other day to discuss and buy some of the items that Kate had acquired for resell and Loren would purchase them to resell to shops in the southern U.S.

About three months after they first met, Loren went to her warehouse in Chicago to fill his truck with the items she had purchased for him at his request. It was getting near dusk before his truck had been fully loaded, then he asked her if she would like to go out to dinner. Knowing that Loren had Lynn, a woman who he called his business partner in Dallas, and knowing that he and his business partner lived together, Kate believed Loren when he said that immediately after dinner he would be heading back to Texas.

They went to a great little Mexican restaurant and ordered dishes of chicken enchiladas and Chile Relleno along with a pitcher of Margaritas. Not surprisingly, when they had finished eating their meal and drinking a pitcher of Margarita's- they were both feeling happily intoxicated. Loren had driven Kate's car to the restaurant because his truck was already overloaded with his purchases from Kate.

Once they arrived back at Katie's house they were feeling really talkative and in a good mood, then Loren decided to stay the night in Kate's 3-bedroom house with the intent of him leaving early the next morning for his home in Dallas.

They continued to enjoy each other's company, which lead to casual playing and, before he could say "party time", Kate was walking up the stairs to the guest room on the 3rd floor, wearing silky pajamas with Loren following close behind. Both of them are still feeling happily unrestrained and still light headed from the Margaritas. The first room off the stairway was small and light in color, furnished as a reading room with a log-made table and chair set with colorful baskets scattered around. Next they entered the guest room that had walls of wooden wainscoting and Indian artifacts, giving the room the feel of a warm and comfortable Montana lodge. The ambience of the room only added to the sexual arousal that was happening between them.

Loren brought out a small package of foil from his pants pocket and found a piece of cardboard to tap a small amount of the white powder on, then he gently cuts the powder with his jack knife making fine lines of the white powder. He then pulls out a dollar bill and rolls it into a straw. Kate has never done this powder before but is open to new things, especially fun things, and anyway she trusts this guy, Loren, quite a bit.

Kate puts her nose down to the rolled bill then bending down farther she snorts a line of the drug, with Loren following suit. Within a few minutes Katie feels very light, sensual and comfortable, and then she and Loren kiss for the first time and the kiss envelopes them with overwhelmingly erotic and liberating force. The kissing feverishly continues and becomes more intense as if their bodies seem to be blending as one through the meeting of lips and tongues alone, then Loren puts his hand inside of Katie's skimpy pajama bottoms and starts caressing, making the intensity and desire within her rage to an even higher level. She wants him to enter her so much, but he keeps caressing her with his hand and saying with a quiet lust in his tone, "I'm going to drive you up the wall", which he is doing, and she's saying, "Oh, please Loren please go inside me, please!" It seems like eternity that he caresses her- the feeling of desire building in her is to the point of being overwhelming. She is thrusting her hips wildly in involuntary passion and she whimpers to him, "please fuck me now!" Then he enters her and, when he does, they look into each other's eyes and the two of them had the most wonderful and intense physical connection between them that either of them had experienced ever before, for her, feeling the long hardness of his penis thrusting inside her and for him, the silky moist feeling of her soft, warm, moist flesh inside- so smooth and soothing.

He makes love to her over and over intermingled with passionate kisses throughout the night and when she becomes sore; he bends down to her vagina and licks her soothingly, and then begins to penetrate her again and again and again. Her orgasms are incredibly intense and so wonderfully long the whole night through. The sex and the cocaine seemed to be never-ending that night. At one point in the middle of the night while Loren is penetrating her, she says in a fit of passion, "If I say I love you I don't mean it," only because the feel and presence of him inside of her is so devastating wonderful that she is losing control of not only her emotions but the breathless words coming from her lips. Her physical passion is at the highest peak she has ever experienced- ever! Several times during the night Loren said in his masculine passion, "You are the sexiest bitch I've ever fucked."

Then Kate would in turn say, "Yes, I'm a bitch, please don't quit, and whenever she would orgasm again, she would say, "fuck me again and again, oh please don't quit" and when she became sore, he would bend down and sooth her with his tongue again, and then enter her again with full thrusts of passion and make her come more and more and over and over until she is almost senseless. Almost everything they were doing together was pure physical pleasure and probably the most physical enjoyment that two adults could ever experience together as one. Sleep was not even in the agenda that night, only sex, wonderful, pure, raw sex!

When daylight approached they still hadn't slept but it was time for Loren to be on the road heading back to Texas- where his home was with Lynn. Both Loren and Katie left the attic after they dressed and walked downstairs to the first floor to enter the Dining Room. Kate sat on the edge of the dining table with Loren standing in front of her, touching the edge of the table with his body between her spread thighs, and he looked into her eyes with both of them lovingly attaching to one another in the same moment. After a minute, Loren only nodded his head just once and then he walked out the door on his way back to Texas- his home- and to the woman with whom he resides.

Over their time together, their sexual attraction remained very strong but grew into a heart-wrenching monster which was not sufficiently potent to keep them from separating on a regular basis. They would part for a while but he always came back to her eventually and she always accepted him back- just hoping that someday he would love her as much as she loved him. Love to Katie was illustrated by the act of sex itself, she knew of no other kind of love. That was the only time she could really feel close to a man....

...Kate was still standing there with the broom in her hand in Loren's shop, where she had been the past 20 minutes reminiscing about how she and Loren had spent their first night together. When suddenly Loren was right behind her and she still doesn't notice him until he speaks in her ear, "what's going on?"—which makes her jump in surprise, as she had been in such deep thought that she didn't hear him come down the stairs or even hear him walk into the room. Kate jerks around and looks at him, noticing that his eyes are a little glazed and quite red, not from sleep but from smoking pot or something else.

He looks at the floor, which is now mostly swept, and smiles at her. But he is also standing next to the worktable, right by the stack of receipts, when his eyes focus on them. Right on the top of the stack is the receipt with the scribbling written on the back, with the scribbled side up.

Loren picks up the paper, looks directly at Katie with a questioning look then stuffs the receipt in his pants pocket. Then he looks again at the floor and says, "Good job Kate, thanks a lot." He then walks away toward the back of the shop without saying another word, opens the large back door and then pulls out his cell phone and auto-dials a number. Kate can just faintly hear him mumble something to the person who answered the phone.

3

THE DINNER

Loren came back into the warehouse after this last phone call look-ing anxiety-ridden and somewhat crazed due to his eyes being glazed and red. He announces suddenly, "We are going somewhere and you'll have to get changed. I'm taking you out to dinner--go get ready, I'm hungry and would like to leave right away." He didn't even make the dinner engagement sound like something he really even wanted to do- more like a hated obligation that had to be fulfilled.

Kate asks, "Where are we going to dinner?" Loren just stared back at her with an angry look. Then he says, "What the hell does that mat-ter anyway, why do you have to know every detail?"

Kate looking directly back at him says sarcastically, "Because Loren, is this a dressy place or just casual?" Then adds, " What the hell is wrong with you anyway, it sounds to me like you think you're doing me a favor by taking me to dinner, and frankly with your attitude, I'd just as soon stay here and eat some of the food that I bought this morn-ing at the market. I really don't even feel like going out to dinner with you right now."

Loren replies with a calm and more civil voice, " Katie, I want to take you to dinner- the restaurant is a surprise, just dress casual, the clothes you have on are pretty dusty from sweeping and, by the way, I want to thank you again for sweeping up my mess, I appreciate it."

Katie just turns and walks away from Loren with Rex following right behind her, as the dog is probably thinking that once upstairs Katie will give him a treat, which is her normal routine. So both Rex and Kate go up the steps so she can clean-up and change clothes.

Loren remains downstairs in the workshop and as Katie gets to the top of the stairway landing she can hear Loren again talking to someone on his phone. As she is already upset with Loren about the bungled way he invited her to dinner, another partially concealed phone call by him is even more irritating to her than ever. She just can't let go of it and, as she starts to change her clothes, she mutters to herself sarcastically, "I better hurry up so we can get to the glorious dinner that I'm going to be sharing with Loren". But first gives Rex his treat.

About fifteen minutes later Katie emerges down the stairway in black slacks and V-necked black sweater, her face clean and rosy, her light brown hair attractively pinned up so that a few trickles come down the sides of her face. When Loren sees her, his eyes have a slight glimmer in them as he can't help showing that he likes very much how she looks tonight and his mood changes rapidly from anger to lust. Loren says to Kate with a sensual look in his eyes," I hope that tonight you don't plan on sleeping much." Katie flushes a little, and turns her back to him and gently presses her buttocks into his groin area and sways against him just oh so slightly. She says nothing but the look on her face when she turns back to him says that she and Loren are now on the same wave length. Loren opens the front door holding Rex back so he doesn't get out the door, then Katie sidesteps around Rex and Loren and walks out the door with Loren close behind her.

The dark night air outside is damp and cool, which makes Kate glad she wore a sweater. Loren shuts and double locks the door as he does every night whether going out for the evening or staying in. Loren then says to Katie, "We're taking my truck tonight." Usually they'd take her jeep when going out in the evening because it is in better condition and gets much better gas mileage.

Katie doesn't say anything as she gets in the passenger side of his black truck after Loren unlocks it. They drive towards downtown taking Jefferson Avenue at first, and then she is lost because she doesn't recognize the rest of the streets as they near the cityscape.

The Arch is beautiful in the daytime, but at night it is spectacular! To Katie city skylines, especially at dark, are awe-inspiringly beautiful and the architecture is magnified because of all the wonderful lighting within and surrounding the edifices that come into her view. Her artistic eye is able to appreciate the way everything that is lit up has gone through a lot of thought for embellishing particular areas of St Louis.

St Louis also has many wonderful sculptures in and around the city. "A city of Arts," Katie whispers softly to herself as Loren's truck moves past the Arch. Once downtown Loren turns onto Market Street. Earlier Katie had been hoping, and then just now realizes that they are going to Key West Cafe located in Union Station.

Union Station is a phenomenal representation of early 20th century architecture that for a long time lay in dreadful condition until the right buyer purchased the building and renovated it. The new owner kept everything original that could be saved intact and tastefully brought the grand building back to life. At that moment they discovered that there was no parking available on the main street in front of Union Station so Loren turned the corner to park on a side street.

Then Loren loudly said, "Oh, I just noticed Jack Colbert getting into his truck over there, he was with me the other day and he forgot his briefcase in my truck". Then Loren quickly swings half way around in his seat and reaches into the section behind his seat and lifts out a brown leather case. "Kate, I'll be right back, just wait here." Loren quickly parks and opens his door then gets out and walks into the alley diagonally across the side street from where their truck is sitting.

Katie's thinking, "Gee how could Loren have seen this guy's truck, let alone see an alley, it's so dark in this section, especially since the street light closest to their truck is burnt out."

Loren is away from the truck for only a couple of minutes before he is back minus the briefcase. He walks over to Kate's side of the truck and opens her door saying, "Let's go get something great to eat. How about starting with oysters on the half shell? Come on Katie; let's really have an enjoyable night." His mood seems wonderfully uplifted.

Katie gets out and they cross the side street together to get back to Market Street and then walk up the one block to enter Union Station. As they are walking on Market Street, Katie notices a dark Lincoln Town car passing by. She thinks to herself, "that sure looks like the car that was at the warehouse the other day", but doesn't say anything to Loren. Once inside, the interior of Union Station's huge grandeur hits all of Kate's senses and she forgets everything else.

Loren leads her to the Key West Cafe, as they walk in the door and the maître d' asks if they have reservations, Loren answers, "Yes, for two, the name is Loren". The maître d' says "Follow me please". Loren and Kate are seated at a table that is fairly secluded.

Immediately Loren asks Kate what she would like to drink. Kate always being slow in ordering, after hesitating, decides on a Margarita-Frozen, lots of salt on the rim. Loren orders a Sam Adams and an order of oysters on the half shell for an appetizer. The night seems light and golden. After two drinks each and a second order of oysters their appetites have diminished, so they each have a small Caesar salad while talking and enjoying each other's company.

Katie's happy and thinking, "At last our relationship is the way it should always be, or mostly anyway. Loren does open up to me some times and maybe he'll start doing this more. It's times like this that I always remember and makes me want to be with him."

On the way home from dinner Kate casually asks Loren who Jack Colbert is and Loren just says, "Oh, an acquaintance of mine who needed a ride home the other night, his truck broke down and then he forgot and left his briefcase in my truck."

Although mentally questioning his answer, Kate asks no further questions as she wants the evening to remain pleasant and cozy, and hopes Loren feels like having more of the frenzied sex they had really been getting into. Katie is more than ready and she can sense that Loren is too. On the way back to the warehouse they stop at a liquor store where Loren purchases a pint of tequila and some lemons, which signals to Katie that tonight will likely be a very lustful and sexual night all night long. They are both still feeling the light effects of the drinks at Key West Cafe as they enter the warehouse. Rex greets them as if they are long lost friends, then all three move upstairs to Loren's room. Loren immediately turns on the television, not to watch it but for the low light effect turning off the volume. He soon removes all of his clothes, like he quite often does whether Kate is there or not. He is a very comfortable being naked as he is a very free spirited person in this and many other ways.

Then Kate seductively removes her clothing and puts on a man's white shirt leaving it unbuttoned to just below her breasts, which is intentionally quite provocative as she has a dark sensuous beauty mark located between her breasts that, when revealed along with just the rounded inner curves of her breasts exposed, will make almost any red-blooded man totally stand to attention. After watching how Kate has gracefully adorned herself with his white shirt, Loren sits down at his chair next to his computer then opens a small folded paper to reveal some very fine white powder. He asks Kate to bring over the lemon wedges with the tequila and salt, which Kate brings to him while barely being able to contain her arousal knowing a full night of physical plea-sure is just beginning. Kate likes becoming subservient at times like these; it is a sexual role she loves to play with Loren and is a strong sexual turn-on for him as well. She sets the plate of lemon wedges, booze & salt in front of Loren then sits down in the chair facing him already enjoying the anticipation of what comes next.

He says to her, "Kate, I found this stuff, (meaning the white pow-der) stuck in a book while straightening my bookcase. I don't know how old it is, but let's try it and see."

To Kate this powder looks pretty fresh and so does the clean folded paper containing it. But she isn't about to say anything about it, as she trusts Loren enough to know that he won't give her anything that will kill either of them.

Loren takes a razor and separates some of the fine powder into 4 lines. He then takes a rolled bill and hands it to Kate. She takes the rolled bill and holds it up to a nostril and lowers her head to where the bill just touches the edge of one line of powder, and then she inhales in her nostril deeply while moving the bill slowly down the line until the line has completely disappeared into her nose. It burns her nose momentarily but it only takes seconds for her to feel an incredible rush that almost knocks her over, but then immediately following the rush she feels extremely relaxed with a feeling of well-being inside and out. She hands the bill to Loren who does the same thing himself with the other line.

They both take swigs from the bottle of tequila, licking the salt first, then the taste of booze followed by lemon. This brief intake of drugs & booze is making them both feel relaxed in every way.

Loren nods his head down towards the last two lines of powder on the table while saying, "It's gonna melt". He says this twice before Katie asks him, "What do you mean it's gonna melt?" He responds, "If you don't do your line soon, I'll do it for you!" Katie immediately takes the rolled bill and snorts the 2nd line and almost by the time she lifts her head she is feeling euphoric. Loren follows suit with the last line. Both are wonderfully high and both are really getting into each other as the sexual heat is growing rapidly between them.

Kate sits back in the chair and half closes her eyes she is so relaxed. She takes her hands and touches a breast with each hand, caressing them slowly, the feel to her is sensual, her nipples become hard and she takes her hands and unbuttons one more button of her shirt, she senses the effect that her movements are having on Loren who is intently watching her. Opening the shirt more she exposes one breast and a bare shoulder. Loren moves forward in his chair and puts his mouth on her nipple and sucks, at first gently with his goatee slightly prickling her tender skin, than very hard causing her slight pain. He then sits back and says to Katie, "Unbutton your shirt more."

She is virtually hypnotized by him. At his command, she unbuttons the remaining buttons- except the last one, all the time never diverting her eyes from his.

Loren takes his hands and grasps each breast and massages & squeezes them real hard and rough, then puts his hands on the back of her head and pushes her head towards his groin area, bringing her off the chair and into a kneeling position in front of him. Then he commands to Kate in a dominant, low-pitched voice, "Suck me".

Kate slightly opens her mouth enough to just put the tip of his cock inside, gently circling her tongue around the tip, the warmth and wetness of her mouth on his penis makes Loren gasp and makes him even harder.

Loren, who is still holding her head, pushes her down farther until Kate's mouth is completely full.

Katie does not resist. As she is sucking him she starts fantasizing that he is her master and she is his willing slave who wants, actually needs, to please and love her master in every way he desires. Her sucking makes Loren gasp again, the feel, the warmth, the wetness and tightness is euphoric to him. He lets go of her and tells her to stand, and Katie obeys while keeping her eyes submissively focused downward as she stands in front of him. He looks up at her from his chair confidently knowing that she belongs to him. She is his slave.

With her standing, Loren unbuttons the last button of her shirt and opens it fully exposing both breasts taunt and warm and round with nipples so hard and pointed. Loren then tells her to spread her legs so he can look at her. Katie is feeling embarrassed, but she submissively does as she is told. Loren looks at her and takes his hand and firmly lays it flat upon her entire vagina area, the warmth of his hand almost makes Katie organism. She senses his hand being very strong, warm and protective—an amazing turn-on for her!

Loren's eyes scan the room until he spots what he is looking for, the long rope that has been carefully looped over a hook by the door. He hands the tequila to Kate and she automatically takes a swig as Loren opens the folded paper and sprinkles out more powder on the table and carefully draws 4 more lines with the razor. They both again snort one line each, then the others. Loren gets up and walks over to get the rope then carries it back to where Kate is sitting now very relaxed. He orders her to stand-up - she stands. Kate is a little taller than Loren when she faces him as he takes the one end of rope and brings it around the back of her neck and over her shoulders then crosses the rope between her breasts then around her back coming in front under the breasts. He keeps wrapping the rope around her breasts until they are bound tightly from bottom to top and between them, then he wraps the rope once around her waist and then tightly at the top of each inner thigh to exaggerate her vagina the same way he'd done with her breasts. The rope is very tight and slight hints of blue are showing in the skin color of her breasts. He then takes her arms and binds them behind her. Katie loves the feel of Loren touching her during the whole process of him binding her. When he has finishes tying her- he asks her, "Katie, who are you?" Katie giggles and says, "I'm Katie." Loren says more sternly this time, "Katie, who are you?" Then Kate looks down to avoid his eyes and says, "I am your slave."

"Yes Katie," says Loren, "You are my slave."

With both of them still standing, Loren tells her, "Get down on your knee's now." Katie does as he commands, Loren is very hard and thick in front of her face and Kate knows what she has to do. She submissively puts her mouth on him and sucks, the warmth and wetness is electrifying to Loren, the feeling is an incredible turn-on for him and his power over her energizes his masculinity even more. He pushes her away and pulls her up from underneath her arms, then pushes her backwards unto the bed and takes her legs in each hand and spreads them very wide. His hand goes into her and she is so wet and warm that he immediately kneels down in front of her and pushes his penis into her as she squirms beneath him. He then puts her legs up over his shoulders and fully thrusts into her and continues thrusting as each time goes deeper and deeper.

Katie comes and then in ecstasy she comes again in unison with every few thrusts of his penis. She is so wet, so hot and so swollen inside, all connecting with the intoxicating love she feels for Loren. She is overwhelmingly filled with a wonderful variety of sexual- sensual thoughts and pleasures. Loren pushes harder, his strokes growing increasingly urgent, then Katie screams in ecstasy at the moment Loren gives one climatic push and stops deep within her and shutters and moans a deep moan as his wetness and her wetness meet inside her. This is the ultimate of all mutual pleasures, Loren has her, he owns her, and Katie eagerly and lustfully does just what he wants. He stays in her a long time finishing the flow from his penis, and then collapses on top or her but lays for only a short time before he quickly rises and leaves the bed. His silent thoughts are, "Never, never get too close."

Katie remains lying on the bed where she can actually see her legs quivering from exhaustion. Her body is wet and with perspiration and she feels too weak to get up. But she also has a warm glow from the feeling of total satisfaction produced by the incredible sexual experience she just shared with Loren. Katie cannot sleep though, for whatever drug or combination of drugs and booze she had taken will not let her sleep. Most of the early morning she lays half in and half out of sleep, but before she doses off she realizes Loren is not in the room. She assumes that he is down in his workshop, but she does not bother to see where he is, she just lays quietly in physical exhaustion until she passes out.

4

A MURDER IN THE MIDST

I t is still early and the sun is just coming up. With a cup of coffee in hand Kate makes her way down the stairs with legs feeling wobbly and weak, her head a little wired from just being with Loren the night before, and the white powder hadn't quite worn off yet either. When she's down stairs she finds Loren is nowhere to be seen. She checks the back door and looks outside. There is no sign of Loren but Rex is on his chain and quietly resting. She walks back inside to the front door calling Loren's name but hears no answer; she goes to unlock both locks on the front door, to find that only one of the locks is actually locked. Kate opens the door and sees that Loren's truck is still there, but her jeep is gone. She finds her keys are missing realizing Loren has taken her jeep some place. He has never done this before, there were only a couple times in the past that he borrowed her jeep, but he always asked to do so in advance.

Katie went back up-stairs to find her cell phone to call him. But just as she was dialing his cell number, she could hear Rex barking loudly in the backyard. She looks out the bathroom window and sees Loren parking her jeep at the back of the warehouse. The jeep has one long white scratch going almost the whole length of it on the driver's side.

Loren had unlocked the backyard gate and drove the jeep into the backyard on the cement driveway then he got out of the vehicle carrying a large paper grocery bag that is half full but crumpled closed so Kate is unable to determine its contents. Loren then walks outside the gate to the dumpsters located just down the street next to a housing project and throws the bag into the dumpster. Then he walks back into the yard and shuts the gate. After he chains and padlocks it, she watches him just stand there silently, kind of staring into space for a few seconds before he walks over and inspects the scratch on her vehicle. At that moment he looks up and sees her watching him from the window.

Loren walks to the door then comes inside leaving Rex chained. When he sees Kate and before she can say anything, he explains to her that she was sleeping so soundly that he hated to wake her, and that he just borrowed her jeep to go to "The Courtesy", a breakfast joint, for a coffee since he couldn't sleep at all.

Kate doesn't say anything so Loren continues talking, "I parked the jeep on the side street and when I came out of the restaurant and saw your vehicle damaged, I was really angry". He stopped talking for a moment as if thinking of something, then added, "Someone must have sideswiped it while I was inside. It was parked just down the street where I couldn't see it from the windows. Whoever the bastard is that did it, didn't have the decency or something else like no auto insurance to come and look up the owner of the vehicle. They just took off. I'm sorry about this Kate, I'll have it repaired quickly."

Later that morning a wrecker came and picked up the jeep and took it somewhere to a garage to do the repairs. Kate asked Loren why they didn't just drive it there. Loren replied, "I convinced them to throw in the wrecker service--I know some of the mechanics who work there. So why bother driving when it can be done for you at no added cost?" That was all he said, so Katie just left it alone.

The day progressed fairly slowly for Katie because she is so tired from the night before and still can't sleep. So she sanded and stained on the cupboards for Loren just to keep busy, while Loren, who is even more silent than normal, putzed around the shop not really accomplishing much either. After eating a small meal, they went to bed early to get the deep restful sleep they missed the night before.

Early the next morning Loren is up and in deep concentration composing an e-mail on his computer. A little later Katie got up and starts brewing a pot of coffee. She is feeling good after a night of restful sleep and is in a cheery mood like she is most mornings. She is really looking forward to the coffee as she never really functions very well until she had that first cup. She needs some private time every morning to write out chores that need to be done and journaling events she wants to remember. Then she usually jogs or does stretches to energize herself. She drinks her first cup of coffee in Loren's room quietly sitting on his bed then takes her second cup out into the larger warehouse room where there is more space to do her yoga stretches. It is pouring rain outside, so her usual jog in Lafayette Park can't be done this morning. "Maybe tomorrow I can run", she says to herself, taking her last sip of coffee before starting her stretches.

Kate returns to Loren's room after exercising and she is feeling energized and ready to start the day. Her mental alertness and physical energy are always at their peak after working out. However, today Loren is watching the local St. Louis news on television; he seems to be in deep concentration watching the news coverage about the murder of a woman in the city. Kate catches only part of the newscast - the part about the woman being beaten to death. Instinctively, she feels shock and sorrow for the murdered woman, but she didn't catch the name of the person, which seems unimportant as Katie knows so few people in St. Louis. The newscast closed with the words, "The investigation is under way and that the police were looking for the victim's ex-boyfriend."

Loren turns off the TV right after the news story and says, "Katie let's go get breakfast somewhere, I'd like to go back to the 'Courtesy' and just see if any of the regulars there noticed a vehicle sideswiping your jeep yesterday morning. Not that it makes much difference, but I'd just like to know if anyone saw it happen. You know how it is, you just want to know, and I'd sure like to talk to the person who did it."

Katie dressed in work clothes so that when they returned from breakfast she could start working immediately on what she hoped was the last of the sanding and staining of the cupboards. The cupboards should have been completed before she even arrived in St. Louis, because they were to be installed last week, and Loren still had to seal them lightly then lightly sand some more between the coats of lacquer before the cupboards could be installed. "No wonder he doesn't have much of backlog of work", thought Kate to herself, even worse, "I hope he isn't getting a reputation for being undependable".

When they arrive at the Courtesy, Loren asks a few of the regulars "If they noticed someone sideswiping Kate's jeep yesterday morning". No one saw the incident happen so Loren just lets it go, but one of the Courtesy regulars, an older bald-headed man, speaks up, "Gee, I was here yesterday morning, and missed everything, I didn't even see you here either, about what time did this happen, anyway?"

Loren turns slightly blushed saying, "I was so tired when I came in I didn't look at a clock, although I know it was pretty early." Kate feels that Loren wasn't exactly telling the truth, but also thought it was probably because he didn't want to mention that he was probably still feeling the buzz of the white powder and booze. They both had the breakfast special of 2 eggs, bacon, hash browns and toast, Loren's eggs were cooked over easy with wheat toast, Kate had eggs scrambled and no toast.

Kate picked up the STL Today newspaper and found the news story about the murdered woman on the second page. The woman's name was Susie Brenkenridge aged 42, who lived at 304 Tucker St. in St. Louis, her body was found at the bottom of the basement stairs. The autopsy showed she died of head trauma with numerous lacerations to the head, neck and upper body. Her death occurred in the early morning hours. A neighbor, who didn't want his name mentioned said," he had talked to her the night prior around 8:00 p.m., and she seemed nervous and in a hurry," then adding "he later heard a vehicle idling and then a scraping noise in the middle of the night. But he did not get up to investigate only because there were so many odd noises at night in his neighborhood that he has just gotten used to them." The police are trying to locate the victim's ex-boyfriend a Dale Robbins, last known address 246 Nebraska St. in St. Louis. Anyone knowing of his whereabouts were asked to notify the St. Louis Police Department, he is wanted for questioning- concerning the death of Susie Brenkenridge."

Katie is afraid to imagine the terror this woman must have gone through before her death. Loren is also reading the sports section of the newspaper when Katie interrupts his reading to ask him to describe the Tucker St. area. He simply responded, "It's a long street Kate, depends on where the location is." Loren's face though seemed a little tense in his response to her, which Katie interprets as Loren's frustration from not finding out who had scraped her jeep.

As they are walking out to the parking lot of the Courtesy, the same Lincoln Town car that she had seen in the alley behind Loren's storage yard, pulls up into the lot. The passenger window is rolled down a little and it slowly moves just past Loren's truck pulling into a parking space a few spaces away. After a glance, Loren tells Katie, "I'll be right back, here's the keys to the truck please get in and wait." Loren then walks over to the driver's side of the town car to talk to the driver. Katie couldn't see much of Loren's conversation but she is starting to wonder what is going on, something just seems a little strange and out-of- place.

Loren's conversation is brief and then he comes back to the truck and heads back to the warehouse. In route the conversation is minimal, which is quite often the case. All that Loren tells Katie is what he needs for her to do today besides the staining and sanding of the cupboards. Then casually adds, "I have got to make a trip uptown for a couple hours, I'll be back as soon as I can. I know it will take you a little more time than that to finish the cupboards, but if you should get done with them sooner, just do the couple of other projects that I mentioned, you know what to do Kate."

Loren left for uptown within five minutes after letting Katie into the warehouse, Rex had been chained outside since before they left for breakfast, so the first thing that Katie did after returning was to make sure Rex has fresh water and food. She would love to let him off the chain to give him a little more freedom, but Rex is an escape artist, his body is fairly large but he still finds some way to crawl under the chain link gate. It seems physically impossible but it happens every time! The last time that Rex escaped was the last time Katie came down from Chicago to visit Loren. Rex disappeared longer than usual and Loren was very afraid and upset of what happened to his dog. When Rex did return, Loren told Kate, "From now on when he's out in the yard we'll have to keep him on the chain or he'll end up getting hit or disappear", so at least for today while Loren is gone Rex will be on that chain.

Katie found the 150 grit sandpaper and started sanding the cupboards. She felt an eeriness from being in the shop by herself, and kept herself busy sanding and listening to jazz on a local radio station. The couple of hours that Loren said he would be gone is now running overtime, Katie had finished the sanding and most of the staining. She came to St Louis to be with and to work with Loren on these projects, but not to do them all by herself! Katie's patience completely disappears when she sees that Loren is an hour and a half late and loses interest in doing any more work today. It is time for a break in the backyard and to sit down by Rex—she needs company and decided Rex does too. Of course, Rex is happy and excited for Kate to spend time with him, especially when she pulls a couple of dog treats out of her pocket. After petting and talking to him for a few minutes she goes back inside. She uses her cell phone to try to call Loren, but he has his phone shut off as the voice mail came on immediately.

When he finally returns at around 4:00, Katie is fuming, not only had she finished the cupboards and the other chores, but she had cleaned Loren's downstairs bath so it is at least sanitary again. For more than the last 2 hours she had alternated between sitting and pacing the floor and she had tried calling him several times but never got an answer. "The least you could have done is to have the decency to leave your phone on", she says with anger.

Loren looks tired, all he can say is "I'm sorry; I must have forgotten to turn it on." Then he slowly drags himself up the stairs and speaks the words," Kate, I need to lie down for a few minutes, please excuse me."

It dawns on Katie then and there that if she is going to enjoy herself while in St. Louis- she needs to do some things she enjoys such as visiting the St. Louis Botanic Garden, the City Museum plus a few other places, with or without Loren. She really loves him, but it is ridiculous the way he has been treating her. Yes, she could go back to Chicago, but she'd regret it because she really wants time away from home and she really misses Loren when she is away from him for too long of a time.

She doesn't care if he wants her to work tomorrow or not. Kate has within these last few minutes decided that tomorrow she's going to visit the Botanic Gardens. At the moment it is only 4:30 P.M. and is beautiful outside, a perfect 70 degrees, the rain had quit mid-morning and the sun is shining- but yet she'd been in the shop 90% of the day.

Kate went upstairs to take a quick shower, reminding herself while showering that she'll have to clean the upstairs bathroom very soon. It is pretty disgusting to use the way it is right now so dirty and all. She then put on a pair of baggy shorts, t-shirt and her running shoes then went downstairs with Loren's keys in hand to let herself out without disturbing Loren, who is upstairs in a deep sleep and all Katie wants to do is run.

The warehouse is only 4 blocks from Lafayette Park and Kate dearly loves this park. It is the oldest Park in St. Louis, a fact she had learned from Loren. First she ran the entire perimeter of the park on the side-walk about 1-mile altogether, avoiding running into others who were primarily walking their dogs, then she went through one of the gate's that is located at each of the 4 corners of the park, then ran the diagonal path that leads to a lovely pond and around the pond where just to its right is a magnificent old stone bridge with a small rock-lined stream running beneath. At this point Katie slows to a walk to enjoy this beautifully wonderful little secluded area, which is so serene, so therapeutic.

The rocks lining the stream are Missouri rocks, their formation is similar to Lava Rock, very rough in texture with big holes and ruts in all of them, the effect of the rugged stones next to the slow- running stream, the beautiful plants and lush vegetation compel Kate to slow her pace even further. It is beautiful, tranquil, and a great place for someone with a troubled heart to bring her thoughts together. Kate could not resist the urge to sit down on one of the rocks just up enough from the stream that her feet wouldn't get wet. She thought, "This is so different than Loren's room with blinds always pulled shut and his backyard encircled with an 8 ft. chain link fence with barbed wire on top". Kate promised herself at this moment that this beautiful place would be her place to get away whenever she needed time to herself while in St. Louis. It is so close and so beautiful and until now, undiscovered by her.

She sat there for a few more minutes but knew she had to return to the warehouse, she had taken Loren's keys without him knowing it and he guards his keys with his life it seems. If he awoke and found her gone with his keys she was sure he'd be pretty upset, plus she forgot to write him a note. Although in her mind, this was good for him, maybe it would make him realize how she felt today when she couldn't reach him by phone and he was so late. Katie just did a slow jog back to the warehouse just in time to see Loren open the front door and stand in front of it on the sidewalk starring at her as she came slowly running up to him.

"Where the hell have you been?" Where are my keys? Did you take them without asking me first?" He almost threw these words at her with anger in his voice. Kate was a little short of breath, still was able to calmly stop just short of running into him, looking at him while catching her breath, she coolly said to him, " I'm sorry- I suppose. I'm tired and am going to take a nap." " That's it," she fumed to herself as she walked around him to enter the warehouse, "That gives him a little of what he's given me today." Then Kate immediately ran up the stairs to avoid any more conflict with Loren, at least for the moment anyway.

They had the small red tomatoes, sliced green pepper & canned salmon that night for dinner. Little was said by either of them at the table, although at least in Katie's mind, she thought Loren was no longer angry, although he seemed anxious and concerned about something- but she had no clue as to what he was concerned about, Loren is always quiet and keeps his thoughts mostly to himself but he is generally laid- back, not anxious like he has been since this trip down.

He did let her lay down with him for a while that night, his back to her, her body molded into his, with her arm laying over his side and around his stomach and he with his arm holding her arm in place so she wouldn't move. This kind of closeness is always so special to Katie and so rarely happens. Neither of them are used to sleeping with anyone- to really sleep that is, so Kate slips down to her air mattress on the floor after a while as she is restless. Loren seems so tense and distant, like he has a lot on his mind lately. She wishes so much that he would open up to her- she wants to share her thoughts with him and needs for him to want do the same. Her love for him she knows is much deeper than his love for her. In the night another dream came to her:

THE 2ND DREAM

First there is a mist and nothing can be seen clearly. Then the mist begins to clear revealing the appearance of a curved tunnel that goes both up and down similar to a car ramp. At the end of the tunnel is a small restaurant. Katie enters the restaurant, it is full of people but she notices a booth with a short man sitting alone. She asks him if she can share the booth. He nods a yes, she sits down across from him, and soon two other men enter the restaurant and walk over to her and grab her by the arm and take her away. As she is being dragged down the tunnel she sees a dim light coming from somewhere and can hear women screaming, terrifying screams of anguish and pain, she is dragged into a large overly lit room with exercise machines, then she is forced on to a moving treadmill and right over her head is a large man with red hair which is long, wild and frizzy- this man is raging mad and he is right above her on a bicycle machine in mid-air, his anger is directed at her. She can sense he wants to kill her, he is pedaling the bicycle with great strength and the machine he is riding is drifting closer and closer to her head. She falls off the moving treadmill with a violent thud, landing on her knee then jumps to her feet running. She escapes through the tunnel and then the tunnel materializes into the interior of the high loft of an old wooden barn, she runs to the end wall of the barn and finds a door, she pushes the door open and uses a rope to get down to the ground and into a barnyard.

It is a dark & chilly fall night outside and the moon is full. She knows she is being chased, she must move fast. As she runs through the barnyard she can hear many children playing in an open field to the left of her, she can just barely see their silhouettes; their playing and voices have an eerie sound to her. She sees the outline of an old fence with wooden posts topped with barbed wire. On the other side of the fence is a dried up cornfield not yet harvested. She runs and hurriedly climbs the fence shaking with fear and then as she enters the cornfield-- her dream ends. Then she awakens.

5

2ND HOME

Katie woke up from last night's unsettling dream which was disturbingly similar to the dream that came to her just before she travelled to St Louis to see Loren. The two dreams were so bizarre and vivid that they did not drift from memory as dreams so often do. Normally she would remember the experience of dreaming but not remember the contents of the dream or only sketchy parts of the dream. However, inexplicably these two recent dreams remain solidly fixed in her memory in frightening detail.

Although still troubled by the dream, Katie greets Loren with the most cheerful "good morning" that she can muster. She had developed this routine during her marriage in dealing with her husband who was unbearably irritable just about every morning, then later in the marriage, most of the day, until Kate left him after 8 years because of his inability to change and unwillingness to seek medical help for his acute depression. Loren is busy on his computer and watching the morning news on television at the same time, and doesn't hear Kate's greeting. She starts brewing a pot of coffee and thinks about having a morning run as it is already looking like a beautiful sunny day. Even with the blinds pulled the sun's rays are streaming in pleasantly through the cracks.

Kate intently watches the final spurts of the brewing process then pours her first cup of coffee. She quite enjoys this quiet morning ritual. With coffee in hand she quietly steps into the large warehouse room to do a little journaling before running. After 2 cups of coffee and writing a few lines of a poem she's had in mind, Kate then changes into her jogging clothes and is about to leave but stops at the door and asks Loren to lock the door behind her, which he does without a question or comment.

As Katie starts her jog this morning she notices two police vehicles pulling out of the alley that adjoined to Loren's backyard. "Occasionally, one police car can be seen in that alley, but never two", Katie thinks to herself as she continues to run, then quickly puts it out of her mind as she rationalizes that a problem at the housing project next door may have required extra police. Katie's run is smooth and easy that morning. There are only a few early morning dog walkers and a couple other joggers, as she virtually has the park to herself. On the way back to the warehouse she begins to think of the dream, then shrugs it off, thinking such thoughts are just the result of the tension she and Loren seem to be having during her visit. Once back at the warehouse she has to be let in. Surprisingly, Loren is there at the door after the first ring. He must have already been in the shop downstairs to have answered so quickly.

"I have a surprise for you Kate," as he pulls his warehouse front door key off its chain and hands it to her, "I want you to go down to the hardware store just off Jefferson and get a key made for yourself."

Katie is pleased and stunned; this isn't like Loren at all! To Kate this means he wants her in his life more completely and wants to have a more open relationship. As usual, Loren is a man of few words, but his giving Katie a key to his place means a lot to her.

Loren gives her directions to the hardware store which, of course, are precisely accurate. Katie, still in jogging clothes, is provided Loren's truck to drive to the hardware store on Jefferson to have a key made. Driving back she feels a little guilty about going to the St. Louis Botanic Gardens today, but she really thinks it is best for both Loren and herself; they each needed to have their own space and, frankly, there isn't much for Katie to do until Loren puts a coat of sealer on the cupboards before she can start fine sanding them. Besides, right now the fall colors at the Garden are very beautiful and if she waits much longer she will probably miss some of the prettiest fall foliage.

After Katie parks the truck in front of the warehouse she smiles as she uses her own key to let herself into the warehouse. She discovers that Loren is in the midst of a conversation on his cell phone and, as usual, when she comes near him while he is on the phone, he walks a distance from her to keep his conversation private. This bothers her but she goes upstairs without a word and takes a quick shower, which again is a reminder that she'd better clean the bathroom soon, "Maybe this afternoon when I return from the garden", she thinks to herself. Kate dresses quickly as is her normal routine. Also, she's certainly not one to dilly-dally around fixing her hair or putting on the miniscule amount of makeup that she wears. She dabbed a little blush on cheeks and mascara to eyelashes, a comb through her damp mid-length hair and as quick as that she is ready to go, or as she would sometimes say with spunk-- "Lets Rock and Roll." Kate doesn't mean to show drama it just comes naturally to her, just the same as her showing the intensity of her feelings, and wanting to know everything there is to know about all things that affects her life--that is her nature. She isn't a gossip-not even close to it, if a friend or family member tells her something in confidence she keeps it to herself. Judging the morals of other people is hard for Katie to do. "No one is the same, nor created exactly the same, and every individual is unique." She has said these words often, especially to people who want to put someone down. Katie knows that she won't be getting any award for being an angel because she isn't one, but that everyone deserves peace. She went back downstairs to the shop where Loren is tinkering with the paint sprayer that he needs to use to seal the cupboards. She walks up to him and gives him a light sweet kiss on the forehead and thanks him for the key.

Loren then says to her, "Katie this is your second home, you are always welcome."

Another stunning event just took place in Katie's mind and is difficult for her to process. She is thinking to herself, "First, I am given the key and now it's my second home, is Loren really missing me so much when I'm away that he is now letting down his guard or is there something else?" These questions Katie knows she should keep to herself. She is afraid if she asks Loren "why"; he might renege on the key, the second home and even possibly send her home that very moment.

Katie looks at Loren and asked, "Do you need me to work today, because if you don't I thought I'd go and spend part of the day at the

Botanic Garden, as it's so beautiful outside and the fall colors are probably fabulous there?"

Loren responds, "No, go right ahead and enjoy yourself, you've had to put up with my negativity since you've been here and probably would like to run away from me like you normally do. Have a good time Kate. You have got the key to let yourself in if I'm not here when you get back, don't you?"

"Yep" said Katie with a smile. "I'll see you later." Katie walked out and walked down to the corner to catch a bus to the gardens, since her jeep was still in the shop for the repair."

Upon her arrival the impact is immediate--the St. Louis Botanic Gardens are gorgeous as usual; and all the surrounding beauty puts a smile on her face. Then Katie thinks briefly about Loren. Last fall the two of them had come here together to be close to nature, however, Katie could tell when at the garden that November day that Loren was not interested in being close to her. As time past he seemed to be covertly distancing himself from her through his limited and somewhat derisive conversation, the disengaged look in his eyes and his general aloofness from her, a pattern of behavior he had repeated many times before, particularly after periods of shared closeness, involving laughter, tenderness and intimacy. He seemed to do this every time the relationship seemed to be getting too close, in his own mind, anyway.

On the other hand, Kate is seeing her relationship journey with Loren as very frustrating and repetitive--one or two steps forward- then one or two steps back. Kate's friends would say to her- let go of him Kate, he's no good for you. But Loren's occasional burst of intellect would keep her interested and his mysterious ways were an intriguing attraction she couldn't seem to resist- Katie needs diversity and Loren clearly offers her that.

Katie had borrowed Loren's membership card to the Botanic Gardens—allowing the bearer a free pass, one of the luxuries he bought himself every year. She walked slowly past the trees and plants looking at the beautiful colors that fall always seemed to bring. She strolled by the set of pools where huge water lilies grow, and the bronze statues of dancing nymphs stood high above the waters of the pools, Kate then took the path that led to the Shaw House and Mausoleum where Mr. Shaw's remains are entombed.

She just stands for a moment—the trees and the fall foliage are magnificent all over the Gardens as far as the eye can see. Then Kate takes the path that leads her to the Chinese Garden, and in that particular garden, off to the side is a small-secluded area where a huge and most wonderfully simple stone table & benches sit nestled in some flowering bushes—her favorite spot in the Chinese Garden.

Katie wishes that these were in her own yard. She loves to garden and is an artist by trade and upon sitting at this table for the very first time her curiosity could not be contained. She started investigating how an artist and craftsmen could make this huge stone top sit balanced and level on another rock. Bending very low with her head under the table, almost on hands and knees, she sees the secret and starts planning to someday build her own stone table in her own backyard... She walks over the white marble Chinese bridge and gazes longingly at the small pond and stream on the other side. Katie then continues on to the large Japanese Garden and walks slowly around the lake before returning to the bus stop to take herself back to Loren's place. The trip has been physically invigorating to her and, as usual, refreshingly therapeutic to the soul.

The bus ride to and from the garden requires only two connecting buses to accomplish the trip. Katie is anxious to see Loren and wonders if he would have enjoyed seeing the Botanic Gardens with her. Upon her return to the bus stop nearest to the warehouse, Katie notices that Loren's truck is parked outside in front of the warehouse. She walks up to the warehouse door and lets herself in with a smile while thinking about the "miracle" of having her own key.

Loren is nowhere to be seen in the shop, so she looks upstairs, still no Loren nor Rex, so she walks back down to the shop and then quickly steps toward the back of the shop. Usually when Loren is working in the shop on a beautiful day, like today, the back door is left wide open; today it is shut and Katie starts thinking maybe he went with someone somewhere in that persons vehicle. Then she looks out the windows of the back door and just beyond the fence there is a rental van backed up to Loren's trailer. She could see only hands and arms loading something into the van from the trailer, because the van is so close to the trailer indicates all doors were open before the van was backed up. Whatever is being loaded is in 5 gallon white plastic buckets, which are being loaded very quickly.

As Katie opens the back door it makes a loud screeching noise because of its large size and poor condition. Immediately at least two male heads, possibly three, quickly pop out between the van and the trailer, the men have startled looks on they're faces. This all happens so fast it makes both Katie and the men momentarily freeze in their tracks. If there was a third man he ducked his head never to reappear again.

Loren quickly squeezes out of the back of the trailer and walks briskly up to meet Katie who is on her way down toward the vehicles. Loren is very out of breath but breathlessly says, "You have to go back in now Katie."

"Why?" Katie responds with a very puzzled look.

Loren has to think for a few seconds like he is trying to think of something to say and says, "These guys are in a hurry, they are late for an appointment already, we've got to hurry, I'll tell you about it later."

Kate asks, "Can I help?"

"No!" Loren says too loudly- "Just go back inside." Then, as if from a second thought, Loren hurriedly says, "Katie we need ice badly, please run over to the store and pick up two bags, now if you can, O.K.?" Loren is anxious for an immediate answer and is acting very tense and hurried. "I'll get the ice now Loren," Kate replies, "I'll be back in a few minutes," knowing that this is what Loren wants to hear.

Katie immediately leaves- very shaken about what just took place at the shop. Something very dark is going on- she feels it in every bone in her body and it scares her. All the uncertainty surrounding Kate is making her feel that she needs to slow down to think about the events and possible dangers swirling around her and Loren. She needs some time to try to understand what is going on, what to do and where to go. For several minutes she walks the isles of the store in a half daze trying to piece together something of what just happened. Not knowing why, she suddenly feels an urgency to get out of the store so she hurriedly purchases the ice and walks back to the shop feeling very confused.

When she gets to the shop she is even hesitant about using her key then, just as she is turning the lock, Loren rapidly opens the door with a very concerned look on his face. "What took you so long?" He asks with a firm voice. From his tone, Kate senses that his question is not an expression of his concern about her safety but more an inquiry as to what she was doing that caused her trip to the store to take longer than expected. She did not answer Loren immediately, partly due to being dazed from the events of the afternoon, but also to try take in the whole warehouse scene.

She observes that the van, men and white containers are gone. That's what Katie hoped would happen and is probably the unconscious reason why she stayed so long at the store; she just wanted them to disappear.

Katie just tries to stay calm and not to show concern. She shrugs her shoulders as if everything is normal and says, "They were short of cashiers at the store and you know how slow they are anyway, there must have been 5 people in front of me at the checkout." A bald faced lie, but it seems to calm Loren and end the uncomfortable conversation for the moment. For her own safety Kate feels she must maintain her normal routine and act as if she has seen nothing unusual. The problem is she knows that whatever was being loaded into the van is probably very illegal, and this knowledge could be of great danger to her- if anyone suspects she really understands what she saw.

That night Katie could barely eat, and made the excuse that she felt like she was coming down with the flu or maybe a bacterial thing she picked up at the Gardens, or on the bus or something.

Loren didn't talk much except once trying to make a lame excuse of why he and the men in the van were in such a hurry to load those heavy pails and his fear that Katie would have hurt herself if he had let her try to help move the pails.

Loren's comment about her strength didn't sit well with Kate. She thinks to herself, "He damned well knows that I can lift heavy objects. Who in the world has been helping him move those heavy cupboards! "It sure wasn't Rex", she thinks to herself, a little steamed that Loren would even make up such a comment.

After dinner Kate went to bed but could not fall asleep, so she tried reading but that didn't work, so she then tried watching television but that didn't work either. Her mind is just swirling with all kinds of sinister scenes-- most involving illegal drugs and violence.

The problem with Kate, and she knows herself well, is that her head and emotions can go overboard quickly sometimes leading her to make a mountain out of a molehill. Because of Kate's creative mind, sometimes just normal thoughts get blown way out of proportion if the situation and timing aren't just right. Katie wants with all her heart to believe that the situation earlier today involving the van and trailer is just one of those instances. She wants so much to be able to trust Loren.

It seems to take hours before she half-falls asleep. While lying there in the darkness she senses that Loren is just pretending to be asleep because of his stiff pattern of movements which seem different tonight. Katie also thinks of just getting out of the area by going back to Chicago, but that's not possible at the moment because her jeep is still at the auto repair shop being fixed. She hasn't asked Loren how long it will take to have it repaired because she has just been contented being with him, but now circumstances have changed. Kate wants no part of illegal drugs and feels very much at risk. If Loren is selling them and is busted by the cops while she is staying at his warehouse, she could easily be considered an accomplice which would subject her to possibly a heavy jail sentence, along with Loren. Kate is very angry that Loren has put her in a perilous position like this. But again, what if it is just her mind blowing everything out of proportion? Tomorrow she will need to find a way to subtly ask Loren when the jeep will be repaired without raising a red flag about her fears and contemplated get-away. By the middle of night she knows she wants to go back home to Chicago, whether her fertile mind is exaggerating the threats facing her in St. Louis or not. Kate finally falls asleep but her night has been tortured and mostly sleepless.

6

THE STALKER

Katie awakens at 8:00 a.m., which is unusually late for her, yet she remains groggy from the mostly sleepless night. While starting to do some light stretches she hears Loren down in the shop running his table saw. She then notices he had already made a full pot of coffee and appears to have drunk only one cup so there is plenty left for her. This morning Kate needs a lot of coffee to help clear her head to try to deal with where her life goes from here since Loren may be an entirely different person than he appeared to be up until now.

She then walks downstairs to where Loren is working, trying to look very relaxed with a smile on her face and a warm look in her eyes, which is not easy for her under the circumstances. Before stepping off the last stair she notices that his coffee cup is empty, then she says, "Good morning —would you like more coffee?"

Loren seems relieved that she is still talking to him and he responds, "Yes, I really could use another cup". Kate takes his cup upstairs and quickly returns with a full cup for him. After having a couple of sips of coffee, she then tells Loren that she is planning on running this morning- late or not. When she mentioned this - he frowns a little then said "but I need your help right away". Kate is non-committal then excuses herself to go upstairs to change clothes.

Kate takes her time donning her work clothes because she was really looking forward to some time to herself and running always helps her clear her head. Whenever she prepared a "to-do" list for the day she never actually included exercise because that was just a given—she

would exercise. It is definitely the top priority for her own well-being-
it even topped her artwork. She finished dressing at a snail's pace.

When she did come downstairs, Loren asks her to sweep the floor.
In reality the shop floor didn't need sweeping. This morning is the first
time even a little sawdust could be seen on the floor since she swept it
just two days ago--and Loren is not a clean freak. It seems the events of
yesterday are starting to intrude on her today. Her mind unconsciously
senses that Loren is watching her and is uneasy that Kate could separate from him and talk with someone about what she saw Loren doing
yesterday. After she finishes sweeping the shop floor Loren says to her,
"Let's go get some breakfast, I'll bet you are as hungry as I am."

Katie responds, "Sure lets go, I am hungry and need some fresh air,
since I won't have time to jog this morning." as cheerfully as she could
muster, then added, "Maybe if my work is done early this afternoon I
can go for a run, huh?"

Loren looks at her with gentle questioning eyes, trying to disguise
his true feelings, then stammers as if trying to think of something to say,
"Sure Kate, but only if we get done with this work, I'm so behind, well,
we'll just have to see O.K.?"

Once in the passenger side of the truck, Katie thinks of her jeep,
but doesn't dare ask about it because of the tension Loren is showing
right now. She wishes she knew the jeep's location then, on her own,
she could try to find out directly from the auto-shop when it would be
fixed and be ready to drive. If she could locate that shop hopefully, the
office help at the auto-shop doesn't feel the need to confirm her plans
with Loren.

Loren pulls the truck into a parking space at the Courtesy and says,
"Katie, one of these mornings I want to take you to a restaurant out by
St. Charles, they have the best omelet's, but frankly I'm short of money
and we're going to be way too busy trying to catch up on the cupboards
to even think of going there today. Maybe next week after the cupboards are installed."

Katie says nothing to Loren but thinks quietly to herself, "Next week,
I wonder how long Loren thinks I'll be staying in St Louis anyway?"

They enter the restaurant and sat down at one of the back booths where they usually sit, if available, and then both ordered the same 2-egg special. Kate and Loren each picked up sections of the newspaper, Loren reading the sports and Kate the main news. On page three there were photos following the story about the woman who was murdered three days ago. One photo shows the victim, Susie, who has red hair, is average looking and with eyes which appear to have large dark circles around them and a second photo of the ex-boyfriend who still had not been located. The story said that both Susie and her ex-boyfriend were known drug users, and that she had been charged recently with possession of a small amount of methamphetamine, but was out on bond and due to go to court next week.

It was reported to police that the ex-boyfriend had fled the state and possibly was hiding somewhere in Oklahoma or Texas. Both Susie and the ex-boyfriend were being investigated by the city police who had reason to believe that both of them were involved in selling large quantities of street drugs. The article ended with a request to readers to send any information or leads about either the victim or ex-boyfriend to the St. Louis Police Department.

When Katie looked at the newspaper photo of this woman, Susie, and noticed her eyes, she was sure she had been doing hard drugs for quite a while and/or had lived a very hard life generally. Katie was feeling genuine sorrow and empathy for her because it was likely she had been a victim at some point in her life. At the same time Katie thought to herself, "If this woman had been selling large quantities of drugs, like the police believe, then she has produced many other victims by her ruinous acts involving the distribution and selling of meth and other narcotics. Kate mentioned the article to Loren who seemed so mesmerized by the sports section that he seemed to not even hear her, or didn't want to for some reason.

When they finished breakfast and were driving back to the shop, Katie got up the nerve to ask Loren about her jeep, "Loren, just by chance do you know when my jeep will be done and be brought back to your shop?"

Loren answers, "When I asked them how long it would be the other day they said they had two vehicles to finish before they could start yours. That's all I had asked them, when we get back to the shop remind me to call them to find out when they expect it to be done. I'd call them now but I don't have their phone number with me, ok."

Katie was somewhat relieved, it sounded to her like he was being straight with her and soon her jeep would be back in her possession.

Loren's cell phone rang as he was unlocking the door to the shop, Katie walked in, leaving him on the sidewalk to take his call. She went out to the back of the warehouse to make sure Rex, who was chained, had fresh water and food. When she came back inside after making Rex happy, Loren was already busy putting sealer into the paint can for his paint sprayer. Loren has facemasks for both he and Katie, which is important as the sealer is toxic to breath.

The first of several cupboards to be sprayed have eight doors attached. Before putting on his mask Loren asks Katie to hold the doors open so he could spray the interior first, then she shut the doors so he could spray the exterior. They worked quickly, sealer dries fast so it definitely takes two people to do this properly. After the first cupboard is finished and refilling the spray can a couple times, they go down the line and do all 6 of the units, interiors first -exteriors second. The fumes in the building, even with the large back door open, had become over-whelming. Both Loren and Kate step outside for a while to get away from the fumes and fill their lungs with fresh air.

While sitting outside, a red truck pulls up next to the alley and a man gets out and walks through the open gate into the yard. Loren greets him and says, "Kate, I'd like you to meet Jack Colbert, he's the one who left the briefcase in my truck the other day." Katie says "Hi" then comments on what a nice looking truck he has. Jack replies "Yes, I replace my trucks every other year because I put so many miles on them."

This made Katie wonder what he does to run up so many miles on his trucks so she asks him. Smiling, Jack replies, "I buy out commercial businesses and factories that have gone out of business and resell the inventories at less than wholesale to whoever wants to buy the items, I travel pretty much all over the United States, but only if the business wanting to sell to me warrants my time and efforts. So far it's paid off very well." What do you do for a living Katie?" Katie hesitates to say for a second, because since the big recession her business has fallen off tremendously and the first things to quit selling it seems are always the artistic and luxury items. After a pause, Katie just says jokingly, "Well, I'm not sure anymore considering the economy and all, actually I'm an artist and I'm in galleries in Chicago and California at the present. But art is hard to sell right now. But I'm doing o.k."

Loren then steps into the conversation telling Katie, "Jack and I have some business to take care of, please excuse us for a little while will you Kate?" Then Loren did something he almost never does, he gives Kate a hug and pat on the butt.

"Boy" Katie thought," he's really trying hard to stay on my good side."

Both men walk inside the fume-infested building almost like there are no fumes at all, although, Loren coughed a few times on the way in. They are in the warehouse only a few minutes before they come out both acting concerned about something, but don't express what's causing the concern. Kate senses it wasn't the fumes that bothered them but something much bigger.

That afternoon after Jack departed, both Loren and Katie fine-sanded all the cupboards and then put the first finish coat of lacquer on them with the spray gun. "Loren wasn't kidding when he said they're really working today," thought Kate. It was 7:30 P.M. when they finished, both of them exhausted from the work and kind of ill feeling from the fumes, as the masks helped only a little. They ordered pizza that night and both fell asleep before 10:00 P.M. But before they fell asleep Loren apologized for forgetting to call the auto-body shop about her jeep. She appreciated his apology, but she had to admit that she had totally forgotten about the jeep herself because they had been was so busy the whole day. Usually it is only Loren who is so absent-minded.

Very early in the morning when it was still dark outside Loren slipped down into Katie's bed and held her firmly, it was a masculine warm feel to her, at first she was tense because her feelings are so knotted up as to what is really going on with Loren, but she realized quite quickly that him holding her was because he needed the human contact of being with her, not of greed, but of needing to be close to someone.

It was so seldom that Loren did this- just holding her, because lately their sex had changed so much that softer feelings were not even part of their lives, only hard raw lust.

Katie rolled over to face him, he kissed her face gently, first her lips then her forehead and nose and soon his tongue was in her mouth probing. The kiss turned into a hotter feeling that made them both want more. Katie loving to give pleasure hungrily kissed Loren's neck, then chest, stomach and her face went down in his groin area. Katie is so warm from being under the blankets and this warming plus the natural hotness of her arousal made Loren intensely pleasured. Katie put her mouth on his penis and sucked gently, Loren moaning very soft and deeply, Kate's intensity of what she was doing made him pull her mouth off him, as he wanted this to last a while longer.

Loren kissed Katie's breasts and then each nipple he put between his teeth and gently nipped before sucking, then he kissed her ribcage, then stomach and into the v part of her inner thighs. He put his mouth on the soft, damp area and opened her with his tongue and used his tongue to lick and kiss her clitoris. Loren was driving her wild and all at once her buttocks moved upwards off the bed with exotic tension as she came. Loren continued to try to kiss her, but the feeling was so intense that it was unbearable for her. She brought his face to hers and whispered, please go in me Loren, please- she needs him inside her so badly he is driving her crazy.

Loren's so hard and thick, his thrust firmly inside her. Her wetness and warmth making him become larger yet; he pushes hard, long and deep strokes inside her, both of them loving the ecstatic feel. There are no ropes, nor whips, nor chains needed, this is pleasure they both had been missing for too long. Man to woman, woman to man. Katie climaxed over and over, her verbal words and the tensing of her drawing tight inside made Loren realize what he was doing to her. Then Loren pushed so hard inside and stayed there very stiff and intense as he came, pulsating hard and long. Katie at that moment, without even thinking, said very softly, "Loren, I love you so very, very much."

They just lay and talk lovingly, something Loren seldom ever did after having sex. After a good while, Katie decides to get up and make coffee, the sun is just coming up around 6:30 A.M. and it is such a relaxed morning that they actually spend the morning together instead of separating to do activities apart like they usually do.

Katie says to Loren around 8:00, "I think I'm going running for a while, my missing exercise yesterday just makes me yearn more for it today." She then adds, "Last night makes me yearn for more of that in the near future, too", she is smiling a genuine smile because her eyes show the happiness she is feeling.

Loren looks at her with kind of a kidding but firm look and says, "I think that you could wear me out, Katie." In reality, this morning was kind of a twist of what we usually have been doing in bed." He also adds with a more serious tone, "Don't let it go to your head, Kate."

Katie finished her second cup of coffee and changes into running clothes, while sitting on the edge of the bed and putting on her shoes and socks Loren asks her where she plans going jogging this morning. Katie answers, "Where I usually run around Lafayette Park once or twice, then through it sometimes. Loren, have you ever walked the interior of that park? It's really pretty. Did you know there is not only the pond, but a stream that runs through there too? I love it there-- it's kind of a therapeutic haven right in the middle of a city." With that she jumps up with lots of enthusiasm and spunk and starts to walk out the door saying as she goes, "See you later."

Kate got all the way downstairs before realizing she had forgotten her keys so she went back up to get them. As she enters the room, Loren is just auto-dialing someone's number on his cell, but when he sees her come in, he clicks off the phone. He asks, "Did you forget something?"

Kate just nods holding up her key after she picks it up off his table, smiles at him and heads for the door saying, "I won't be gone long." She is out the door and has it locked it in seconds. The sun is shining and it feels like it is 65 to 70 degree' already on this early autumn morning. She thinks to herself, "I'm glad I'm here running as it's only in the 40"s at home this morning." She started jogging with a real good rhythm right away; sometimes it takes a block or two before she can build up this type of easy-flowing form. "It must have been this morning's start with Loren that is making life so wonderful at this moment," she thinks silently with an inner warmth flooding her mind.

She has crossed the large intersection of Jefferson and Lafayette and only has a couple of more blocks to go before entering the park, her rhythm is perfect- when she got to the first corner of the park she slows her pace a little, as she has decided to run the circumference twice today, instead of just the usual one time. She feels great and just loves the moment of freedom she has as she paces along.

She runs the East side of the park and notices the red truck that was at Loren's shop yesterday is sitting in a diagonal parking spot next to the park facing her as she runs. Jack Colbert, the truck's owner, is sitting in the truck talking on his cell phone and, when he sees her, he just waves and continues to talk on his phone.

Kate waves back but keeps running, she runs the remainder of the park's circumference and as she is rounding the corner where she first saw Jack, he is still sitting there engaged in conversation. Again, they both wave at each other and both continue doing their own thing.

After running twice around the outside of the park, Katie runs the diagonal path inside the grounds. First, she goes to the pond then jogs to the West of it and as she rounds the curve she comes to the stream and bridge. Again, like the last time, when she is here she slows her pace to a walk--this is her place to relax and contemplate

Sitting on a stone above the stream like she had the other day Kate found not the quiet solitude that she had the last time she was here, but the eeriest feeling that she is not alone. She looks around subtly trying not to draw attention and sees no one. "Must be my imagination again," she murmurs to herself. She heard a twig break close by but still sees no one. Again, she feels uncomfortable so she stands to leave when she sees a silhouette of a person on the knoll hidden amongst a few trees and bushes, seemingly looking down at her. Because of the knoll, distance, trees and other vegetation she can't tell if it is a man or woman, but the build of the person from this distance sure looked like a man to her.

Kate feels at that moment that someone had been watching her the whole time she has been sitting by the stream. She immediately starts jogging in the same direction as she had come into the park on the diagonal road, the opposite direction from where this person is standing. She tries to keep a good standard rhythm- to make it look as if she is just jogging- but on the inside of her she is scared- very scared, and she wants to sprint to get out of the park!

It isn't until she is almost back to the shop that she realizes that whoever the person was standing behind the tree was in close vicinity to where Jack Colbert's truck had parked just outside the perimeter of the park. She ran hard the rest of the way to get to the front door of Loren's shop, breathless as she is- she is able to get the key in the keyhole with the first try then goes in shutting the door quickly then leaning against it to catch her breath. Then, to her surprise, who is standing there right in front of her but Loren-- just ending a conversation on his phone, which occurred right after she'd leaned against the door.

Loren smiles at her and says, "Did you have a good run?" He seems genuinely relaxed and this, in turn, helps Katie relax a little.

She responds, "Yes, I did, until I thought that someone was stalking me, then I became a little scared and ran back here."

Loren just laughed at her in a gentle way and says, "Katie, that park is pretty safe during the daylight hours, I sincerely doubt if anyone was stalking you, you know how your imagination runs overboard sometimes. Did you see this so-called person following you?"

Kate replies, "No, I didn't look back, I was afraid to, I just ran as fast as I could once away from the park." Maybe your right though, my mind does go overboard sometimes doesn't it," then with spunk she adds, "I'll be damned if anyone is going to keep me from running there, I'm going back tomorrow morning to run. If it's just my imagination then I'll overcome that problem too, by just being there again- won't I."

They both finely-sanded the cupboards again, to prepare them for the final coat of lacquer. "At last!" Katie says out loud. Then Loren expresses to Katie how much of a help she has been to him. This, of course, makes her feel good as she really appreciates receiving some recognition and a thank you from him. They both donned the masks before spraying the lacquer to help avoid inhaling the toxic fumes. Once finished Loren and Kate went out to the yard, leaving two huge fans running in the shop to ventilate and de-fume the large room as fast as possible.

Loren quips, "As soon as it's safe to walk in there, why don't we clean up and take the rest of the day off to do something fun? How about going to one of the vineyards outside of town and enjoy the scenery and a bottle or two of good wine." This sounds wonderful to Katie, it would be the first time on this trip that they actually got out together to have fun.

It seems like quite a few minutes, to Kate anyway, before they could enter the building to go upstairs and get cleaned up to go out for the afternoon. When Kate thought it was safe she entered the building- still smelling some fumes –but not too bad though, then she looks back towards Loren wondering why he isn't coming in.

7

VISIT TO THE VINEYARDS

Kate goes right up the stairs then quickly undresses and steps into the shower. The shower is quite refreshing and she lets the fine spray just splash against her back for a minute relieving some tightness in her neck and back. During this brief respite she thinks about Loren's behavior the past few days, including the excessive time he has been spending on his cell phone. She thinks to herself, "I've never seen him on the phone like this—it's really getting ridiculous!" By the time Katie has finished showering; Loren is then just arriving at the top of the stairs still wearing his work clothes.

Loren walks into the room as Katie is drying off, and he kiddingly says, "What's taking you so long."

Katie keeps the kidding going by saying, "Are you going like that?" giving him a comic head to toe going-over with her eyes. He laughs and starts stripping off his clothing then steps into shower. As he is showering Kate, still unclothed, puts on face cream, body lotion and a nice fragrance. In a few minutes Loren steps out of the shower dripping wet while standing on a towel that he uses as a floor mat. He pauses for a moment to watch her, and then catches her eye with a smile. As they are both naked, Kate could tell he is having thoughts about not going anywhere, except maybe closer to a bed.

Knowing his thoughts, she immediately says "Oh no! No, no, no, let's go out first, and then come back here and then---we'll have an unforgettable time in or near the bed or wherever we land," she says laughingly, then adding," I think we both need to get out of the city and go to the vineyards, they are so beautiful to visit especially this time of the year.

Can we go out west out by Augusta or Defiance, where you've taken me before? It's gorgeous out in that area." Loren replies, "OK, that's fine with me, but tonight lady"- then he pauses-it won't be all roses and that lovey stuff; it will be our kind of sex. O.K.?"

Kate smiles and as she slowly walks out of the bathroom, butt naked, she turns her head around and blows him a kiss.

They are on the road in no time taking Hwy 40 W to Interstate 94. The traffic is starting to get busy especially on Hwy. 40 in the city, but once out in the country, the traffic is much lighter. The hills are beautiful, and resplendent with the colors of autumn. Once Kate and Loren are in the country they silently enjoy the ride and beautiful scenery. After a while Loren breaks the silence, "the weather is so warm and sunny this is gonna be a great time, I'm pretty sure of it anyway, huh Kate?" Kate just nods her head.

Once they arrive at Kate's favorite vineyard they select an outdoor picnic table overlooking the Missouri River Valley, the scenery is breathtaking. Loren orders a bottle of Seyvel- a fruity wine, which is quickly served and they both sip from their glasses taking in every hill and valley and all the autumn colors-- -the beauty is overwhelming! After the first bottle is empty, they order a second bottle plus a roast beef sandwich to share. Loren does this often because he likes sharing food with Kate, he doesn't do it to be cheap, but he genuinely enjoys sharing sustenance with her. Kate likes doing it too as it makes her feel a closer bond with Loren.

Occasionally Loren looks down at his cell phone to see who has called, he must have it on silent mode and is recording messages as they come in. Only once did he have to excuse himself to make a phone call.

The roast beef sandwich and the second bottle of wine are served to the table, which they share together along with a beautiful afternoon. They have some occasional small talk-- about some birds flying by and then later a cloud which changes shape by the wind—but mostly silence after the sandwich is eaten. As they relax, Kate thinks of her relationship with Loren. He is being a little more gracious than usual, which gives Katie hope that the "real"- lovemaking of the night before has gotten to him. The sex they have been having lately is far from loving- it is hardcore sex, which Kate likes sometimes but all she has ever wanted from Loren is his friendship and love, not really a commitment, just his love and friendship. Both words, "love" and "friendship", have broad and equivalent meanings to Kate. In her mind, you had to have one to have the other. It has sometimes been tough when she visits Loren in St Louis. Only having one room to share together is hard for the both of them, because of the lack of space, plus she is used to her own personal conveniences which she leaves at home like her computer and her books, etc. because to her bringing even some of these belongings for short visits is often more of a hassle than doing without them. Two bags are plenty for her; traveling as light as possible is Kate's style.

Both of them are feeling the pleasant effect of the two bottles of wine and they talk for a bit about whether to order another bottle then decide not to, then they chat some more about their enjoyment of the afternoon. They have stayed at the Vineyard quite a long time and the sun is starting to set. They are relaxed and continuing the good conversation when Loren asks her, "Did you enjoy the stream this morning at the park Katie?"

Katie immediately says, "Yes, it's my favorite part of the pa---park" she stutters over the word park because her mind is racing to try to understand how Loren even knew she was at the stream that morning? She hadn't said a word to him about being in that particular spot. Kate looks at him with a questioning look and asks," Loren, I never told you I was down by the stream-how did you know that I was there?"

Loren's face turns somewhat red—he stammers and it takes him a second to gather his thoughts before saying, "Yes you did Kate, you know how you can sometimes talk a thousand words a minute, you sure did tell me you were down by the stream."

Katie knows it's not so- this time he can't t use the excuse of her blowing things out of proportion, she had only mentioned the stream once to him a couple of days ago, not since, because she knew how much Loren loved natural environments, possibly even more than Kate. She wanted to take him to the park to see the wonderful stream, the stones and the enchanting bridge. She knew he would love it and it is so close to his warehouse, but she knew she had mentioned this beautiful spot to Loren only once—but not this time.

She became silent almost immediately; Kate is starting to feel pangs of paranoia again. She knows now that someone is watching her and that Loren is somehow involved. "Why?" Kate asks herself silently. In reality, it takes her very little time to realize why. She was witness to a malefic event two days ago involving the loading of those mysterious pails in a rental van. A series of bizarre events have followed.

On the way home they were both silent excepting for one question that Katie asks, "How much longer is my jeep going to be in the repair shop?"

Loren quietly answered, "I don't know."

When they reach the shop Katie doesn't really want to go in but she feels she has no choice. Without her jeep she can't go anywhere, plus even prior to her departure for St Louis her funds were already short due to the economic recession and her artwork not selling as it had been before. Loren had mentioned in one phone call that he would pay her hourly for working in his shop but hasn't mentioned anything about paying her since she arrived in St Louis. Tonight she feels trapped; she knows that Loren is lying to her about the stream in the park, and he knows that she knows he's lying, making being together and the whole situation very awkward and uncomfortable. Also, she is starting to understand why, since the van incident the other day, he has been showing more tenderness and patience to her than he normally does. Kate thinks to herself, "Probably even the sex they had that morning was concocted to have her warm up to him." Too many things just don't seem right to her. Katie is totally silent now, not asking questions or telling Loren what she is thinking or planning to do, but she knows as soon as her jeep is back in her hands she will be leaving for home, pronto.

Once they are at the warehouse door, Kate waits for Loren to enter the building first. When she walks in behind him she proceeds toward the upstairs trying not to show any nervousness. At the same time Loren remembers he had left Rex on the chain outback and goes out to retrieve him. When Katie enters Loren's room alone, she looks around at every detail of the room in the context of what she has seen the past few days--and is hit with some starting perceptions. Loren doesn't appear to be actually living here, meaning he had a second hidden life somewhere else and she is being used for a reason unrelated to helping him do the woodworking and casting countertops and fireplaces of stone. As her mind is churning, questions keep coming to her about the van—"Why were the men so startled when she showed up unexpectedly? Pails of what? Why would anyone be so concerned about plastic pails of what? She searched for every "good" answer she could think of but none of them had the ring of truth under the slightest scrutiny. Of course, the inevitable answer is "illegal drugs-- large amounts of illegal drugs! What else?" She knew it all along- but Kate didn't want to let herself believe it, even though she instantly knew it in her heart when she witnessed the loading incident. Kate whispers to herself alone in the room, "Love is blind and this love is bullshit."

Then she kept thinking silently, "Jack Colbert was here yesterday, conducting business alone with Loren, when in the past when someone had a business negotiation with Loren, he would almost always conduct such business in her presence. That has changed now. During her 5-day stay 100% of the phone calls received by Loren prompted him to ask Kate to leave the room or he would excuse himself and step away from her for privacy. All she wants to do is go home now, and is nervous about a possible confrontation tomorrow morning when she talks to Loren and demands that her jeep be returned to her, finished or not. If it isn't finished, he can reimburse her one way or another to get it fixed when she back in Chicago. It is drivable as is. The repair is only for dent and paint damage. As she waited, Kate's fear started to ease up a little, thinking that Loren would let her go without much of a fuss- "they are at least friends after all, aren't they?"

Loren is taking a long time to bring Rex upstairs which, in some ways is a relief for her to be away from him, but in others it makes her wonder what he is doing? Like making another call seems likely. Just at that moment Loren arrives upstairs and acts as if everything is fine, that nothing has happened and he seems more relaxed than usual.

Rex is thirsty and hungry in that order and proceeds to indulge himself and Loren asks Katie if she would like a cold beer? She responds

"No, I can still feel the wine a little bit and I'm starting to get a head-ache, 'Thanks anyway."

Loren just shrugs his shoulders, walks over to the ice chest and grabs a cold beer dripping wet, opens the can and started drinking the beer slowly as he walks over to start his computer. After sitting down he hits the start button then stares at the screen for several minutes. After a while later he speaks up, "Boy, Katie you sure are quiet tonight, what's wrong?"

Due to Kate's inexplicable obsession with Loren, just the sound of his voice is almost soothing to her and seems to relax some of the ten-sion that she feels. She drops her head then sits silently thinking for a moment before saying, "Loren, I need you to be very truthful with me," then hesitates again before continuing, "What were you guy's loading the other day from the back of your trailer into the rental van?"

There is more silence before Loren responds to her, "We were load-ing special glue that I had picked up two weeks ago while in Atlanta, the men you saw were one week late in picking it up and it was urgently needed for a big commercial job here in the city. You know, I was down in Atlanta to deliver some architectural pieces that I had sold. These guys paid me well to bring the glue back, it was like a double bonus for me, I made good money on my sale plus I got the opportunity to bring back the glue besides. What's wrong with that? Why do you ask me questions like that, what's the concern anyway?" Loren's voice is start-ing to rise like he is becoming irritated.

Katie doesn't care if he is irritated, and then asks another question, "Why were the vehicles in the storage yard so close together and why were the men in such a hurry?"

"Damn it!" Loren screamed at her, "Why can't you just be satisfied with what I said, why keep coming up with more questions? Damn it Kate." Then he stomps out of the room slamming the door behind him.

Kate sits there silently for a while, she has no idea if Loren is down-stairs or if he left the building and drove somewhere. Rex had followed him out the door and neither one came back. Kate isn't interested in watching television, or reading, or just sitting, or whether she stays or leaves the warehouse. She just needs something to do because there is no way she can go to sleep now. The bathroom is filthy- so she decides she'll clean it. She starts with the sink, getting rid of old razors, discarded wrappers, etc. Then she cleans the shower from top to bottom, and then she looks at the deep window sill that holds much of Loren's personal care belongings. "By the look of things, the last time this bathroom had been cleaned had to be over three months ago, if not longer," she thinks to herself.

Kate starts by removing all the products off the windowsill like mouthwash, toothbrushes, after shave, etc. and as she is almost finished clearing everything off, she notices a bullet on the windowsill, one lone bullet- a fairly large one. In her mind she thinks the bullet was for an expensive gun or a law enforcement officer's gun, but she is just guessing- she really has no idea. "OK, stop", Katie mumbles softly to herself, "I'm going overboard, that's what I'm doing. I have no idea- about any of this, this is all just really confusing. Leave it alone right now, Kate, it's all just driving you crazy." Katie gently places the bullet with all of Loren's other personal items, then scrubs off the sill and wipes all his toiletries before she puts everything back on the sill except the bullet, which she hides deep down in her suitcase under a stack of clothing.

Loren never did come home last night and she has no idea where he and Rex have gone. All she knows is she wants to go home tomorrow morning. Finally she is exhausted and falls asleep, then in the middle of the night a dream comes to her.

THE 3rd DREAM

A grassy knoll appears in a city park, a blanket is spread upon the ground just at the top of the knoll, Loren is on the blanket in a half kneeling position, with his head close to the ground and he is blowing large amounts of white powder from his nose out on to the blanket, over and over powder is being blown from his nose-- and as he is doing this a large group of people, especially women, are running toward him to get some of this powder. He gives a portion to them all.

8

ALMOST A HIT & RUN

The dream awakens Kate with a start, her head is perspiring and she feels clammy all over her body. It is dark, still in the middle of the night, and all is quiet in the building but she can hear two hookers outside on the sidewalk arguing. She can tell they are hookers from the coarse words being spoken and the fact that they are arguing over how to divide their crack cocaine. They love their crack.

In the past Loren had mentioned to Kate that if hookers are outside late at night to be extra quiet, because these "ladies of the evening" are known to put bricks or rocks through windows and, if they know you are home they will ring the doorbell, then if you answer they ask for money, and if you don't give them money- they will quite often do damage to something of value on the property. Kate sure doesn't want anyone to know she is there, with or without Loren. She could not go back to sleep the rest of the night and brews a pot of coffee around 4:00 in the morning. She drank the entire pot by 6:00 AM and it is still dark outside.

Last night was torturously restless for Kate and now she is shaky from too much caffeine. Kate's whole trip seems to be turning into a nightmare. If she just knew where her jeep is located she would go and get it herself, except for problem number 2, she is almost completely out of cash. Basically, she is screwed and she knows it. She has no choice but to wait for Loren to return and then try to convince him to help her get home. It is his fault that her jeep even needs repair. "Where the hell is he," Kate blurts out loud, as her anger and frustration increase every time she looks at her watch.

Then, without warning, the door to the room opens and in walks Loren with Rex at the lead wagging his tail. Considering he supposedly had no place to go, Loren sure doesn't look too rumpled, and in a lot better condition than Kate who had a bed to sleep in.

There is dead silence for a few minutes after Loren shut the door behind him, he looks at Katie who, in turn, looks back at him- both of them pretty unhappy with each other and their body language reflects the obvious. Loren goes into the bathroom to relieve himself, then walks back into the room and sits in his chair and grabs the remote to turn on his television. He does not look at Katie at all; she feels that Loren is ignoring her just to unnerve her, which just adds to her shakiness from drinking too much coffee. Kate gets up off the bed in her nightshirt and walks out into the large warehouse room just to break the awkward tension in the other room. Her main focus is to get possession of her jeep ASAP. She tries to calm herself as much as she can then walks back into the room to talk with Loren. "Loren, I need my jeep back today," Kate says as bravely as she can muster. Loren just looks at her and says, "I'll see what I can do," then goes back to watching television.

Katie is upset, frustrated and needs to get away from Loren so she decides to go for a jog and get some fresh air. She gets dressed in her jogging clothes and leaves without saying a word to him. Because of everything that has been happening, including the incident at the park yesterday morning, she decides to run a different route today. She is just going to stay on the sidewalks of the business district running East on Jefferson St., "it is an iffy neighborhood but anyone who is dangerous is pretty much off the streets by now," she thinks to herself. It is almost 7:00 a.m. and dawn is providing a little light and traffic is starting to flow on the streets too. She is feeling reasonably safe, at least safer than how she felt at Loren's warehouse anyway.

She runs for as long as she can without slowing down much except for crossing the side streets. She runs for about 15 or 16 blocks before making a U-turn suddenly when seeing a group of young men gathered at the street corner about a half block from her. She knows they are probably selling drugs to cars passing by on the streets and she doesn't want to be any place close to that scene. Now heading the other direction back toward Loren's shop she sees coming right at her what looks like the red truck owned by Jack Colbert. He is going too fast for driving in town and as he is getting closer to her he swerves up on the sidewalk right at her! Kate dives over the other side of a short fence surrounding a fast food place just as he swerves and hits a large concrete planter the city had placed on the sidewalk to beautify the area. The truck then backs up and speeds off down the street. Kate's nerves are now shattered and she doesn't know what to do, except perhaps notify the police? She can't prove anything. "Oh my God, that son-of-a bitch just tried to kill me," she shouts out loud knowing that the only witnesses to what just happened are the drug dealers who had already split the scene and who obviously don't want any part of police contact whatsoever.

Katie knows she is in real trouble. She does not have her cell phone with her so she can't call her family in Chicago- which in some ways, may have been a good thing because that's exactly what she would have done, with the result of making her family feel worried. Katie is having a hard time stopping tears from coming to her eyes as she starts jogging back toward Loren's warehouse. She is devastated by the attack that just happened and terrified by what may happen next. When she is about six blocks from the warehouse, she sees Loren driving his truck in her direction and she instinctively starts edging closer to the buildings staying away from the street thinking that he would try to run her down similar to the failed first attempt. Now the tears are really flowing, "A frantic- sobbing jogger", she thinks to herself, "probably the first one in America."

Loren sees her because he pulls over just as she is passing him by. Leaning over inside the cab of the truck he rolls down the passenger window and calls out, "Katie, get in."

"No", she responds, "I can't."

" Why can't you Kate?" Loren asks.

"Because, that's all- just because." Katie is out of breath and struggling with talking and crying, all at the same time.

Loren looks at her with sympathy in his eyes and gently says "Kate, please get in the truck now; do this for you, not me."

She stands there for a moment, trying to think through the confusion of the earlier attack and Loren's sudden appearance, which is very difficult, and she is very scared. Katie slowly opens the passenger side of his truck and gets in with Loren.

Loren does a U-turn in the middle of Jefferson Street and drives back toward his warehouse. He takes Katie's hand in his while driving and squeezes it firmly. "Katie," he says with concern in his voice, "Katie, what is wrong with you?" You have been so different this trip down here, you are not yourself- you are paranoid about everything. You don't trust me---"

Kate blurted out interrupting Loren, "Your friend Jack Colbert just tried to kill me." her crying becomes uncontrollable, saying these words only made her worse.

Loren questioned her "What? Katie get a grip on yourself, what are you talking about, what are you saying?" His face and eyes are showing disbelief to what he heard Katie just say.

Katie again taking deep breaths, repeated, "Jack Colbert just tried to kill me-- he tried to run over me with his truck." Her sobbing has now subsided quite a bit and she seems to becoming dazed from anymore thought or feeling and is almost in shock.

Loren went silent. They are almost back to the warehouse now, stopped at a red traffic light waiting for it to turn green. He never let go of her hand, only holding it gently but with a warm firmness, trying to reassure her that he is there for her.

After they walk back into the shop, Loren holds her, his arms feel so warm and secure to Kate. "Look" he says, " I really think that possibly you are imagining all of this"— Katie immediately gets tense and Loren feels her stiffen, and then he proceeds to say, "and maybe this really did happen, I don't know this Jack very well and today I will get to the bottom of this, I promise, Kate." With that they both go upstairs, Katie feeling numb and dazed but relieved that she has told Loren what happened and that he believed her. They had been friends and lovers too long for anyone to hurt her, as long as Loren is around, anyway.

Once in Loren's room he offers her a cup of coffee which she rejects- knowing that it would only make her shakier. Loren steps out of the room taking his cell phone and returns seconds later. This increases Kate's anxiety level that he left her to make another secret call. Loren sits down with her on the bed and says, "You have got to be exhausted from crying so much and running at full speed when I found you. You must be dehydrated, so at least drink some water or something won't you?" At that moment Loren gets up to go over by the microwave located behind his bookcase and returns seconds later with a glass of water for Kate. "Here drink this, you look like you really need it, then lay down, I promise I won't leave you here alone." Kate looks at him numbly but with hopeful trust in her swollen eyes and, did as he asked, taking the glass in her hand, first sipping, then quickly drinking until the glass is empty. She then lies down on the bed, starring up at Loren who is standing over her with concern in his face and then all at once her eyes rolled back in her head and she is out.

Loren immediately clicked a number on his cell phone and says to whoever is on the other end of the conversation. "She's out. I have got to move fast." There is a silence because the other person is talking, then Loren says with anger in his voice, "I know that her seeing us the other day was not good and I understand the repercussions of something like that, but you guys were told to leave it alone, she would have soon forgot what she had seen, you sure as hell were not to try to kill her.

"She isn't a liar and what she told me is the truth, one other woman has died this last week, because of our stupidity now you've to tried killing Katie too. I care a lot for her and don't want to see her dead or hurt, there are other ways of taking care of this problem, leave it up to me for Christ's sake." Loren clicked the phone off then immediately puts his mind to work on what to do next. He has already been through this thinking process extensively and he knows there is only one strategy he can think of to save Katie's life, which means getting her away from the city or get her involved in some way, so she won't talk, if he has to.

That's how he became involved himself-- owing money to someone-- who in return needed favors done by him for a payoff. It isn't as bad as you would think most of the time, but when a woman is beaten to death and you are partly responsible then it's really bad. He needs to get Katie away from here or involved without her realizing what he has done to her.

He cares for her, her life is worth much more than dying for something she wasn't even part of in the first place. Loren had become tough, real hardened, it shows in his eyes. But Katie is a hope of light for part of his soul.

Loren immediately calls the auto-body shop and left instructions to have Kate's jeep returned to his warehouse. It takes only about 20 minutes for the jeep to be driven there. His phone instructions he left for them, "Park the jeep out back on the blacktop driveway, the gate will be open, just back it in and leave. Someone will be in to pay you for repairing and hiding it for the few days you've had it at your shop. No receipt needed--its cash." Loren then hangs up.

While waiting for the jeep to be delivered Loren injected Kate with a shot of Heroin, realizing the dose of liquid G he had put her in the water was short lived -but acted fast, with this other drug she would be knocked out for quite a while, although he might have to stop and inject her one more time to get her to the destination that he has for her.

Loren whispers to her, "Katie, this is for your own good." then he adds, "I'm sorry." He knows she can't hear anything he said, but he means what he said. He checked her pulse, it is slower than normal but he knows she will come to eventually. He gathers a few clothes for her as fast as he can plus the other equipment he may need to hide her at the location where he is taking her. He throws everything into garbage bags, he then takes the items down to her jeep and loads them in the back. Then hurriedly he runs upstairs and bodily picks her up, she is dead weight and Katie is not a petite woman, a little taller than he is and probably weighing around 145 to 150 pounds. He hefted her up on his shoulder and slowly, agonizingly carries her down the stairs, which he fears are too long to make it down safely. Rex is nervous realizing that something isn't right but trusting his master he follows, but is afraid to lead.

By the time Loren reaches the bottom of the stairs he is exhausted and breathing heavily. He is almost half way to her jeep parked in the back and he knows he can't stop for both Katie's sake and his. He needs to get her out of St. Louis.

Loren moves a little faster once he is down stairs and on the flat ground. Once at the jeep, he leans her against the fender, then takes his free hand and opens the front passenger door. Then carefully, but quickly puts her in the front seat, belting her in and then lowering the seat to a reclining position and she continues to sleep. He had wanted to drive his truck, but it doesn't have as many conveniences as the jeep, such as fully-reclining seats and tinted windows which provide the privacy Loren needs for this trip. He then opens the back passenger door and Rex jumps in enthusiastically. Loren is glad that that he has vines covering his chain link fence, which make it difficult for anyone to see inside the yard, and easier for him to load Kate in privacy even in daylight. He locks the jeep doors and runs upstairs one more time to get some things he'd forgotten, including his camera and miniature camcorder. "These item", he thinks to himself, "are the most important items to take, how stupid of me to almost forget them." With the cameras in hand, he gets in the jeep, backs it out of the drive just outside of the gate- then padlocks it shut. Then in short order Loren is heading South on 55 leaving the City of St. Louis. Katie doesn't stir for about the first hour, and then she starts to move a little in her seat, her body is sort of jerking in reaction to coming down from the heavy dose of drugs.

By now Loren is off interstate 55 and on a two lane secondary road. He pulls over at a roadside parking area and stops, opens the back of the jeep, then pulls a needle, syringe, spoon and more drugs from a small paper sack behind the spare tire. Loren returns to the front seat of the jeep, then puts the powder in the spoon bowl, and proceeds to melt the powder down with a lighter underneath the spoon, then injects it carefully into the needle so not to form bubbles- he finds a vein in Kate's arm at the inside bend of her elbow and pushes the needle into her skin injecting the liquid from the syringe into her vein. She lies perfectly still during this procedure. "Thank God" murmured Loren softly.

He is back on the road immediately obeying the speed limit, which is almost mandatory because of the narrow winding pavement going up into the hills. "Only another 50 miles to go" Loren thought to himself.

Upon arriving at the cabin, which is about 5 miles down the river from Riverbend, Mo., Loren looks at Kate who was still in a deep-drugged sleep. He gets his key to the cabin out of his pocket, unlocks the door and walks in to prepare a room for her, in the effort to make moving Kate from the jeep to her room as easy as possible.

The cabin is clean- always clean-for many occurrences which happen here quite frequently. He first set-up the cameras in her room and then makes sure the ropes and gag are on the side of the bed before he goes out for Kate and carries her in. She seems to weigh even more than when he carried her out of the warehouse.

Rex jumps out of the jeep and immediately finds a tree, then another then runs after lots of scents helter-skelter. Rex seems to know this place well.

When Loren lays Kate gently on the bed he pauses and feels remorse about the change her life is about to take, "At least for a while, anyhow, "he mumbles to himself. He had been secretly filming the sex bouts they had been having at the warehouse, but even that is going to change, as she will soon be a slave to drugs, the easiest way to get someone under your control.

Katie is out for another hour before coming to, when she awakes she has a horrible headache and feels nauseated. She is very groggy and the room is dark, and this disorientation only adds to her fears. She tries to get up by trying to lift her legs off the bed which is proving very difficult because they feel incredibly heavy. She starts crying out loud for Loren who, upon hearing her goes immediately to her bedroom and by her side. Kate tries to sit upright and in doing so vomits down the side of the bed. Her stomach hurts intensely - and she can't figure out what is wrong with her.

At first she thinks she had fallen asleep on Loren's bed at the warehouse and has become very ill somehow. It is dark in the room, and once her eyes adjusted, something just doesn't fit. Loren had always kept his shades pulled, but there were two windows in his room, now there is just one. Katie then starts to panic- this is not Loren's room, "Oh, my God" she screamed "Where am I, what have you done to me, you Son-of -a bitch." Loren just looked down at her with sadness in his eyes, as he'd witnessed this before with other girls.

"Kate," he said softly," Katie, if I hadn't had done this something worse was going to happen to you, this is for your own good."

Kate is still screaming at him "What do you mean for my own good? How can something so disorienting and so nauseating be good for me or anyone else?" "Where am I." after that statement, she immediately vomits again.

Loren bent over and picked her up under her arms and half and walked half carried her to the bathroom, setting her on the floor next to the john so she wouldn't continue to make the mess that was happening in the bedroom. Loren then looked around the bathroom, and carried out the razor and scissors in his hands and shut the door and locked her in the bathroom. Then he carried a bucket and a clean rag into the bedroom and proceeded to clean up her vomit. "I deserve all of this" he said out loud. She deserves nothing of what's she's getting. God, this is gonna change her and not for the better." God, I wish this never happened, any of it."

Katie started screaming from the bathroom, Loren ran and unlocked the door and watched her as she went into convulsions. He held her head with his finger behind her tongue so she wouldn't choke. After a little while Katie just collapses in his arms, and he hugs her hard. She became so still he feels compelled to inject her with another dose of drugs, this way she will relax and also stop her from being sick to her stomach, until the next injection is needed. Loren thinks to himself, "I hate that I have to do this."

9

HOSTAGE

Loren holds Kate comfortingly for a long time on the bathroom floor. For a man who had become to routinely treating Kate with cold discourtesy, and as of the present put her very life in jeopardy, he still feels curiously drawn to her and treats her with warmth and care even though she's oblivious to his presence. Loren has been addicted to methamphetamine, for a while now. "That's how this whole mess started." he said quietly to himself. He had been seeing another woman on the side and she introduced him to meth, not that Loren wasn't already using other drugs, he had been experimenting with them for years, but meth quickly captivated him and rapidly became his drug of choice. In his opinion- it gave him the ability to see life more deeply, most of the time anyway. Loren was a "brain", a thinker and a dreamer, and talented--he could build fine pieces of furniture and effectively design complex architectural structures, but he also developed a dark talent for assembling the required materials and ingredients for producing methamphetamine.

Loren's introduction to meth quickly led to a wild and very erratic lifestyle. The drug he produced initially was harsh with impurities, and would make the users very jittery, anxious and unable to concentrate on any one subject for more than a few seconds at a time. Undeterred, Loren continued reading available information to come up with alternative ingredients and procedures to refine the meth. Within a short period of time he made some improvements and started producing meth for himself and for his friends. He became "established" for producing a good product. Then he was introduced to a rich and powerful man in the city, who many would call a mobster, as the majority of his businesses are outside the law.

Loren was invited to meet with this powerful man at one of his businesses and, at the end of the meeting he was offered a job- to produce meth- for the black drug market. Loren had doubts and concerns but he has needed a high paying job for a long time. Over the past several years he was recognized as an artist and, like many artists, he is financially broke. Yet he hesitated to take the offer at first then, with some apprehension, accepted working out a deal with this man. Soon thereafter he opened a profit making lab and, because of its success, his boss fronted him more money to open more labs in different parts of Southern Illinois and Missouri by employing others to do the lab work with the requirement they follow Loren's instructions- explicitly.

Business was lucrative and, not surprisingly, in working with this powerful man and his people greed came into play prominently in the new meth business just like the man's other businesses. The number of labs were put into operation rapidly, a few failing but most were instant successes. Loren sincerely felt sorrow for the fate of some of the people who were introduced into his business affairs, but others he really didn't give-a damn-about because he saw them as bad apples just making another mistake.

Susie Breckenridge, for instance, was introduced to meth by her sleaze-ball boyfriend, Dale. She already had chemical imbalances in her body which led her to take antidepressants, and the meth combined with her prescription medication only made her more anxious and confused. Her boyfriend already had established connections with the mob and brought Susie into the business to do small errands and eventually to sell the drugs on the streets. Because she was a whiner and sometimes was a little too talkative with the wrong people, she had been warned to shut up at times in the past when it became known that she had talked with outsiders about her employer's businesses and products.

Loren had even gotten concerned enough about Susie that he borrowed Katie's jeep to go to her house one night to admonish her to keep her mouth closed about her employer. But, upon arrival at her home, he found her brutally beaten lying at the foot of the basement stairs near death. He couldn't help her, nor even touch her to give her human compassion, for fear of leaving finger prints. All he could do was get the hell away ASAP.

Loren was shaken badly by Susie's murder and upon leaving her driveway he scraped the entire length of Katie's jeep on the driver's side on the neighbors white picket fence backing out of the driveway. The driveway was narrow, it was dark, he was in a hurry and the damage to the jeep just topped off a very bad scene for Loren. It was the first, and he hoped the last, time he would see a woman beaten lifeless. That night it became clear to him that the value of an individual's life to the men he works for means nothing-if they perceive that individual to be a threat to them in any way. Susie had always listened to Loren in the past and she would have done it this time too- if given one more chance. Now she was dead.

Katie is starting to stir. As Loren looks at her, he is having mixed feelings. He is addicting Katie to heroin but that addiction will allow him to control her, which is the only way he can see to save her from meeting the same fate as Susie. He has been waiting to give her another dose of heroin but he did not want to wait too long as she had reached the stage of addiction by becoming sick every time she came down off the drug and she would remain sick until another dose was given to her. He doesn't want her to be sick, he really does care for her wellbeing, and believes that putting Kate under his control through drug addiction is certainly better than seeing her dead. Heroin is the drug known to addict a person very quickly and to keep the user drowsy, whereas meth keeps the user awake and moving.

He has been giving her larger doses just to keep her lethargic. Later he plans to lower the doses, so she just feels good, and not so drowsy. After that at some point Loren knows he will change her drug to one with fewer side-effects if she survives this, he hopes she will listen to him, she usually does. He waited until Katie started to gain semi-consciousness and moving quite a bit on the bed before giving her another small injection. This enveloped him in sadness but is what he firmly believes he has to do.

Then his cell phone rings. It's his boss, which is not surprising because he has been calling Loren more and more frequently and directly reflects the fact that Loren has become a premium asset to his boss and his group of thugs. Not only are they cashing in on the meth labs, but laundering most of the money thru him to put into viable the purchases, such as gold and expensive antiques, made off the drug money in different storage units around the city of St. Louis. They also had taken over a cache of porn sites on the internet thru Loren's extensive research and uncanny genius.

This is where Loren, although reluctantly, has been planning to put Kate. He didn't want her on the streets as Susie had ended up, and besides Katie and Susie were total opposites. Susie had been introduced to street life as a teenager, whereas Kate had not. Kate's body is well toned and she is very good looking and can be quite sexy when she wants to be. "She would be paid well, he'd see to that," thought Loren as he is hearing the fourth ring of his cell phone.

" Hello " Loren answers, then silence as the other party speaks" Yes she's here, knocked out at the present." then another silence as Loren listens- then replied " Look everything will be fine, have I ever messed you up before? You jumped the gun on Susie and now we'll have to cover that one, if you'd listened to me in the first place we wouldn't have to cover up, would we?" Plus Susie was good at selling on the streets and she was just a little problem that could have been managed, so we lost on that one big time." Loren's eyes grow hard and cold when these calls came in, lately his stress level is higher because the more the gangsters see him perform in their businesses, the higher their expectations become of his skill and intellect. The only positive he sees is that he has gained more power & money than he ever expected from all the successful financial endeavors which have occurred since he met the powerful man. The phone conversation ended as abruptly as it began.

As Katie slept, Loren undressed her and laid her in different poses to photograph, just innocent, but very sensual and seductive body poses. God she looked good to him, but he dared not do what he wanted to do, because she might come to consciousness, at least partially, and he didn't want to be engulfed in the bad scene that could create. Meth made Loren very horny, which he enjoyed but it also could be frustrating at times when he couldn't satisfy his heightened libido. The photos- if some of them turned out as well as he expected, would be used with head titles to open a new porn website introducing her to the porn market.

Katie is lying on the bed; very much in a deep mental haze. It is dark outside by the time Loren is finished with the photo shoot, Katie is still knocked out and it is obvious to him that it is too early to give her another drug dose so he decides to leave her in her room alone for a while. He shuts the door to her room and locks it from the outside. Then he checks on Rex, who is now lying on the front porch of the cabin- worn out from his exploring and hunting all day-is being well behaved.

Loren then switches on the television just in time to see the St. Louis news broadcasting that Susie Breckenridge's boyfriend had been arrested in Oklahoma and is being returned to St. Louis for questioning about her death.

Loren isn't hungry but he hasn't eaten in a long time so he has a look in the pantry and refrigerator and finds them almost empty except for peanut butter in the pantry and a partial loaf of bread in the freezer so he is able to make a sandwich. The main provision in Loren's cabin is down to a few bottles of booze and a cache of assorted drugs. He needs to develop a plan to get groceries tomorrow which will involve leaving Kate here alone.

Loren is in a quandary and Kate has been caught up in events beyond her control. Under his "protection" she is going to have to be here for a while, for hope of safety. She's seen too much and being a naturally curious person has inadvertently led her to life-threatening trouble. After she witnessed the containers of meth being loaded in the van, men have been watching her like they had done with Susie when she was first suspected to be a threat to the powerful man and his businesses. After some surveillance, it was decided Kate was also too much of a risk to remain alive, resulting in the scene on Jefferson Street where Jack tried to kill her with a vehicle. Loren said in a low voice to himself, "These guys are getting too stupid, too nervous- too fast."

Katie partially awakens in the middle of the night and is very groggy and disoriented, her room is pitch black, her stomach hurts like hell and she feels like she is on the verge of throwing up again. She lay back down because of shear weakness and instinctively closes her eyes. Groggy or not she knows she urgently needs to do some thinking." Where is she, is anyone else here, where is Loren?" These are the first of many questions she desperately needs answered. The sharp pains in her stomach are so intense that they almost divert her attention from the reality that she is a prisoner in a chilly, damp, dark room somewhere- unknown. How long has she been like this? She remembers being sick in the daylight, but it is now dark."

She is afraid to scream or even move, in fear of who might respond. She trusts no one including Loren, not, after what he has done, especially Loren! "Don't cry" she whispers to herself as tears run down her face. "Think! Focus! Think! Focus!" she whispers over and over to herself with her eyes closed in the dark silence. After a few minutes, which seem like hours, she opens her eyes and tries to adjust to the darkness.

After a while her eyes can see the outline of a darkened window, the curtains had been pulled shut tight, but the moon is almost full so moonlight is faintly visible along one edge of the curtain. Shakily using her hands she feels her way around the bed to get her bearings, as the darkness even prevents her from knowing the size of the bed she has been lying on. This is the most conscious she has been for a long time, how long she didn't know.

She is now able to focus on getting out of the room that confines her, without regard to where she is, but she just knows she needs to get out. Her stomach is suffering the most terrible knotted-up nausea and pain. She is having to devote all of her strength and concentration to refrain from vomiting, just the noise of her throwing up could bring someone back into her room. For her on safety, silence is of the utmost importance.

She is able to lift her leg and slowly move it toward the side of the bed, then is able to slide her body toward the side and, as she slowly pulls the covers off of her, she realizes she is completely nude. Then groping with her foot she tried to feel for clothing on the floor with her hands still on the bed. No clothing, her foot is touching only floor. She slowly lowers herself to the floor to a kneeling position then is able to search with her hands for anything that feels like loose clothing. She reaches a chair or settee, or something similar, she couldn't tell in the darkness so she kept feeling until she determined it was a chair. On top of the chair she felt lose clothing or cloth of some kind, she just hoped to God it was her clothes, which would eliminate one problem in her current predicament.

Kate started feeling intense queasiness in her stomach again, she lay there in spasms trying to repress it and could even feel vile liquid come up into her mouth, but she was somehow able to keep it from going any further. She swallowed and laid still for a moment then she was OK again. "What did he give me?" she thought to herself. She reached up and quietly pulled down the clothing articles off the chair next to her unto the floor. She realized, after a quick feel, that these items they were her jogging clothes, the last clothing she remembered wearing. She quietly pulled on the shorts, then the t-shirt- and started groping for her shoes and socks, feeling under the chair, she then realized it must be a settee as it was too long to be a chair, then she found one sock then another, but her shoes are still missing. Kate knows finding her shoes is essential to her escape. She is planning on running for miles- sick or not- and the terrain is likely to be difficult and probably impossible without shoes. She did know one thing, she had never been in this room before in her life – with or without Loren.

On her hands and knees she crawled quietly as possible so as not to disturb anyone, then she heard a noise that came from the other side of the door. Almost immediately she realized it was Rex, he must have heard her moving in the room. He is sniffing at the door and just knowing the way he is, the next thing he'll start doing is scratching at the door to get in, just like he does at the warehouse. His keen sense of smell and hearing will realize it is Katie who is in the room and he, of course, will get excited and want to see her. Katie went completely still. Total silence is the only thing that might possibly keep Rex from getting excited and making a racket.

She has no idea where Loren is, but she is guessing that he is in the house or building somewhere because Rex is always with him. She needs to get out of this room as soon as possible as it is just a matter of time before someone comes walking in to check on her. There is silence for what seemed like a long time and finally Rex seems to have gotten bored and moved away from the other side of the door. Katie waits a little longer sitting still before once again trying to find her shoes in the darkness. She proceeds to silently crawl and grope until she finally finds the running shoes, shoved under the bed. She feels other items under there also, but her interest is only the shoes as she carries them silently creeping over to the only window then peeking out between the curtains and her eyes open wide. In the moonlit night all she can see in any direction is a massive forest of trees. She panics inside, thinking silently," Oh, my God, I have no idea where I am."

Kate tries to visually scan the outdoors area and is also looking to see if anyone is in view. As her eyes adjust to the moonlight, in addition to seeing lots of trees she sees sloping ground with bramble. The porch light appears not to be on. "That's good", she thinks to herself. Then another stomach spasm hits her. She takes a deep breath and holds her stomach tightly as if that would relieve the severe pains. After a couple of minutes the pain fortunately goes away as it did before.

She slowly stands up and pushes herself between the curtains and gropes the window to see how it opens. The moon light helps her to see that it is an old type window with the lock in the center between the two panes of glass. She tries to open the window lock but it is rusty and probably hasn't been used for a long time and at first she can't make it budge but after pulling with her fingers for a little while, she is able to get the lock slowly in the unlocked position. Holding her breath she reaches down and finds two pulls to gain leverage for pushing the window up. It is hard to push, and she is getting more frightened that a lot of noise will be made trying to open this window. Kate takes her time and moves slowly, at first there is a lot of resistance then it opens more easily, she discovers there is no storm window or screen that she has to deal with. At last, things are going her way! She had gotten the window open wide enough to easily squeeze through its opening.

She bends over and puts one leg through the opening and then bending further she gets her body through it but she still isn't touching the ground outside, although she knows she's on a first level, the window must be a little higher than usual or that part of the house is on a downward slope. As she is getting her other leg thru the window she can hear Rex at the door, this time whimpering. She releases her second leg and falls to the ground then immediately gets up and starts running without knowing where she is going. The crisp fallen leaves are making crackling noises as she runs over them. Then she realizes she has to locate a road.

10

THE ESCAPE

By now Rex is fully awake and barking like a guard dog in the middle of a jail break. Kate is standing behind a large tree, a relatively safe distance from the house, at least for the moment. She can hear the door to the room where she had been confined banging open and sees a light go on, then heard Loren shout loudly in anger, "Son of a bitch."

All this time she remains standing behind the large tree being still, silent and vigilant, waiting for her next opportunity to run. She knows she has to move fast yet silently, which is difficult because of all of the dried leaves on the ground. Knowing her time so close to the cabin is limited, she starts tiptoeing from behind one tree to the next as fast as she can, trying to minimize the crackling sounds of dry leaves under foot. The next thing she is aware of is that Rex has been let out and is running about trying to pick up scents from the ground, which is his normal behavior but could easily put Kate's whereabouts at risk.

Loren follows Rex outdoors toward the expanse of trees with a flashlight, running the beam of light through the trees quickly at first, then he slows down the movement of the light to try to either catch a glimpse of her or to just pick up a clue of the direction she is heading.

Through the expanse of trees Kate sees the lights of a pick-up truck being driven by, which eases her mind a little, she now knows where the road is located to get away from these woods has just been revealed to her. The road is gravel, she could tell by the sound of the tires as the truck moved. She needs to get to that road, and already has a plan developed to hide in the trees near the road when she sees headlights of oncoming vehicles. Kate is thinking she could travel easily this way because the road is lined by trees on both sides. Then the truck came to a screeching halt down the road a bit, and then backs up to near the front porch of the house. She could hear a man talking to Loren, and she continues to move as quietly and as quickly as possible because she realizes this is her best chance for escape while Loren is occupied in conversation.

The road is just to her right and she keeps edging toward it tree by tree. Then she heard the man say, "Just checking to make sure that you weren't being broken into since that's not the vehicle you usually drive." Loren thanked him and told him a quick good night, before the truck drove on.

By now Kate is right next to the road, she turns right and stays in the trees until she is about 150 yards from the house. She can still see the flashlight beaming around behind the cabin close to the window that she climbed out of.

Without warning she is startled by a wet nose touching her arm--- it's Rex, who is so happy to see her! Kate stops abruptly and gives Rex a quick pat on the head and whispers breathlessly, "Go home, go see Loren", at this point she keeps on moving in a half walk- half run. The crunchy noise of leaves could still give her away from this distance, so she gets onto the road and starts running " thanking the God above for an almost full moon to guide her. But Rex still isn't leaving her side, he must think that he is having a great adventure. Kate keeps running and murmurs breathlessly over and over for Rex to "Go see Loren, go home Rex, go home.."

All at once Loren whistles for Rex and Rex picks up his ears, looks at Kate and turns and runs back toward Loren's whistle. What just happened makes Kate feel uneasy because Loren probably thinks that Rex found her and saw that Rex returned to him from the general direction of the road that Katie was at.

Kate starts running faster, which causes pain in her stomach and she feels weak, but she has to run as long as she can hold out. Then she sees the car, with lights on, backing out of Loren's place. She immediately dodges back into the trees still running full force.

Loren is driving slowly toward her direction, with Rex running beside her jeep. Loren knows exactly what he is doing. Katie is crying again while she is running with tears streaming down her face. She is terrified! She can't get too deep into the woods because of all the thick bramble, Rex at this point runs right up to her. Loren slams on the brakes of the jeep and veers the front end into the woods until the headlights are shining directly on her and Rex.

Loren jumps out of the jeep and runs after her. She could out run him normally, but she is so tired, weak and her stomach hurts so intensely that she could barely stay upright as she ran and it was not long before she could hear him right behind her, then he tackled her with ease. They both fell into sharp branches and dried leaves. She was laying there crying and fighting him off the best she could until he slapped her hard across the face. She just lay there, recaptured and numb.

Rex is bewildered. Loren hoists her to her feet, both of them breathing hard from running and fighting, he then half drags her to the jeep, and she continues fighting as much as she can but to no avail because of her weakened and sick condition. He pushes her in the front passenger seat and climbs over the top of her in fear of her trying to escape again if he went around to the driver's door. He held her body tight against him, partially crushing her as he pressed her into the gear shift lever between the seats.

When they reached the cabin, Loren pulls her out of the jeep and drags her to the front of the cabin then inside. Slamming and then locking the door as he went, he drags her and pushes her on to the couch screaming "You fucking bitch", then he hits her again across the face. He is mad and he is scared because had she gotten away, that may have put his own life in jeopardy as much as hers is in jeopardy now.

After hitting her he realizes what he had just done and did an emotional turn-around. Looking down at her he feels a deep remorse for what has happened, as Kate is innocent of any wrong doing and he is fully to blame for her current problems. He only wanted her to come to St. Louis to spend some time with him, engage with him in their kind of sex and to help with the cupboard project. This has all gotten totally derailed, because of his dealings with the mob. In honest reflection, Loren thinks to himself, "Now he's hitting Katie for no reason, has drugged her enough to kill an elephant, he's kidnapped and traumatized her to supposedly save her life, and, the hell of it is, she is completely innocent, an absolute victim of circumstances beyond her control."

Katie lays there starring up at him, traumatized, filthy dirty, clothes torn, scrapes and scratches all over her body and tears running down her face. She is numb, and now cold, as her clothing is not warm enough for this chilly fall night, but while she was running she never felt the cold. She can't talk, but only look at Loren, this man she had loved so much. The feelings of hurt, confusion, betrayal and distrust are now so deeply embedded in her that he could have pulled out a gun and shot her on the spot and, at that moment, she wouldn't have cared and probably would have welcomed it.

Loren could deeply feel her pain and this prompted him to sit down beside her on the couch to attempt to give her comfort. He tried to hold her but she crouched away from him. Rex came scratching at the door, and Loren looked at Katie hesitantly, with a slight warning in his eyes as if to say" Stay right where you are", then he got up and let Rex inside, relocking the door afterwards.

Rex bounded over to Kate, happy to see her, happy to see them together. Kate's stomach pains have vanished and she is hungry, but is too upset to ask for food. She just keeps her eyes downward diverted from Loren, who may be almost as upset as she is at the moment.

His life could be on the line now if matters with his boss and his associates are not handled properly Loren doesn't know what to do with Kate. Giving her drugs in large quantities is not a solution he wants to accept anymore, but something has to be done with her to keep her and possibly him alive. Loren re-positioned himself over to the table next to the window where he props up his feet on a chair to watch television but he looks disinterested and restless. Every few minutes he would flip through the channels showing his restlessness full tilt.

Katie is watching him out of the corner of her eye knowing that sooner or later he is going to do something to her, she had no clue as to what, but she knew it was coming.

Loren's restlessness is adding to her already anxious mood. Kate knows that given the right chance she would again try to escape, and she also thinks that Loren realizes this too.

He knows her all too well. Loren then walks over to the cabinet and pulls out a plain metal box with a lid, then takes the lid off revealing various drugs mostly in packets with some packets larger than others. Katie has no idea of what is in the metal box that Loren just pulled out of the cabinet.

Loren selects a small packet and mixes it with water in a glass. Taking it over to Katie he said, "Drink this," she became sarcastic saying to him "That would be suicide, wouldn't it?!" She wasn't about to drink something again that came from his hands, especially now- realizing that the last time she remembered anything was before drinking water that he handed her back at the warehouse in St. Louis.

Since they hadn't spoken since her capture, she still had no idea how long she had been drugged. One day, two days, three or four? She still has no idea where she is either. Knowing that he wouldn't tell her, she didn't even bother to ask.

Loren was becoming agitated, and again demanded," Kate, drink this now." She screamed back, "Hell, no I won't drink that Loren." He walked over to her closer and said real quiet and with a danger in his voice she did not recognize. "Now Katie, then added almost as firmly, "All this will do is knock you out for a while, it will not hurt you." Katie screamed again, "It made me very sick to my stomach, I will not drink this shit." Loren said, "It isn't this that made you sick it was something else. So drink it right now." He was right in front of her on the sofa, holding the glass close to her face when she took her hand and slapped the glass out of his hand, spilling the contents on her, Loren, the sofa and floor. His face became angrier, he needed to make her go to sleep because he hadn't slept for close to 48 hours and needed sleep himself, it is difficult for him to think in this condition.

He once again tried to sit down to talk to her when all at once Katie asked him "Loren, why is all this happening to me? What have I done that I should be treated like this?" Her voice has a softer edge this time and she is now sincerely trying to figure out why all this chaos is happening and his moving closer to sit down by her sends the signal that maybe they will be able to have genuine communication.

Loren sat there for a while just looking at her like he wanted to say something. He would start to talk, then go quiet; it took a couple tries before he could reveal to her some of the why's she was asking. He at last spoke, weighing his words carefully, "Katie, your curiosity and my ignorance has created a problem that has escalated into something larger than either of us could have imagined. What I'm trying to tell you, and please don't ask any questions even after I'm done trying to explain because I will not answer them. Things have already been blown way out of proportion, and I can't tell you much, but because I know you well enough and trust you thoroughly not to repeat this to anyone (he stressed anyone) I can tell only some of what you want to know, although these answers will be vague just because they will have to be, lives could be at stake here, both yours and mine." Loren continued, "Kate, the day you witnessed us loading pails in the van, you witnessed something you shouldn't have seen. Granted I'm involved in some business dealings that can be life threatening to people who interfere, which seldom ever happens. But what must have happened is one of the two men helping me load these pails told the boss that you walked in on and saw an activity going on which has made them all nervous- you were watched by them, not me, although I was told you would be watched, but no one said to me that they were going to try to run you over," Loren continued, "I never would have let you go out of the door that morning if that was the case, I was told you would be tailed, that's all. The pails contained illegal substances which I won't discuss with you, I'm sorry, but it's for your own good- it's important not to know more than that. The only reason that I drugged you and brought you here was to keep you in safe hiding with me, I knew that you would not come after the incident on Jefferson Street. Kate, please do not try to leave again, I know how hard headed you are and all, but you need to stay with me and do as I tell you. I'll try not to make it hard on you, but please stay for your own safety. These guys will chase you down and find you if you leave. That's all I can say Kate, and what I've just told you is of utmost importance to keep exclusively to yourself."

Loren can't bring himself to tell her he planned to get her addicted to drugs to control her or how he planned to use her on porn sites. He knows the bosses would allow this and not kill her only because they would be making money off her. However, he can't tell her these things because he will probably still have to carry out these plans, but only if he has too, What he believes for certainty is, Kate is only safe with him and she can't go back to Chicago, for probably a long time.

Katie listened intently to Loren as he spoke, her adrenaline pumping and halfway understanding that most of what he said she had already suspected. She now also knows that her safety at the present and at least for the near future can only be fulfilled by staying with him. Katie-who always wants to know everything, had a very hard time not asking questions, and she had many of them, but knew Loren meant it when he said-"Don't ask questions, I cannot and will not answer them, lives are at stake here." She knows he meant their own very lives.

They both fell asleep on the sofa, Katie on the inside and Loren on the outside, huddled together in warmth and security. Rex is now at ease, sleeping beside them on the floor.

PART TWO

FOR THE LOVE OF MONEY

11

The ring tone from Loren's cell phone abruptly awakens Kate and Loren from their deep, much-needed sleep. It was unusual for them to sleep this close in proximity, especially on a sofa- but the distressing circumstances of yesterday made their closeness feel quite comforting to both of them. Loren finds his phone lying on the floor just underneath the front of the sofa, becoming awake and alert almost immediately. Few people have his phone number and the people who do call usually want to talk business only. He didn't leave the room this time, but answers the call with Katie in his presence. Loren speaks into the phone. "Yes she is still with me."

Then a pause, "Yes- she is sedated and sleeping, and causing no problems so far." With those words he looks at Kate and winks and then puts his finger to his lips in the sign to be silent. His face changes into a frown as he listens carefully to what is being said to him. After listening his reply is simply, "It will get done." Then the call is over.

Loren gets up from the sofa and steps over to the coffeemaker to pour himself a cup of stale cold coffee, which is the last remaining coffee in the cabin. Putting the cup in the microwave he heats it then moves back to the sofa and sits beside Kate offering to share it with her, while apologizing for the coffee being stale and being the last drop they have in the cabin. Katie takes a sip of the scalding coffee and, upon it touching her tongue; she realizes it is more like espresso- very strong and concentrated. Then she carefully hands the coffee cup back to Loren.

He takes a sip of coffee, looks Kate in the eye and says, "I have something very important I must tell you." He pauses and weighs his words before proceeding, "Kate there has been trouble back in St. Louis, nothing to do with you, but something else. I need your full cooperation in this, please do what I ask you to do, it could mean my life if you don't', and eventually could be yours too when they find you, which sooner or later they will. I have to go back to the city within a couple hours; I'll be back late tonight. I can't take you with me, I told them that you are sedated heavily and I really don't want you back in the city at all right now. I'm trusting you to not leave here, it would be a tragic mistake, and this is not a threat but just a statement of reality."

"I know you can leave when I'm gone, but please don't. Notifying any authority would make it a death sentence, because neither of us knows who can be trusted. I am sorry for doing this to you. I don't want to drug you again, and I think it's no longer necessary. I trust you, just bear with me and please trust me. I hope to God I know what I'm doing and that this plan will work for both of us." Loren ended his talk by putting his arm around Kate's shoulders and looking straight into her eyes, he is hoping she really understands the seriousness of the tragic mess that is overtaking them.

Loren starts making arrangements to depart within a half-hour of taking the phone call from St. Louis, including leaving Rex with Kate. As he is about to step outside he gives her a hug and she kisses his forehead in the little ritual she always does when they say their goodbyes. After everything that has happened, Kate has serious apprehensions about how much she should trust Loren, but her inclination is to give him the benefit of the doubt, based on the realization that he had the power to drug her and keep to her captive at the cabin and declined to do so. On the other hand, she has no doubt that he wasn't exaggerating when he said their very lives are in jeopardy. He drove her jeep making a right turn out of the driveway, which made Katie think, with a slight laugh, "at least I was headed in the right direction last night".

Kate decides to take a shower after Loren left, as she is filthy from her escape attempt of last night. The shower feels good but she doesn't want to linger in the small bathroom for long- in fear that someone might try to enter the cabin. Kate with her hair still damp and Rex, as a good companion, sit on the front porch watching the morning clouds slowly moving above the trees and the countless number of autumn leaves fluttering down from the trees to the ground, each leaf landing in gentle silence. She could hear geese, a large flock of them, flying overhead but she couldn't see them because of the forest of tall trees blocking her view.

Rex got up and left his marks around different trees in the area surrounding the cabin, but most of the time he seemed content just to be near her side. Kate thought to herself, "Maybe dogs can sense something that people really don't realize, maybe Rex feels he needs to be here for me right now, to sort of be my protector." He certainly gave her away last night though, showing who he really loved, his master, Loren, of course.

Katie has worries about Loren and his trip to St. Louis; she wants only good things to happen for him. Regrettably, he has gotten into business with criminals and is starting to lose control of events. He didn't tell her anything about why he had to return to the city, all he said was there is trouble and she didn't question him, as he'd asked her not to.

She is getting anxious just sitting on the porch and being unable to think of anything other than bad things that Loren may be facing in St Louis. After a short while Kate decides to go back inside the cabin, with Rex following close on her heels. For the first time Kate really looks around the room where she had been locked up. She notices right away that it has many more conveniences than Loren's warehouse room ever did and is also very clean. The furniture is fairly new, just lightly used, but she senses that most of the pieces must had been new when they first arrived at the cabin.

The kitchen is a real functioning kitchen with a refrigerator, stove, microwave, etc., all the modern conveniences that most new homes have. At the warehouse Loren's room has only a refrigerator that doesn't work, with an ice chest to replace the fridge, and an old beaten up microwave oven with a defective timer that has to be manually shut off. She then starts opening cupboards to find something to eat and all she finds is a jar of peanut butter and a half-used frozen loaf of bread in the freezer. There isn't even coffee, Loren wasn't kidding when he referred to "the last drop of coffee" earlier. "Well damn" thought Kate, "today could be a very long and hungry day!"

With an empty stomach that is getting increasingly difficult to ignore and the lack of alternatives in the pantry, she makes both herself and Rex a peanut butter sandwich, tearing Rex's sandwich up into bite size pieces so he can eat it more easily. He is as hungry as she is as he shows by devouring his peanut butter sandwich pieces almost instantly. After a moment, Rex goes into some loud lip smacking and head shaking, which makes Kate laugh when she realizes that Rex has gotten peanut butter stuck to the roof of his mouth and doesn't know quite what to do.

Kate doesn't know how far she is from civilization, a village, a gas station, or even a house. She has no money to buy anything anyway, and her uncertainty about strangers makes her very uncomfortable, and it's possible that even someone here- wherever here is- could be watching her. From what Loren said during his phone call, the men who are monitoring him and her have the message that she has been heavily sedated so, as she thinks about her situation, fears for her own safety increase and she instinctively moves toward the interior of the cabin, away from windows, where she plans to stay until Loren returns. Not knowing what else to do, Kate says a prayer toward the heavens, "Dear Lord, please let Loren be safe." She then proceeds to look around for something to do, a crossword puzzle or just anything to keep her mind occupied.

Loren made it to St Louis in record time. He drove well over the speed limit, but watched continually for cops to avoid a speeding ticket, but more importantly—as he had learned from his boss and the boss' henchmen—keep a low profile so as not to raise any type of suspicion about yourself involving anything at all.

In the phone call earlier he was informed that Dale Robbins had been released and was no longer a suspect in Susie's murder, but the "club", the name Loren's boss often used when referring to his business organization, was pretty sure that Dale had "talked" while in custody.

Also, the vanload of Meth, which was camouflaged under glue and was delivered to a storage facility in Chicago, has been stolen out of the storage unit and no one seems to know its current location.

None of this is good news, because Loren is directed to be a' tough' some times and today is probably going to be one of those times. He knows the boss wants to meet to talk about problems and what needs to be done by whom to solve the problems, which is what Loren hates most about being in the club. But he can't say no--there is no one who can say no to this group--unless they don't care about staying alive.

Once he arrives at the St. Louis city limit, using his cell phone he places the required call to meet up with the boss. Within a half hour they meet at Loren's warehouse using the back yard for their entrance which is the usual routine. The boss 'Lincoln Town Car isn't driven to the shop today, but his Cadillac SUV is driven instead. There are the three of them-- the boss, Frank, his bodyguard, Joe, who is Franks life-long friend and Loren, they all enter the warehouse, with Loren shutting the door behind them. Frank is dressed as usual, wearing a short sleeved button down shirt and black slacks and his body language revealing a man who is very disturbed and on the verge of losing his temper, which is known to be quite volatile and sometimes violent. He looks at Loren and snarls, "First things first damn it, I told you not to let her visit you, but you let your penis rule your head, now she is a threat to us, and I don't give a shit that you say it is just sex that keeps you together. Bullshit Loren, I'm not stupid! We checked this broad out a long time ago, she has brains and stupidity mixed together and she doesn't fear much, meaning that she could talk to the wrong person and we could all end up in prison, and you probably won't live long enough to make it to prison. Get her in line and keep her in line or you'll never see her again!" And second, that son of a bitch Dale is an idiot! While he was being interrogated by the cops he let out a little about who might have killed Susie, by telling the cops she was selling drugs for some guys. Dale will have a fatal accident in the very near future, he's been nothing but a pain-in-the-ass for me since I've known him, and he's the one who brought Susie into this- who was just as nuts as he is!"

Loren said, "How do you know that Dale talked to the cops?"

Frank replied with a sarcastic growl," Shit Loren, you should know by now we have friends on the force, some are just small cops, but some hold senior positions too. I can't believe that you're that stupid to have to ask a question like that. By the way, the records regarding Susie's death will quietly be changed in a few weeks from murder to accidental death as soon as it becomes old news."

Frank continued, "Third and most importantly- the stash of meth has come up missing in Chicago! It was definitely delivered and put into a cube van which was garaged in a storage unit, someone I know personally was there when it was stashed, but it's all missing now, it was going to be distributed to three cities --Detroit, Chicago & Milwaukee. Someone must have hot-wired the cube van, and had cut-off the lock to the storage unit and then they just drove off. We believe that another club up there must have been clued in that it was coming, and voila, easy money for them. When we find out who it was--easy will never exist for them again, and we will find out! Frank's speeches are normally rambling and threatening and he continues, Loren you figured the street value to be around 2.5 million, right?"

Loren nods his head yes while saying, "That's a conservative figure, somewhere between 2.5 to 3 mil depending on the geographical area and the local economy." Then Loren asks, "So you think it was another gang that took it huh?"

Frank answers with more impatience and anger rising in his voice, "It's the only people I know who would be stupid enough to do this! We know it wasn't for a fraternity party, for God's sake, of course it was another gang! The two guys who picked up the stuff from here we know and trust, it was someone else who tipped them off but we don't know who yet. Right now what I know is that you, Jack, us, and the two men in the van are the only ones who knew the planned day of the pick-up and the planned place of delivery in Chicago and that we're out a minimum of 2.5 million!" Then Frank gives another order, "I need for you to get Dale taken care of, maybe a brake line job or something. He drives real fast, and I'm thinking maybe at the track having his brake line cut, you know who to talk to about it or do it yourself, just make sure it looks like an accident. This has to be done within the next couple days, I hear he's drinking heavy right now, and he has a big mouth- so it's essential to get it done quickly, you know-him being drunk and driving can easily lead to death. Also, I may need for you to go to Chicago, but not yet, we're trying other methods for getting the drugs back or, as a alternitive, getting payment in full from the assholes who took it." Then Frank asks, "Where is this woman Kate right now?"

Loren re-states what he said on the phone, that he had sedated her enough to keep her completely under for the next 18 hours, meaning he has to return to her before too long.

Frank looks at him and delivers a stern warning, "You must either get her under control and keep her under control, or we will take over matters ourselves, I'm not kidding one bit and you know it."

Loren nodded looking Frank in the eyes, not showing any of the anxiety he is feeling. His mind flashes to the incident occurring shortly after he joined the club when Loren learned the lesson that an order given by Frank, or by someone designated by Frank, is to be followed and not altered, and that lesson was accentuated with a loaded gun pointed to his head.

Loren replies, "Dale will be taken care of, and Kate is under my thumb", which satisfies Frank at the moment.

With that they split-up Frank and Joe drive away out the back gate of the warehouse as Loren clicks on his mobile phone to call the auto-body shop. Loren hears the call connect, "Yah, Jeff –this is Loren, how about meeting me at Fairmount Racetrack. I need a little help with something," there is silence as Loren listens then says, "North gate at 8:00, see you then."

After Clicking off the phone- he steps to his room to retrieve Dale Robbins' phone number, one that hadn't been important enough to put in his phone contacts list. He calls Dale Robbins, but no answer, "Damn it" thought Loren, "This means having to go get him out of Terry's Bar-- I'm sure he's already wasted by now." Loren looks around upstairs to see what stuff would be useful so take back to the cabin, where he feels he needs to be. He knows his time in St, Louis is short and he quickly looks for items that are the most needed at the cabin, realizing such items, if they are going with him, have to be loaded now. Loren grabs Kate's suitcases and a few clothing items for himself, more film and a few other odds and ends. He loads everything in the back of the jeep then backs it into his yard locking the gate before he hops in his truck and headed for Terry's Bar.

Terry's is on the corner of Jefferson and Cherokee St. just a mile or two from the warehouse. Loren found ample space to park, which is not surprising as this area has come on hard times and many people down here don't own a vehicle and only use public transportation.

Dale's old beat-up, rusty and dirty truck is parked out front on the street, so Loren parks his truck right behind Dale's truck. As he walks into Terry's Bar he hears Dale's loud mouth even before he sees him. He is sitting at the far end of the bar next to an old man who has been drinking his life away longer than he can remember. Loren frankly can't stand Dale. He is a braggart who is especially irritating because he has absolutely nothing to brag about- he is generally useless and constantly over-promises and under-delivers on what he says he can or will do. Now with Susie dead, Loren feels no qualms about what is going to happen to Dale, though he wishes it wasn't he who has to choreograph Dale's accident, but he has no sympathy for him because if it wasn't for Dale, Susie never would have become involved in the club and now she is dead because of it. Now Loren has done the same thing to Kate- for different reasons- she has entanglement with the club and now Kate's life is under threat because of it. This made Loren dislike himself and loathe Dale even more.

Loren walks over and sits down next to Dale on the vacant bar stool just to the left of him, he then looks at Dale and nods a hello and signals for the bartender to bring a round of drinks for Dale, the old guy sitting to Dale's right and a beer for himself.

Loren notices that Dale is drinking whiskey and, from what Loren had heard, when Dale Robbins is drinking whiskey he's usually wasted, meaning don't bother to use him for help or he'll screw up the job.

Dale is only used for little jobs anyway like making sure the prostitutes are given small gifts of crack if they work a little longer on a certain night or he does manual labor like unloading trucks of goods purchased with laundered money. Generally, Dale thinks of little more than his next drink or being high on his meth. He has used many women to get something to eat or a place for him to sleep, but never helped them- Susie included.

Loren made small talk with both men, and slowly sipped his beer wanting to remain fully sober for the job ahead of him. It is only 4:30 in the afternoon and Loren doesn't want to have Dale at the track any earlier than 6:30 to 7:00, so he has a couple hours he has to spend with this jerk before they have to leave for North of St. Louis where the Fairfield Race Track is located just inside the Illinois border.

Loren sees a newspaper on a nearby table and walks over and picks up the sports section of the newspaper just to catch up on the latest general sporting news, and to kill some time. After a few minutes he turns to the racing form in the sports section. After looking at the racing form for a couple of minutes he interrupts Dale's drunken conversation with the old man and says,

"Dale, I've heard there is a real good horse running tonight with surprisingly high odds." This makes Dale's ears pick up because he knows that Loren has connections and he could use some easy money. Loren then adds, "The third race", as he pointed at the schedule. Dale looks intently at the schedule with squinted eyes. "He's probably seeing double right now," Loren thinks to himself.

As he looks up from the schedule Dale asks, "Which horse?" Loren baits Dale by saying, "I'm not at liberty to say as it is still about 4 hours until the race, but if a person just happened to ride along with me, then they might just find out the answer- let's say- just before the betting window closes on that particular race."

Dale, not being the brightest crayon in the box following years of drug and alcohol abuse, immediately became Loren's best buddy for the afternoon. They sat at the bar, Dale doing most of the talking and drinking, and Loren trying hard to look interested while tuning out the blather and slowly sipping his beer.

After almost two hours, but too early to go to the track, Loren says to Dale, "Listen I'll meet you over at my warehouse, drive over there in say about 15 minutes, we'll take my truck to the track o.k.?"

Dale wants to follow him immediately as he fears he'll be left behind and miss out on the big pay-off. After giving Dale some assurances, Loren convinces him he has a couple things to do before he can go to the track. Then it's agreed, they will meet at Loren's warehouse in fifteen minutes.

Dale parks his truck near the gate at the warehouse about eight minutes later. Loren is outside with the hood up on his truck, swearing loudly as Dale walks up to see what's going on. "Son of a bitch", my truck just quit," looking directly at Dale, Loren continued. "Sorry Dale, looks like we can't go tonight, I can't figure out what's wrong with the truck, but we sure can't get to the track without it can --? ". Loren didn't get to finish his sentence

When Dale interrupted, "I'll drive my truck, but I need to buy some gas and I'm out of money."

This is what Loren had been hoping to hear. Loren comments, "You sure this is o.k. with you?" You've been drinking quite a bit and I don't think you can handle another DUI,"

Dale responds, "You can drive my truck then, as long as I make money at the track, its fine with me."

This is the other answer Loren had wanted to hear. Loren quickly says, "I'll stop and buy some gas on the way."

When Loren jumps into the driver's seat he is careful not to touch anything but the necessities, door handles, steering wheel and light switch. Loren stops just off 55 going north toward the racetrack to get a few bucks of gas for Dale. Then he proceeds to drive further north into Illinois to the Fairmount Racetrack with Dale, who is "sitting more quietly now, probably because he hasn't had a drink in a while", Loren thinks to himself.

It is 6:30 when they arrive at the track and it's getting dark. The bright lights at the track are illuminating the whole area and, as usual on Friday night, the parking lot is filling up fast. Loren has a permanently-assigned parking spot next to an old storage building which is very convenient although the lighting is poor around the storage building, which could be considered a security concern by some people. They get out of the truck and lock it and Loren puts the keys in his pocket. The parking spot is located on the North side of the track and they enter at the pay gate right where the horses are stalled just before the second race. After going through the pay gate Loren walks over to the stalled horses and carefully examines each horse in its individual stall. There are nine horses running in the first race which is starting in ten minutes.

12

AN ACCIDENT

The racetrack is buzzing with anticipation as crowds of people are standing and talking at various locations around the race track grounds and the stadium is filling quickly to near capacity already. There are always promotions at the race track on Friday nights including one dollar beer and a free food buffet on the third floor. Consequently, it is never a surprise to see extra-large crowds of people at the Friday night races.

Loren always prefers the clubhouse, but not tonight because he has arranged a meeting with his friend Jeff at 8:00. The trumpet sounds to begin the parade of horses to the race track. Loren informs Dale that he does not have a strong pick for the first race and that Dale is on his own if he wants to bet on the first race. Loren buys a beer from a vender and begins sipping it but doesn't place a bet, while Dale places a one dollar bet on a horse named King Alabare, which turns out to be a loser. After the first race, Dale starts getting fidgety and pushes Loren to tell him the name of the winning horse in the third race, which is irritating to Loren who just ignores the question.

It is now 7:30 and the second race is going to begin in a few minutes. Loren has to make a couple of phone calls, so he excuses himself from Dale, but makes sure that Dale can see him in the crowd as he makes his phone calls so that he doesn't get panicked that he might miss out on the third race which is starting soon. Dale nervously watches every move Loren makes to ensure he does not lose sight of him in the crowd of people.

Loren's calls are going to be brief, in which the first call is delivered almost in code when he states, "Accident will be completed tonight."

Frank, who is on the other end, listens and understands completely, then grunts an acknowledgement before hanging up. The other call is to Jack in which he tells him to "Never, ever do anything as stupid like you did on Jefferson street with the jogger", which Loren delivers in a hard-edged and threatening voice. Then he hangs up. Jack knows exactly what Loren means.

At 7:50 Loren walks over to Dale and tells him he has to go out for a few minutes and is going to miss the third race. Dale's face drops in shock, then Loren reaches in his pocket and hands Dale two twenty dollar bills to put on Killarney Kathy to win at twenty to one odds and also gives Dale a twenty dollar bill for himself to put on the same horse. Loren looks Dale in the eye says, "I'll be right back, after you pick up our winnings just wait here- don't take off with the money", which he says in a slightly threatening voice, just to make sure that Dale knows he will be returning.

Loren is walking out the North gate at 8:00 when he sees his friend Jeff driving up just as the trumpet sounds signifying the third race is about to begin. Jeff follows Loren's lead as he drives his truck slowly over to Dale's truck and parks close by it. Jeff proceeds to cut most of the brake lines and does some other tinkering with the brakes in Dale's truck, leaving just enough braking capacity to hold for a few miles until Dale gets to the Freeway.

Loren then confirms with Jeff that he will need a ride back to St Louis after he returns Dale's keys to him, because he obviously won't be riding back with Dale after Jeff completes the modifications to Dale's truck. While Jeff is cutting and tinkering with the brake lines, Loren is busily wiping all of his finger prints off of the truck. By the time they are through with the truck there are only two or three races left on the program. While Jeff and Loren were working on the truck in the parking lot they could clearly hear the sounds coming from the race track, including the crowd cheering or moaning or sometimes gasping during various stages of the races. They could also hear the announcer over the loudspeaker urging race fans to "place your bets" between races and describing each race as it was run. In particular, Loren listened to the third race, in which he heard the announcer excitedly say, "No.3

Charlie's Way finishes first with No.9 Killarney Kathy coming in a close second."

Once the brakes on Dale's truck have been carefully calibrated for disaster, Loren goes back into the stadium to locate Dale. Jeff waits out by his truck for Loren to return as instructed. When Loren finds Dale, it is obvious that Dale is inebriated, upset and hot under the collar. "You sure as hell screwed up on that race!" Dale yells at Loren, who is trying to act unaffected by Dale's crude comment and diffuse the stares he is getting from nearby people whose eyes have been drawn to them by Dale's angry outburst.

Loren takes Dale aside as quickly as he can and says in a low voice, "Shut up, you are drawing attention to what needs to be a private matter. O.k., there was a screw-up, we can't pull off a win 100% of the time--and I'll talk to the boss and tell him he was wrong, o.k.?" Loren has no intention of talking to anyone about this- he is just saying verb age to quiet and calm Dale, who is acting drunk, loud and angry, the way he usually does when things don't go his way.

Just to pacify Dale a bit more, Loren digs into his pocket and pulls out another twenty dollar bill and says, "Look-it, I'm sorry our horse lost, probably more than you are, here's twenty bucks for your efforts. Also, this woman I've been seeing is here and she wants me to spend time with her tonight. You know, the fuck-your-eyeballs out- kind of night-- can you make it home o.k.by yourself?"

Dale is calming down now and, while looking at the twenty dollars in the palm of his hand, says I could go for some pussy myself."

With that Loren turns around and walks out of the North gate and gets into the passenger side of Jeff's truck and then they drive back to St. Louis.

Meanwhile Katie is waiting at the cabin and its feeling like a very long day for Kate. Patience is not one of her strengths and she is becoming more anxious, paranoid and confused as the hours go by. She is a "doer" and waiting for Loren to return makes his absence of several hours seem like days. By noon she is beside herself with cabin fever and, to take her mind off of things which she can't control, she decides to busy herself by dusting and sweeping the cabin.

She starts in the main room which is one large living area encompassing the kitchen, dining area and living room. As she is dusting she opens the cupboards to do a thorough job inside and out. When she opens the cupboard in the living room, there is a metal box with the lid only partially closed. She pulls the box off the shelf to adjust the lid and, in doing so; she discovers many packets of various pills and powders within the box. As she quickly inspects the packets Katie grows pale and feels sick inside as the realization hits her that she has found a large cache of illegal drugs. She is not really too surprised to find illegal drugs but the large quantity is a surprise along with it being located here in this cabin? She is confused and scared and immediately replaces the box back on the shelf, shuts the cupboard door and then backs away to the farthest point in the cabin from the cupboard then just stares at it.

After an unknown period, she steps out on the front open porch for a breath of fresh air, wishing she could remain outside, because the cabin is making her claustrophobic. However, within a few minutes she has a new problem—the woods have eyes! She is having intense feelings of paranoia about remaining outside as she fears someone is watching her from the woods although she hasn't yet seen anyone. But within a few minutes, her fear becomes too intense so Katie steps back inside and sits on the sofa, her mind racing- as she tries desperately to decipher her fears, both real and imagined, and determine just what should she do.

The drugs she just found this afternoon brings back to her consciousness the reason she is even here-- a prisoner, for witnessing drugs being loaded in that van the other day.

Should she leave now while she has the chance, she could be miles from here by the time Loren returns? She is thinking seriously of doing this when Rex walks up to her and touches his cold nose to her hand bringing her instantly back to reality. She put her arms around him and bending down gives him a kiss on top of his head, while tears trickle down her face. Kate speaks quietly to the dog, "Oh, Rex, I'm so messed up and confused. I love Loren very much, but I'm losing all trust in him by the minute. Rex, what am I supposed to do?" Knowing he can't answer her nor help her she still needs to verbalize her thoughts to him, hoping in some way that can help to give clarity to her confusion just hearing her thoughts put into words. Rex just looks up at her with mournful eyes, and seems to communicate empathy for her feelings of fear, frustration and pain. Katie, with Rex at her feet, sits on the sofa for a long time just trying to figure out some sort of an escape plan- or how she might really fit into Loren's life.

Because of the trauma that Kate had endured in the bedroom where she had been held captive, she has delayed re-entering the room partly because of the fearful experience and also because she wants to keep her feelings about Loren as positive as she can and, if she re-enters this room, her feelings toward him might revert to feelings of dismay and betrayal. In any case, she knows she has to go back in there to deal with her doubts and confusion. Kate's mind is racing, "Why would he keep so many drugs around a cabin? Why would his true living quarters in St. Louis be less equipped for everyday life than this cabin and why didn't he bring her here before? He knows how much she loves the outdoors. It is as if he is leading a double life."

She finally has her nerve and walks toward the bedroom but hesitates before opening the door. Then after hesitating she goes in, which is the first time she sees the bedroom in the daylight. Numbness envelops her as she looks around the room. Two of the walls- one to the side and the other wall at the headboard are mirrored from floor to ceiling, as is the ceiling itself. The room is decorated in plush reds and soft blacks on the bedspread, pillows and drapery. The settee is made of a soft, supple red leather. The black and white harlequin floor tile gives the room a significant richness and voluptuousness. This room is definitely designed with passion in mind- it just exudes it. Kate walks around the room evaluating its contents, which is all high quality and expensive.

Since the day that Kate met Loren, Loren never once in all that time ever talked about or even hinted about the existence of this cabin, yet he has a key to the cabin and the man last night in the truck who stopped did so only because he knew the vehicle in the driveway did not belong to Loren. All of this makes Katie believe that Loren owns this cabin and all of its contents.

Kate is jolted and hurt by the implications of what she has seen. The drugs in the other room and the design of this bedroom leads her to obvious and shocking conclusions-- Loren is leading two separate lives, and she's not the only woman in his life, which she had only suspected until now. Then Katie's eyes spot something sticking out from underneath the bed and she kneels down to see what it is-it's the shoulder strap of a camera case. She reaches underneath and pulls the camera case out onto the floor, revealing a case with quite a bit of wear on it, which contains what, appears to be a new, high-spec camcorder. She then peers under the bed again, adjusting her eyes to see in the darkness beneath the bed, where two more cases are located. She pulls them out one at a time and opens them revealing another camera which is digital and the last larger case is full of assorted sexual pleasure devices with bondage straps, handcuffs and other objects for sexual games and endeavors.

Kate gets up off the floor leaving the items lying where she scattered them, and walks out of the room and closes the door. Her mind is racing- "I need to get away from here", she says out loud then raising her voice in anger, and "I need Loren out of my life. He is not who he says he is—he's a stranger to me! I'm crazy to even be here and to believe anything he says to me! What a jerk, what a liar!" Kate then becomes silent. Her mind is in a state of confusion and she is basically a prisoner not knowing who to trust, nor where to go- or even where she is.

Her biggest drawback at this moment is not having a landline phone installed at the cabin, because her cell does not work in this remote location. She is alone, confused and very scared. Kate walks back outside but this time she walks around to the back of the cabin and sits down with her back against the outside wall. She looks out into space as she tries to think of a plan to escape once Loren returns, and is hoping that when he does returns, he drives her jeep here instead of his truck.

The sun is filtering through the trees warming her and helping her loosen the tenseness inside of her enough that she is starting to possibly see light at the end of the tunnel. Kate has developed a plan. She can hear birds singing again and then she hears Rex whining and scratching, which reminds her that she forgot to let him outside with her.

Loren is driving like a maniac trying to get back to the cabin as fast as he can. All he can think about is Kate and how she may be coping with everything that has happened to her, including being drugged, being made captive and then being left alone out in the middle of nowhere for an extended period. In the back of his mind he is also thinking of the look that Dale gave him as they parted at the racetrack, just a stupid drunken look, but not one that justifies him dying. Loren's mood sinks to another low- which happens every time he is called in to do a job like this, being a tough. However, this time is the worst job for Loren- because it is likely Dale is dead by now and it is the first time that Loren himself is directly responsible for the death of another person.

He is doing 65 miles an hour in areas where he would normally not risk doing 45mph. The road is paved but narrow and winding and it is very dark because the trees and clouds are blocking out the moonlight. He is anxious- as the minutes seem to be exceedingly long and the odometer miles seem to be going in slow motion.

Kate's jeep handles much better than his truck, "Thank God for that", Loren says to himself. Then, without warning, a deer jumps out in front of the jeep leaving no place to maneuver except veering hard to the left to just miss the deer by inches, then losing traction for a few seconds before regaining control of the vehicle. Loren starts to relax once he reaches the gravel road as that signals that signals he only has 3 more miles to go. Upon reaching the last turn, he is relieved to see lights on in the cabin, then he checks his watch showing his arrival to be1:00 a.m. When he walks in the door Kate is curled up on the sofa sleeping, with Rex at his feet wagging his tail in a greeting. Loren pets Rex's head and wishes that Kate was awake. He wants to talk with her to see how she is and if she still believes what he told her before he left. He knows the cabin holds so many incriminating objects that can be held against him, and he knew before leaving hurriedly yesterday morning that, with Kate being here all day alone she would probably find these incriminating objects and view them and the activities associated with them as threats to her that Loren is with someone else. He now wants to explain as much as he dares about the cabin to her. He regrets he did not explain everything about the cabin to Kate before leaving for St. Louis, but didn't have the time.

As Loren heads over to the kitchen for a bite to eat it is then that he remembers there is no food. "Oh boy", he thinks, "I deserve everything I'm going to get for what I've done to her." He sees the empty peanut butter jar in the wastebasket and feels pretty guilty about everything in general. Loren can't hold in his feelings any longer and walks over by the sofa and sits down next to Kate, rubbing her shoulder gently to wake her. While looking at her sleeping he has amorous feelings for her, but he stops himself because he knows the importance of talking things out with Kate about the cabin and the incriminating items in the cabin right now.

Kate pretends to wake up, as she really wasn't sleeping at all. In reality she couldn't sleep because of the intense anxiety that she has been feeling all day. She yawns as she stretches and then opens her eyes looking into Loren's face- and fakes a smile at him, she is afraid to even let him touch her for she knows how he can schmooze her and turn her emotions around without resolving important issues that may be tearing them apart. The way she feels right now she never wants this to happen again.

Loren takes one look into Kate's eyes and knows she is holding something back from him, which makes him believe that she did find the incriminating items in the cupboard in the living area and under the bed in the bedroom and she is trying to distance herself from him as she has done in the past when he has neglected her in some way. Normally, in these circumstances Loren's instinctive reaction is be silent and just "zone out" or otherwise cut off communications with Kate. However, because of the recent extraordinary events, Loren knows he can no longer keep quiet and has to talk to her now, no matter how tired he is he has to talk now.

He starts by saying, "Katie, before you begin to get angry, which I know you can do with such force that we could never work this problem out, but we need to talk Kate, for the benefit of both of us- and for many reasons. Kate, you know how I had to leave in a rush this m-, I mean yesterday morning, and you know how I asked you the night before not to ask me questions-- well, I need to answer some of those questions now about the cabin especially. I would have taken you with me if I thought it was safe for you, but I know better than to even consider that as an option and I also know that you were here alone for such a long time with nothing to do and you would be seeing many things in this cabin that you would not understand at all." Loren stops for a moment, then adds a comment, "What you have seen within these walls are not me, Kate--just part of my job. I need for you to ask me questions, and I will answer them. Please though- ask, I need for you to do this."

Kate stares at Loren with steely eyes and anger within her almost at a boiling point and then raises her hand and slaps him with all her strength across the left side of his face leaving a red line that colors his entire jaw line, and with her fists she starts beating on his chest and upper body with such fury and strength that he starts to fall off the sofa, while she is screaming at him, " You-son-of-a-bitchin- asshole, you-motherfucker- I hate you. You have screwed me over and over and over and I just lay down like a stupid fool and take it. I want out of here right now Loren, right this minute!"

At this point Loren grabs her wrists and holds them so tight she can't move her arms. Loren knows that her anger is so intense that if she found a gun or knife his life might be in danger. He knows that her anger and resentment are warranted and he has treated her shabbily from time to time since he's known her, but he really does care for her and has love for her in many ways. Also, right now he is dead tired and just needs for her to calm down. He also senses, thank God, that her anger will be short-lived and that tomorrow morning he may be able to have a talk with her.

Loren is actually thinking that the only way to calm her is to sedate her again. But if he does that he knows she will leave as soon as she comes out of the sedation and, if she leaves, she will be dead within days after that.

Loren could feel Kate's tension start to subside as he holds her in place by her wrists. Still holding her, but with lessened pressure, her tension slowly dissipates then Loren takes her into his arms and just holds her, she is silent and so is he, he continues holding her feeling gratitude for life itself.

They fall asleep on the couch, knowing at least for this night they are together, but both being so exhausted that the mutual need to sleep is preeminent over all other needs.

13

REVELATIONS

They both woke up early the next morning feeling groggy after two consecutive nights on the couch together, which had been cozy but not conducive to sound sleep. The level of anxiety for both of them is high, which is not surprising considering the roll-a-coaster sequence of events they had just experienced.

Kate is expecting honest and complete answers from Loren this morning and, if she doesn't get them she has committed to herself that she will take her jeep and leave. However, she continues to have a quandary. Something in her subconscious mind tells her to leave him- whether she is satisfied with his answers or not, but her heart has a mystifying yet unfailing need to trust Loren and have a life with him and even love him. Kate knows she has a dilemma yet the outcome of the impending clash between mind and heart is unknown and her future a jumble.

There is no coffee or food in the cabin, which prompts a couple of apologies from Loren to Kate for this, and he also apologizes to himself silently because he needs morning coffee before he is able to start fully functioning, both mentally and physically.

They spoke little while they dressed as they both clearly recognized their first priorities for the day-- head for the nearest town for a good breakfast and then pick up needed provisions at a grocery store. Riverbend, Missouri is a little village located in the Ozarks, whose residents almost totally rely on the tourism business generated from canoeing and horseback riding enthusiasts from outside the area. The small village is located about a 3 hour drive South of St. Louis, which is right out in the middle of nowhere. But Kate is attracted by the natural beauty of the area, including the rolling hills, the lush forest with fall colors, and clear streams which are visible from the road, and she comments to Loren about the beauty as they drive. As they near outskirts of the village she sums up her thoughts about the area, "This is so beautiful, no wonder people make the extra effort to vacation here." Once in the village, Kate estimates to herself that the village is about 6 miles from the cabin.

They eat breakfast at Chuck's Restaurant ordering eggs, bacon, hash browns, toast- with lots of coffee and with hunger clean their plates empty. After Loren pays the bill they proceed down the street to a small old time grocery store to buy staples to take back to the cabin. Their conversation during all this time is intentionally light and clipped, as both of them know that once back at the cabin- the revelations that Loren will be telling to Kate could make or forever break their relationship. With this in mind, Loren knows from experience that Katie can be stubborn so he has to be very careful as to what is revealed and how he reveals it. Too much information would likely scare her into running and not sharing enough information would likely do the same. As Loren thinks about what he has to tell Kate he is feeling like a man on a tightrope in a high wind without a net.

Once back at the cabin and after putting the groceries away, Loren asks Kate to join him on the front porch. There are no porch chairs, but the steps are a comfortable place to sit and talk and it is a warm fall morning with the sun shining through the golden trees. Loren knows how much Kate loves the outdoors and is thinking this beautiful setting might help soften what he has to say.

Katie sits down beside him and is still hurting inside but at least not with the intense rage that she had the night before.

Loren's words are soft spoken, "Katie I know how I would feel if I walked into a bedroom laid out like this one is and it belonged to you. I would automatically believe that you are seeing other people. You are not wrong in that thought by far." Upon hearing these words, Katie's face starts to turn red and her eyes hardened in anger, but he stops her from interrupting by raising his hand gently and touching her shoulder, then continuing by saying "please let me finish before you make judgments Kate." " You are not wrong about the room, but it isn't me who actually uses it for sex, I'm usually the one who does the filming." As Loren completes his words, he looks anxiously at Kate hoping she is believing him.

Katie is quiet, then looking him straight in the eye she says, "Huh?" "Filming who?"

Loren hesitates but goes on, "This club I belong to, this cabin was purchased in my name but not by me, nor does the cabin even belong to me, it belongs to the club's owner, and the money is so good in the pornography business that this is what the cabin is used for. Granted I can come here to relax, but have only done so a couple of times since the Clubs owned it.

Katie asked, "How long have have you been coming here, Loren?"

Loren replies, "About a year."

Kate continued, "You actually pay people to come up here to have sex that is filmed?"

"Yes", said Loren not adding any more.

"So that is why I found straps and things like that?" she asks, and then Loren nods his head, "Yes". "Are these men with women, or men with men or women with women?" she asks wanting to know more.

Loren just sighs and says "A little bit of everything. To get to the point, Kate, it actually bores me. At first it was interesting and sometimes arousing, but now it's just a job, that's partially why we haven't had sex as much since you arrived from Chicago. Although if anyone can get to me- it's you Kate, and you have aroused me more times than you think, even this time, but our sex has changed to be sort of like these porn films, and I don't think I want it like that anymore", Loren finished.

Kate's face softened- no matter how difficult it has been for her to believe him at all, she believed what he just said, just by the way that he had said it.

Neither of them talked for a while, both silently taking in the rare sensation that two people feel when they are truly connected in their common emotions. This moment of connectedness was not one of lust or physical desire but one of reconciliation on their spiritual side which engendered feelings of affection and endearment that had not been felt between them for a long time.

Katie then asked, "This club, some or all of its members are really very dangerous aren't they? They are organized crime aren't they? How did you really get involved, Loren?"

He knew she would do this to him—ask questions that he really didn't want to answer because this just made things more complicated and dangerous for both of them. If the boss ever heard of him answering these questions or talking to her about anything involving his activities- there is little doubt that "hits" would be put out on both of them. Also, knowing Kate, once he answered these questions- he knew she'd ask more, that is just her nature.

Hesitantly, Loren said, "Kate, what I'm about to tell you is only between us- when I say to you trust no one- I mean this. Before I say anything more you have to understand that this is a group that I cannot walk away from, they just don't let you walk away- once your in- your in, and the only way out is to stop existing. I'm there to stay Kate, I have no choice, and I'll understand if you want to leave, but right now you can't. I've already been forewarned about you, if you leave my presence now you will become a target and it will be lethal. But I can and will make sure that you can leave safely in the future- as soon as possible- but first you have to do things that make it look like you are under my control. I have some ideas"-Loren then hesitated, his eyes searching Kate's for re-assurance, "I have some ideas to make it look just like that, that you are under my control, but I need your help with this, I can't force you to do anything you don't want to do".

Katie looks at him intensely taking in what he is saying, this isn't the Loren she's known, the Loren she's known is such a free spirit- and doesn't believe in controlling others as much as he doesn't want to be controlled himself.

"It definitely is organized crime Loren, I know this just from what you have said. It is only these kinds of people that don't let you leave, alive anyway, so you let me answer that myself, but how did you become involved?"

Loren said softer yet, "It's a long story and I'll try to shorten it, there is more to this than I want tell you, one time when I needed a little money it was lent to me for a couple of small favors. That's how it started, they started to trust me and realized, I guess, that I had potential to make more money for them, I launder their money. That's where I am right now, I make money for them mostly." Loren really didn't want to say anymore and asked Kate not to ask more questions and to try to be content with what she presently knows. He is hoping that she will understand enough to realize that she has to 'really play the controlled part hard' and stay with him for a while longer.

Loren's cell phone rings and he leaves the porch area away from Kate to take the call. He listens carefully to the remitter of the call not saying much; just listening then hangs up and returns to Katie. Loren's face looks a little sullen when he looks down at her, then not saying a word but walks back into the cabin by himself.

Kate stays out on the porch guessing that Loren probably needs some space from her, and she herself, needs solitude to think intently about how to handle a future knowing what she knows without blowing it all. It is hard for her to subjugate herself to others, and if she can do this for anyone it would only be Loren. But even that is hard for her to do. Loren is the one man in her life she wants to trust. In general it is a major task for her to trust any one man, as she had lost trust for males starting with her father. Although he was a great provider he was also a womanizer and a violent man from Kate's early childhood on and, she being the oldest child and a girl besides made her the scapegoat for much of her father's violence. She learned long ago not to give her heart to a man, but Loren had taken it many times before and he could easily take it again.

Katie's mind had been toughened for a girl who had been raised on a farm in Minnesota; she became streetwise and assertive over the years. She had no choice but to abide by the rules that Loren had set for her today- just as much for him as her, because Kate quite often put Loren's welfare in front of her own.

She went back into the cabin finding Loren on the sofa with his feet up on the coffee table and his hands laced behind his head with his mind off in the distance. He didn't hear her walk in and didn't notice her until she spoke to him.

Kate said, "Hey, we forgot a newspaper today. Darn it, Loren you know how I like to read the news." He said, "We've got a television you know. What's wrong with that?" Kate didn't say much because it's true the tube has the news too. It's just that one of her morning rituals is reading the paper. "Oh, I just miss some of the things I like to do in the morning, speaking of- do you mind if I go for a run or should I say do you trust me enough that I go for a run?" Kate asked.

Loren looks up at her, his mind other places obviously not paying too much attention to what she said and said "Sure". Kate enthusiastically changed into her clean running clothes that were in her suitcase. And said, "I'll see you in a little while." then exited the cabin, turning right like she had the other night when trying to escape from Loren. She started a fast walk for a block down the road just to warm up before jogging. Then she ran for a good mile and is still on the gravel road. In her solitude, the obvious question comes to her again, "where am I". When she returns to the cabin she will have to ask Loren exactly where they are as she still has no clue, except for visiting a village called Riverbend she had never heard of until this morning. When she felt she has run far enough she does a U-turn and starts running back, Kate hears a vehicle coming up on her, so instinctively she gets over as close to the ditch as she can.

It is an old beat-up truck going too fast for the road but didn't come near as close to her as the incident on Jefferson the other day but is, in her opinion passing too close to her anyway, or is she just being paranoid? She keeps running picking up speed and a good rhythm but when the same truck turns around and starts coming back toward her, she is terrified as the truck slows down and stops beside her with an older man at the wheel, she can see most of his teeth missing as he smiles and sticks his head out of his window, and asks her if she is one of them girls from the cabin up the road saying, "You know one of the city girls who come down to visit?" He looks at her with a sly grin showing only a few widely-spaced teeth, most of which are decayed.

Kate looks at him knowing she has to be careful and says, "I don't know what you're talking about, my husband and I are renting a cabin down the road. Have a good day sir." Then she starts running again--now faster, her heart beating rapidly but she's trying not to show fear. After a short distance she stops to listen for his vehicle as it sounds as if he has turned around again and is following her, but to her relief he continues going the opposite way.

When Kate gets back to the cabin, anger is again building up in her, but not as much as the night before. "Are you one of those girls?" she repeats under her breath with clenched teeth, the irritating question from the toothless man. "Boy, Loren has really given me a reputation and I'm not even one of those girls."

Loren is again on his phone when Katie enters the cabin. Fortunately for him her anger subsides while she waits and watches him talk on the phone.

It is close to noon by now and Loren is getting hungry, "Let's go and get a hamburger in town, o.k.?" Katie agrees. On the way to town Katie tells Loren about the incident on the road with the toothless man. "Oh, that's Jake", he says laughing, "Kate, he's harmless. Once in a while he tries to sell me firewood, but the wood is either of poor quality or rotten. As far as the girls are concerned, well think about it- to him these girls are probably real pretty, he has no idea who they are or what they do except that on hot summer days I'm sure he's seen a few sitting on the front porch passing time. Sometimes there would be as many as six of them here waiting a call time for their filming", Loren finished.

Kate is relieved about Jake, but jealous that Loren was in the room with these naked girls. But she doesn't say a word, just sort of fumes inside.

By the time they enter the small town, both of them are famished. This time they go to a different restaurant called Sammy's. Loren tells her the restaurant was named after a retired Army General who had grown up in this town. They both ordered cheeseburgers and milkshakes and as they waited for their lunch Loren tells Kate some history about the restaurant --The building at one time had been a worn out tavern until the General actually brought the old building back to life making it usable again as a restaurant. Without much of a wait the waitress brings the food and it tastes great. Their conversation stops for a while except for comments about their enjoyment of their meals. After they finish and Loren has gotten the check and paid it, they are about ready to leave when Katie remembers to buy a newspaper.

While reading the newspaper during the drive back to the cabin, Katie notices a small article on the third page about a man named Dale Robbins who was found at about 11:00 p.m. last night in his truck wrapped around a tree in the woods abutting Interstate 55 going Southbound. His condition was reported as critical after the high speed accident and his blood alcohol level exceeded the legal limit three fold. Also, the article reported that he was recently interrogated by the St. Louis Police Department about the death of a Susie Breckenridge but was released. His injuries were so extent he is in a coma, with head injuries and multiple serious body lacerations. His chance for survival is critical.

The news article bothers Kate because she remembers the murder of Susie Breckenridge and she can't figure out why the paper mentions her death without using the word "murder" in that article. "There must have been sloppy journalism or a typographical error by the person who wrote this article," she says out loud to herself.

Loren is driving and asks Kate, "What did you say?"

Kate tells him about the article regarding the man, Dale Robbins, and also comments on the sloppy journalist usage of the word "death" instead of "murder". Loren doesn't talk; he just listens and seems a little down. "Maybe he's still very tired", Kate thinks to herself.

When they return, Loren walks into the cabin following Kate; Rex is waiting for them eagerly hoping for a treat. Katie goes to the cupboard and removes a dog biscuit for Rex and gives it to him after he sits, which makes his demeanor change from excitement to contentment.

Silently Loren walks up behind Kate and, while standing close behind her kisses the side of her neck. Katie loves the feeling of sexual warmth when Loren does this. Then he starts to slowly rub her buttocks and then his hands go around to the front to her lower stomach and then up on to her breasts, cupping each with a hand. Kate is becoming intensely aroused as he keeps rubbing her gently then unbuttoning her shirt at the same time so his hands could fit inside to caress her bare breasts and nipples. She turns around facing him and puts her arms around his neck and they just stand there looking into each other's eyes for a minute. They both need this kind of intimacy right now; this intimate closeness feels so loving and warm to them, just the opposite of how harsh and cold the outside world feels at the present. Their lovemaking is gentle and sensual--exactly what they both needed right now.

14

UNINVITED TRIP

Kate slept late the next morning, and Loren is already on his phone in the other room sitting at the table. After their lovemaking last night on the couch in the living area, they had slept together in the bedroom for the first time. Upon getting in bed, Katie had been so exhausted and relaxed; she had fallen asleep almost immediately upon touching the sheets. In the morning stillness she can hear him talking to someone about something in Chicago and then there is silence before he his next words, "Are you sure you need me to go up there?" There is another brief silence, as the other person is speaking, then Loren speaks, "I'll leave here in a couple hours, and I'll bring her with me." Katie just lays on the bed-trying to imagine what Loren is talking about, but whatever it is, he has included her. He walks into the bedroom and says firmly, "We have to go back to St. Louis, then on to Chicago, anyways I have to go to Chicago. I'm not sure why they want you to come back", he then pauses for a thought, then adds "most probably because they just want to see if you give them any sort of suspicious reaction. I strongly advise you not to react, but to act as if you know nothing at all- more or less play dumb to everything. Right now everyone is nervous because a series of unusually heavy things have occurred recently." Get some clothes together Kate so we can get going. The sooner we get there, the sooner I can bring you back here, o.k.?"

Katie looks up at him, with worry in her face, saying, "Loren if anyone else would ask this of me I'd just tell them to fuck off!"

At that, she and Loren packed a few things, and then put Rex in the back seat and they leave for St. Louis, drinking their first coffees of the morning on the road. About 20 minutes before reaching the warehouse- Loren clicks his cell phone and says to someone, "Yeah, I'll be there, give or take 10 minutes. See you then", then hangs up.

This is unsettling to Kate and when they first left the cabin, Katie began to feel very nervous about her safety. Loren had picked up on the stress in her body language and began to try to calm her by first giving her assurance that she is going to be OK because it is unlikely that she will even see his "business associates" and, secondly, "if she does see them, all she needs to do is to act the same, just like she did when they were in the warehouse's back lot the other day--just pretend they are regular guys with regular jobs. Think of it that way Kate. Also, act like you're at my beckon 'n call, whether you like it or not, it's the only way out to get you of this mess I've gotten you into."

This made Katie feel more at ease and she knew she could do what Loren asked of her, that it would work, and she planned to do exactly what he said.

Loren had the back gate unlocked and Kate's jeep backed into the yard before the Lincoln town car pulled in blocking the jeep. Both Frank and Joe got out of their vehicle with frowns on their faces. Loren had already told Kate, "Go and act busy inside the shop, so that they can see you are with me, but try to stay far enough away so they won't try to talk to you. Seeing them first and not having to talk will probably ease your tension if you are approached by them later."

The men walked towards Loren who was pulling both suitcases out of the back of the jeep. Loren stopped and put the suitcases on the driveway then walked over to meet them. They all nodded to each other and then immediately the two men looked toward the shop fixing their eyes on Kate. She purposely looked up at them and said "hi" and then went back to her 'work'. The three men talked in low tones amongst themselves, and then all three turned and looked her way again.

Kate had been watching out of the corner of her eye, feeling that soon she would be approached. She saw Loren reach in his suitcase and show them what she thought were pictures and Frank and Joe looking towards her again and then chuckling to themselves. "At least their mood is changing for the better", Katie thinks to herself.

Without approaching her, the two men got back in the Lincoln Town Car and drove away and didn't wave or give any acknowledgement toward her. She feels relieved that they are gone; both of them give her the creeps and an aura of coldness when in their presence.

Loren locked the gate after their car pulled out of the yard, then closed his suitcase and picked up a few things that were out of place in the yard before going in to see Kate. Unbeknown to Kate, he had just shown his "business associates" photographs he had taken of her nude as he had her posed while she was drugged at the cabin. Kate had no clue that photos were taken of her and Loren had been trying to think of the right time to tell her what he had done and that he has more of the same planned to keep her out of the hands of the two goons who had just driven away. As long as she produced money for them and kept her mouth shut she would be safe. Now he has to go tell Kate the business deal he has to keep her alive.

He walks into the shop and gets right to the point, "Kate, I may have a temporary profession for you."

She looked at him quizzically, "O.K. Loren and what might that be?"

Loren is a short distance away trying to act as blasé as he possibly can, while knowing she might just throw something like a hammer at him, he blurts out the words, "a porn star."

Her brown eyes turn darker instantly, "What did you say"? Then not letting him answer, she bellows, "A PORN STAR"??

Undeterred, Loren pulls some pictures out of his unzipped bag and hands them to her.

Kate looks at them only a second, quickly looking back at Loren saying, "Where did you get these"? Her voice growing defensive like she had been cornered.

Loren tells her how long she was under sedation, starting at the shop in St Louis all the way to the cabin plus a few hours, because he knew she wouldn't go with him to the cabin otherwise. Then while under the sedation he photographed her knowing full well the effect it would have on Frank and Joe making them think she is viable money-making source for them, thence they would leave her alone.

Kate listens without interrupting-- something she has learned in these last few days. She feels like a prisoner and in reality she is a prisoner. Her hatred for Loren's "club" is growing by the minute.

The van load of meth in Chicago has still not been located- nor have the thieves that stole it. Consequently, Loren has been ordered to go up to the Windy City to listen around amongst a few known hangouts to see if he can get a feel as to who might have been in involved in the theft. Usually a couple low-life hoodlums are used to help with jobs like this, so if given the buddy treatment with a few drugs and/or a little extra cash they'll usually talk.

Loren doesn't want to go to Chicago, but doesn't have a choice. He can't very well leave Kate alone in St. Louis because of his mistrust of his fellow business associates. They might just decide she isn't worth the risk and do something lethal with her after he's out of St. Louis, which is exactly what happened to Susie. This means he will spend more money than he would have otherwise because Loren will book a much better hotel room for Katie's sake than he would have for himself traveling alone.

Loren told Kate about the trip to Chicago, without any specifics, it's just a business trip and she is going with him. She agreed without hesitation because she did not want to remain in St. Louis by herself after the incident with Jack Colbert. They showered and changed clothes and left for the Windy City that afternoon with Loren driving his truck instead of her jeep. Loren hopes to return within a couple of days.

When they arrived it was early evening and the traffic going out of the Chicago is jammed up, but once inside the loop the traffic is light. Loren knew of an old hotel that a franchise had taken over on Ontario Street so he drove directly to that location. It is easy to get a room almost anywhere on a Friday night so they stayed at what had been a luxurious older Hotel. Their room is located on the 11th floor and Kate is impressed that a discount franchise would have acquired a hotel of such quality.

Just down the street is a small seafood restaurant located in the basement named Oyster Bay, the seafood is delivered fresh daily and they specialized in the best soft shell crab. Both of them ordered the soft shell crab and an appetizer of oysters on the half shell along with a bottle of white wine from Napa Valley. This was the first night they could relax after the harrowing week prior.

Loren told Kate that she will be on her own for the next day or two and not to be surprised if he doesn't come back to the hotel until the wee hours of the morning- if that. The business he is doing is very tenuous and most of it can only be handled late at night when the people he needs to see come out of the shadows.

Katie doesn't argue with him, she is afraid for him and she knows whatever the business is - it is dangerous and possibly life threatening. She then thinks of how much her hate for Loren's boss and his lieutenants is increasing as they intrude more and more into their lives. Unfortunately, it may be impossible to escape the tentacles of the organization but she silently commits to herself to find some way to do so for both her and Loren. She is thinking in cold and calculating ways and she is mentally putting pieces of a plan together to escape this menace. She is not ready to talk with Loren about her ideas yet but she hopes she will be ready, even if only in little bits at a time, before it is too late.

After returning to the hotel that night after the wonderful meal and wine, as they lay on the bed with the lights still on and while they are fully clothed and just relaxing, Kate said to Loren, when we get back to the cabin I want you to start filming me- with or without other people.

Loren just looks at her- for what seems like a long time before saying "O.K?" in a questioning manner, not knowing exactly what she is thinking and not knowing if he even wants to know.

That night in bed Katie performs sex with Loren, just the kind of sex that would be filmed at the cabin, and afterward Loren thinks to himself, "I don't know how I'll react to her doing this with other men? I don't know if I can take that." Katie is sleeping soundly, but Loren lay awake thinking about his reason for being in Chicago. Loren isn't worried about finding the people he needs to talk to, he is more concerned with possibly finding acquaintances that might be watching him instead and who may be reporting back to the boss in St. Louis, He has to be careful.

And Kate springing the idea that "it's o.k. to film me stuff" bothers him too. He knows that she gave her body to him totally for his pleasure and disregarding her own. As he lies there beside her, he realizes he couldn't bear to share her with anyone.

They slept late the next morning, having breakfast at a restaurant on Michigan Avenue. Loren doesn't need to leave Kate any earlier than 2:00 p.m. - he won't be able to find the caliber of people he needs to see any earlier than 2:00 in the afternoon when some of them start getting out and about. Most of them don't start showing their faces until around dark, but he needs the daylight to do a visual assessment of the area he will be visiting tonight just in case he needs an escape route of some kind.

Kate says to him during breakfast, "Since I'm under your thumb Loren, I would like some money to go shopping."

Loren cringes hearing those words, he doesn't really want anyone "under his thumb' and frankly he is too broke to be giving money to her for a shopping trip. Those words don't reflect the real Katie either, she never asks for anything from him, or anyone else, to maintain her stubborn independence.

Loren removes a couple of one hundred dollar bills from his wallet and hands them to her, just saying, "Spend carefully, that's all the extra that I have."

When Loren and Kate are back at the hotel room and he is getting ready to leave to do his business, the feeling of tension in the room is so thick it could be cut with a knife. They both realize that something could go wrong and that Loren might not return. He told her, "don't call me tonight" and stressed the "don't". When and only if he has a chance he would call her or leave her a message at the front desk if she was out- this will be her only way of communicating with him and knowing he is alright. Katie kissed him warmly and gently on his forehead while standing a moment at the door just before he walked out.

She can't just sit around in the room and worry, she is so afraid of what might happen to him. Kate has seen how dangerous the streets are in Loren's neighborhood in St. Louis and earlier Loren told her that the area of his residence in St Louis looks like a monastery compared to the area where he is going in Chicago tonight. She needs to busy herself, just to keep from going crazy over Loren's fate. As she walks back to Michigan Avenue, only 1 block from her hotel, she starts to feel guilty for asking him for money. She knew he was short of funds. But she has no money to her name and there are a few items she needs to purchase--the items are intended to be a surprise for Loren.

15

FOLLOWED

Loren drove his truck out of the Chicago Loop going west on 290 until he exited at Cicero Ave then, upon turning South, he saw many boarded up warehouses and commercial buildings blighting both sides of the street. He drives slowly through the area getting his bearings and checking out what is happening on the streets.

Loren observes that some of the people he sees have very little connection socially and that legal commercial enterprises on this street seem almost non-existent. As he drives along he notices that street signs are missing on several side streets, which prompts Loren to pull over to take a look at a street map that he has in the truck. Then suddenly out of nowhere a large man with stringy hair like a voodoo doll with a wild expression on his face is walking straight towards him through an adjacent vacant lot wildly hollering at the top of his lungs-- "Are you lost, are you lost, do you need me to help you?" Loren can see that this man is stoned out of his mind on something or simply insane and with this man's "help" he could likely be robbed, beaten and/or killed within minutes. Loren just nodded at him quickly, not looking him in the eye and quickly maneuvered the truck back onto the street and drove away with the wild man standing and gesturing in the middle of two lanes of the street staring wild-eyed in Loren's direction. Within about two or three blocks of that recent fiasco Loren found the area he was looking for.

The area is populated mostly with small, dilapidated wooden houses, severely in need of paint, a couple of brick housing projects, appearing to be built by the government in the early days of its "war on poverty" in the '60s, plus two crusty taverns located side by side. He is looking for a pub called Lulu's, and neither of these bars is named Lulu's so he continues to drive down another two blocks before he finds Lulu's Pub on the left side of the street.

Because of the minimal traffic he makes an easy U-turn and pulls up close to the pub. The iron bars on the door and smoke laden windows are encrusted with bird droppings and other garbage. Loren slowly gets out of his truck and looks in every direction as he locks the truck doors. He notices a man getting out of a beat-up twenty year old car with two companions. The driver barely makes it out of the car before he starts vomiting in the gutter. Loren thinks to himself, "these guys are doing H", which is a natural conclusion as Heroin can make you sick if you need another hit.

Loren walked to the front door of the pub, where it is impossible not to notice four large heavy-duty deadbolt locks that are installed about 6" apart on Lulu's steel front door. "This sure makes my two bolt locks back at my warehouse look like toys", Loren says to himself under his breath.

Upon entering Lulu's he has to adjust his eyes to the dark smoke-filled room, all the patrons' eyes are on him and no one is smiling. Loren's face shows no fear but a calm vigilance- his experience as a tough underdog in life has taught him exactly what to show in facial appearance and what to say and not to say in situations like this. He walks up to the half-empty bar, then after a brief pause the barmaid, a large-boned woman with greasy skin and hair saunters slowly over to him and, without a greeting, asks him what he wants to drink. Loren tells her, "a bottle of Busch". She takes her time walking slowly over to the cooler and returns with his bottle slapping it down on the bar top.

With all eyes still upon him, he takes a long drink letting the beer, which is about room temperature, wet his throat. When he set the bottle down on the bar, he looked over at the other patrons one-by one and as he did this they each one-by one turned their faces another way. Loren had mentally won the first round at Lulu's. He ordered another beer, this time the barmaid talked a little friendly bar talk with him, easing the tension bit more.

Soon he has a new buddy standing next to him at the bar. "Are you looking for someone?" asks his new-found nameless buddy, with a friendly enough tone in his voice.

"Yeah" said Loren" a guy who might still live in this neighborhood, I think he hangs out here on occasion. We are acquaintances from way back."

The nameless buddy says, "What's his name?"

"Jerry" said Loren, "He lived over on Westland Avenue, he's a short white man about my age, likes his women and likes his booze among other things. Do you know who I'm talking about by chance?"

The new buddy thinks for a long time, you can tell he's been doing more than just drinking a beer, his eyes are glazed over and his speech is permanently impaired most probably from excessive drug use. Loren's has seen this so much and it scares him because of his meth addiction. Then buddy holds his finger up in thought, "Yeah, I might have seen him, does he do night work sometimes?

Loren responds, "Possibly, that's when he always helped me."

That was when Loren was accepted by the crowd at Lulu's" not trusted by any means" but accepted from just that one last sentence-the patrons of this bar are all people of the night. Loren is one of them. The patrons seemed a little more relaxed when they looked at Loren from that point on.

"Jerry?" said another patron- this smiling man with two gold teeth glistening right at Loren.

Loren responded by saying, "Yeah, I need to see him, kind of important. Do you know the Jerry I'm looking for?"

The smiling man said, "Maybe I do but I haven't seen him in a while, if it's the same guy I'm thinking he just got out of the slammer and hasn't been on the streets much since he's been out. You know, probably scared he's being watched while on probation."

Loren asks, "What was he in for?"

"Not sure," said the man with the gold teeth, "you know how news gets screwed up on the streets, but I heard he got caught taking some decoration off from some important building downtown one night. He didn't get much time though, maybe a year."

That was common for a drug addict to steal architectural fragments off of buildings for a little money to get just a few fixes. Jerry's habit happened to be heroin.

Loren finished his beer and said, "I'm going looking for him, just in case any of you see him, tell him a friend of his is here from St, Louis, I need to see him, I owe him a favor, I might be back later if I don't find him."

Loren walks out the door, it is still daylight but the light is fading fast.   He got off the street fast as he sees he is being approached by two separate women coming from different directions, they are working women of the street because of their drug habits and he is not in the mood to be approached about a blow job by either of them. He got in his truck and driving down the street there isn't much to see except a few people sitting on their porches, or just standing around doing nothing.

Loren needs to be seen and heard in this area-just in case he- himself is being watched by the boss. He can't figure out why he had been sent to Chicago, what in the hell could he do? Loren is smart but there is only one of him and the boss has many others on the payroll, meaning that this could be a set-up for him, thinking that he had something to do with the disappearance of the drugs. Loren has to be seen- talking around, like he really is putting effort into finding out who pulled off the theft. His next stop is one of the two taverns he had passed before finding Lulu's. The taverns are in such close vicinity to each other and both in the same disrepair as Lula's. He is in one bar for only a few minutes because it is empty except for a couple old drunks huddled together at one end of the bar. The second bar is more interesting, when Loren walked inside there is a heated argument ongoing between two women who seemed to be fighting over an old man. The old man is in his glory over the two women fighting over him and very drunk besides that.

This bar is almost full of patrons with lots of smoke and noise, this combination in such a small room gives Loren the sensation of dizziness. It takes Loren a few seconds to adjust to the darkness and noise, as he makes his way alongside the bar to find a barstool open. He is in luck on the far side of the bar about 3 stools from the end. Loren wedges between the bar and stool, standing and orders a beer. He listens to various conversations going simultaneously, but the two angry women are becoming more aggressive and the large black male bartender with a deep guttural voice tells them to take their problem outside or he will bodily carry them out himself.

Police are almost never brought into bar fights in this area unless somebody is killed first. No one wants the police around; they are considered a threat to the people here.

Loren drank his beer and will be leaving this tavern shortly, as there is just no one in here who can help him with his work here in Chicago. As he is just leaving, the bartender comes barging from behind the bar in a massive rage to throw the women out onto the street, which Loren sees coming and slips out the door in time to avoid the nasty fracas that followed. He gets into his truck and drives back toward Lulu's- trying to take up time, and be seen in the area just in case anyone is watching.

In the meantime, Katie had walked down to Michigan Avenue, the wind had strongly shifted to a northerly direction and the proximity to Lake Michigan makes it feel cold and raw. She really needs a heavier sweater or an overcoat, but all she can do is walk hunched over with her arms folded to try to minimize the chill of the gusty wind. When she and Loren left St. Louis the air temperature was close to 70 degrees and she hadn't given much thought to packing for warmth, but as she is buffeted by the cold wind she is thinking "it's amazing what 300 miles and a change in wind direction can do to the climate—brrr!" She had seen a small adult shop on a sidestreet just off Michigan Ave. She had all the intentions of checking out this shop for articles she normally wouldn't buy, but she was focused on carrying out her plans to screw these people that Loren was in with, and the only way to do this was become one of them. Kate was in her home vicinity now and knew that she could run from Loren easily, but her instincts told her this was the wrong thing to do, more for Loren's safety and her families also. She had heard how mob figures would get even by taking out family members, if they couldn't get to the original person who went against them.

Katie walked into the shop, at first it was a little too bizarre, many of the clothing items on display were pretty wild and held contents of slavery, masochism, etc., but lately life had become bizarre, it took her little time to adjust. When she walked out of the store her purchases were so small in size they fit in two small bags, and Katie laughing to herself said, "And light in weight too." Kate knew exactly what she was doing and was feeling mischievous about her purchases.

Kate found a newspaper stand on the way back to her hotel and decided to stop. She is glad to see a stack of St. Louis Dispatch newspapers and she bought one then continued walking back to the hotel. It is almost dark when she reached the front of her hotel, there were very few people on the cold street, and it is getting colder by the minute then as she is starting to enter the front door of the hotel, she turns facing the direction she had walked and notices a man who she knew she had seen earlier standing on the corner close to the adult store where she had been shopping. She had an eerie feeling while walking back to the hotel that she was being followed but didn't really take it that seriously until just now. Kate is scared but keeps herself calm. Her first thought is, "if I am being followed- this guy must be a professional." Then she hurriedly walks into the hotel lobby and immediately takes the elevator to the 9th floor and then runs up the last two flights of stairs to the 11th floor to her room. "Just in case," she whispers softly to herself locking her door behind her. "I bet that guy is lost on the 9th floor."

She is hungry because she hasn't eaten anything since breakfast with Loren. A short while later she starts to feel safe enough to order food from the hotel's room service. She selects a bowl of French Onion Soup and a House Salad with oil and vinegar on the side. When the order arrives she is careful about opening the door. She looks through the peephole and recognizes the bellman she saw earlier in the day, which allows her to relax a little. After the bellman delivers the food and leaves, Kate is still too distracted with worry about Loren to start eating. She checks the room phone for messages - but there are none- which immediately increases Kate's anxiety level. As she continues to think about her walk to the adult store and her being followed, it has hit her that she was probably followed by someone hired by the goons in St. Louis. Then what about Loren, where is he and is he alright? She knew being in this room would make her anxious and to think and to worry too much, but she has no choice. It is better than being out of the hotel and being followed by a thug.

Katie finally eats her salad. Then she picks up the St. Louis newspaper and starts reading the front page, which is mostly about political stuff and a large article on a new prestigious high rise building that is being built near the Mississippi River in downtown St. Louis. It wasn't until she reached about the fifth page of the main section of the newspaper that she read a very small article about Susie Breckenridge and how a police report indicates that her death was the result of accidental causes not murder. The police report indicates that the bruises & cuts on her body could have been self-imposed as a result of falling down the stairs -especially since the autopsy indicates a high level of prescription drugs were found in her bloodstream.

Kate instantly feels chills going up and down her spine- as she realizes that Loren is dead serious when he says to "Trust no one--not even the police". She read the rest of the newspaper even the obituary, ironically an obit for Dale Robbins is in the same issue of the newspaper, he is being laid to rest tomorrow at a cemetery in Crestwood, a suburb of St. Louis.

Kate thought to herself, "I'll bet thunder and lightning will erupt when the souls of Susie and Dale clash on their way to wherever they are going." Then Kate spoke aloud with anxiety in her voice, "Damn, I wish that Loren would call, I hope he is safe." She then called to room service and ordered 2 bottles of Bud light, one for now and one for later. She wanted to try to calm herself a little bit.

Loren walks back into Lulu's Pub, to find that his nameless buddy had left but the gold-toothed man is sitting at the same barstool as when Loren walked out earlier in the evening.

The gold-toothed man and Loren make eye contact and Loren moves in his direction and then sits down. The man grins a little and says, "I Knew you'd miss us and be coming back. I've asked around for your acquaintance Jerry, but no one has seen him since he got out.

Loren thanked the man and ordered them both a beer. While they shared their beers together they exchanged first names and passed some time talking about nothing much in particular. Loren feels he needs to call Kate and tell her he is fine so she won't worry, although he has a strong suspicion that he is being watched, which he plans to "forget" to mention to Kate. Tonight the reality of his situation has crystalized in his mind. He needs to get busy hustling the streets to portray he is conducting an extensive search for someone, who he knows will almost certainly not be found and will end in futility. He has subconsciously known that the boss' idea would end in futility from the moment he ordered Loren to go to Chicago.

Using his cell phone he quickly called the main number at the hotel and gave his room number, Katie answers on the first ring, and they are both relieved to find the other is ok. Loren only says," I'll try to be back tonight, I can't find the people I need to see, everyone has disappeared and it is useless even being here." He says this in a tone that, if anyone is listening to the phone call, they would think he has really been trying hard to do his job.

Loren reflects for a moment at the bar after ending the phone call with Kate. He just wants out of this area, he knows it isn't safe even if you are a resident here and being a stranger makes it even more danger-ous. He bought the gold-toothed man another beer and parts company by saying, "you know women; they bitch when you're with them and miss you when you leave." They both laughed, and then Loren walked out the door of Lulu's. He is heading for his truck when he notices someone walk out of the pub behind him, a bald white man in his late 40's-early 50's, it struck Loren as being strange because he never noticed this guy in the pub and wondered where he had come from? Loren got into his truck and drove around a few blocks within the area before heading back on 290 East towards the Loop.

16

TIME TO GO

Kate hugs Loren warmly after he closes the door upon entering their hotel room. He is happy to see her too and to be out of the crumbling and dangerous area of Chicago he had been in for the last 8 hours. Loren is hungry from having not eaten all day and asks Kate if she would like to step out and join him for a bite to eat. Kate nodded and says she'll just get a small appetizer while he eats his meal because she'd already eaten. She was in just a t-shirt and panties when Loren came through the door, so she dressed quickly into jeans and the warmest shirt she has so they could leave soon. Once Kate is ready they leave the room, catch an elevator to the lobby, then they step out onto Ontario Street.

Walking down Ontario Street is cold, and the wind is whistling down in between the buildings. They quickly arrive at their selected restaurant--the Oyster Bay, which is close by and the food is excellent. In the basement restaurant they order a bottle of Merlot to help warm themselves, then Loren orders two appetizers to share with Katie and a large fresh seafood platter for himself. When the entree comes, Kate wish's she had waited to eat with him. While nibbling at the cheese appetizer, Kate tells Loren how she felt she had been followed earlier that day. Loren asked her what the person looked like, Kate told him, "A white male probably mid 30's, dressed in jacket and jeans, dark curly hair and about average height". That is all she remembered, she didn't want to stare at the man because it made her nervous, she then told Loren how she got off at a different floor just in case he came into the hotel. Kate smiled and mentioned, "I saw that in a movie one time, I think it really works."

Loren just smiled back at her and remained silent, not wanting her to lose her illusion of having knowledge of streetwise thugs and how they operate, nor did he want to tell her that if she had been followed by a gangster- and he is sure that she had been- that whoever it was already knows the exact hotel room they are staying in. Loren also didn't tell her that he is sure the same thing had happened to him, which would only frighten her more. They finished their meal and each had an after dinner drink, Kate ordered a Smith & Kearns and Loren a shot of Crown Royal over ice. Katie is feeling warm and secure with Loren and, after he paid the tab with his credit card, they walked back to their hotel very hurriedly because of the cold and windy weather.

They rode the marble lined elevator up to their floor and got off to go to their room, when they entered they discovered a room in total disarray, someone had been into their luggage and everything was scattered from the bed onto the floor. Some of the drawers to the credenza are half opened but neither Kate nor Loren had used them so they were already empty as they were. Loren looked in the bathroom to make sure that whoever had been in their room was not still around. Next they looked to see if any of their possessions were missing but they were not.

Loren said, "Whoever did this either was an amateur and in a hurry, or this was done purposely as a warning to us, I'm not sure why but I have a feeling it is my second guess." They just looked at each other, knowing it is time to leave Chicago.

Early the next morning Loren paid for their room and they carried their bags and hospitality coffee in Styrofoam cups out to Loren's truck and pulled out of the parking ramp just in time to see a man standing in the door of the hotel looking at them as they made a left turn onto Ontario Street. Loren didn't tell Kate, but that was the man who had followed him out of Lulu's tavern the day before. Loren knew then that this was a warning to him, that he is being carefully watched. The message being delivered from the boss is that $2.5 million in meth has been stolen and hasn't yet been located and everyone, including all rival gangs and every associate working for the boss, including Loren, is now considered a possible culprit in the heist. If the boss doesn't recover the stolen meth or receive recompense soon there may be some killings to make people talk. Loren knows that everyone in St .Louis is jittery- but he is outraged, this is all going way overboard.

They arrive back in St. Louis Sunday morning just before eleven a.m. It is raining, cold and dreary-- winter seems to have come early. When they arrive at the warehouse Loren parks the truck out front on the street.

They walk to the front door in the rain and Loren unlocks the locks to the warehouse. -The instant that they enter the building Loren senses that someone has been in his warehouse while he was gone snooping around in Chicago. Not saying anything to Kate just yet, he cautiously looks around the room trying not to raise concerns in Kate that things are getting more dangerous.

Katie ran up the long steps to his room as she is needed a bathroom immediately after the long trip. When she enters his room she sees a mess, including papers that had been piled on the table are now laying all over the floor and his clothing is all thrown in one corner helter-skelter. Books that Loren loved and always took care of are thrown on his bed, against the furniture and on the floor. Kate at this point realizes that someone had been here just like in the hotel room in Chicago.

Necessity is the first priority; she uses the bathroom quickly then runs downstairs to tell Loren of what she has discovered, just in time to hear him in a heated argument on his cell phone. Loren's tone is low and angry, "Keep the thugs away, we had a deal, what a waste of your money and time having people tail me, if you think I am double crossing you, you are thoroughly mistaken- I have nothing to gain by doing that excepting for loss of my own money and life." Then there is silence as Loren listens to the other party, Loren's voice softens a bit, but not his strength of tone saying, "Look I know that everyone is on edge. Too many problem occurrences have made us all like this. I have no idea what happened to the contents of the storage unit in Chicago- it was like a needle in a haystack trying to find someone to talk with up there- and I found no one. You know yourself that people hole up, especially on deals this big. If you don't trust me and want me out that is fine, but the problem is no one trusts anyone and I'm starting to develop the same feelings towards you as you evidently have of me. We've made money-quite a bit together and can continue to do so- it's totally up to you- you're the one holding the cards." Loren listens for a minute, his face relaxing a little as he hung up the phone. When he turns around to go upstairs he sees Kate standing there, he has no idea how much she has heard and at this time, after that draining conversation he just doesn't feel like talking to her about anything.

Loren passes her on the stairs where she stood, he is looking very unhappy that she is standing there and heard what he said on the phone. He went upstairs gazing about the room before his eyes focused in anger on books scattered on his bed and the floor-he then went over and with his hands haphazardly scooped the books from the bed unto the floor and laid down on the bed- looking up at the ceiling in mental exhaustion wondering what the hell to do next. His first obstacle is getting Kate out of the picture and that is going to be a hard task to do, he cares for her- her life is now in danger because of him and his business and his very existence in the future are now at stake. He had always told Kate, "My work is the most important thing- nothing else even comes close to my work," and he meant this to include her and her well-being to some degree." She is strong and can take care of herself anyway" he thought to himself," It wasn't his fault she had fallen in love with him." Although he felt guilty knowing the fact that he himself had helped promote the feelings and behavior that Katie developed for him. He would come to her and stay awhile then leave- coming back months later, doing this over and over while she is rejecting other relationships just to go back with him. It has been an unhealthy relationship, especially for her, she devoted her life to him- and he just wanted her whenever he desired her- not on a full-time basis like she yearned for the two of them to embrace.

Loren knew that he had to get rid of her fast for both of them-but how? He knows she can't leave and he also knows that his associates would just as soon see her out of the picture for good- their way.

Katie went back upstairs- not really wanting to after feeling the inner tension that Loren had exuded toward her on the stairway when passing her by. She opened the door to his room hesitantly gazing around at the disaster. She went over and sat on the bed next to him and he in response turns his back to her to face the wall. "Can I lay down by you," she asked him.

Loren wants to say "hell no," but instead with hesitancy says, "Only if you can keep your distance."   Kate's heart dropped a mile. He always does this to her, one moment he is loving and caring and the next he is cold as ice, as if feelings mean nothing to him. Kate instinctively stood up and said, "I'm going for a walk." She left him lying there on the bed. Once downstairs and out the door- she had forgotten that it's raining, pouring actually, so she goes back inside. She is really lost-she wants to go home, just be away from him. The illusion of helping him get out of this mess is just an illusion- she wishes at this moment in time that she had never met Loren- her obsession with him is making her life miserable. Loren will never love her as she loved him. But now if she leaves it might cost her life- she has seen too much and knows too much. Katie just sat down with her back against the inside of his front door to the warehouse with her knee's up and her head down, she started silently crying- "Oh my God, I'm so confused, so lost"- Then losing her composure she weeps uncontrollably but the mournful cries of her dejection are muffled by her covering her face so that Loren can't hear.

17

DECISIONS

Katie eventually lets herself out the back door of the warehouse and after unlocking the jeep she climbs in. Once inside she locks the door and reclines the front passenger seat to a comfortable position. She is feeling lost, confused and has no desire to return to Loren's room, and anyways, in her reclined position she is feeling quite cozy in the vehicle. Within minutes the exhaustion of the day overcomes her and she falls asleep.

Loren is upstairs in his room feeling despondent about the careless way he has treated Kate and the misery he feels from increasingly losing control of his life to a virulent group of gangsters. As always, Loren has an addictive response to such feelings. After a pause he reaches and opens a small packet of grainy powder with a yellowish tinge, he cuts two lines, then he rolls a bill and snorts one at a time, causing a burning sensation in his nostril each time. He believes that meth makes him think more clearly, which is what he needs right now. The meth takes effect almost immediately and makes Loren hyper-active as any source of speed would do. He then focuses on the jumbled stack of books on the bed and floor and decides to put the books back in order on his large bookshelf to bring some organization back into his surroundings. His confusion mounts instead. As he places the books back on the shelves at high-speed, his vision becomes distorted, and many thoughts race through his mind all at once. To get oriented he tries to focus on one subject at a time, the first being Katie- and how she is part of the cause of his feelings of isolation from his business associates. "If she had not come to St Louis, this never would have happened and fingers would not be pointing at me right now," he mumbles to himself. "In some ways she deserves not to be around anymore, it would be the easiest solution. Maybe I should just go someplace else for a while and let someone come in and do what needs to be done, get rid of her."

Loren's fears are taking him down a dark road that could lead to destruction--then he starts laughing and says out loud, "What the hell Loren, who do you think you are in business with anyhow, choirboy's? You're in it to stay- or to leave in a way that you're not ready to contemplate. You just have to get her out of the picture, ASAP." His mind is really racing-and his thoughts are going way out of control. He takes a deep breath and looks around the room, still feeling shaky and anxiety-ridden he focuses on the small shopping bags containing goods Kate purchased in Chicago and had placed on top of the suitcase in the bedroom. Being inquisitive, he opens the bags and finds very seductive items that a woman would wear for lusty sexual purposes only, particularly if she is sexually submissive. Loren immediately just stops and stares after removing the contents from the shopping bags. These garments and accessories are like nothing he'd ever seen her wear before, which makes him wonder if possibly she has a second hidden life, or whether she is involved with other men, or maybe she is having sex with others because she thinks that he is doing the same thing. Then he remembers her saying to him in Chicago, "I'm ready to be filmed". Maybe there is more going on with her than he imagined and just maybe he shouldn't feel the guilt he has held inside himself about her. Maybe she deserves what his business associates might do to her in the near future."

Loren holds the clothing out to look at each garment closely- they sure seem to him like the sexy clothing of a submissive sex slave. Also, he just had an idea that might insure him a rightful position with his peers, but this will take a little more study and talking through. Loren returned to the table where he left his packet of meth, he cut another line then snorted it.

Most of the time when Kate visited, Loren abstained from meth, his addiction though has grown since then. Even though he is well aware of how much she hates the stuff. He used to rely on his marijuana to keep him satisfied while she visited. The difference in the two drugs and their effects on Loren are like night and day, meth brings out animated, confused and sometimes disturbing thoughts while when smoking pot he is usually mellow and layed back. Loren's mood swings can sometimes be extreme and unpredictable when he is using meth. Also, recently he has been having more feelings of paranoia, which is one of the common symptoms from using a stimulant like meth. When this occurs he accuses Kate of setting up blocks against whatever it is that he is trying to do.

Katie awakens aching a bit from being scrunched into her jeep all night. The rain had quit and the sun is shining brightly into her vehicle. She opens the door and gets out- wondering where Loren is and why he hadn't come to check on her, maybe he had- but let her sleep, or maybe, she thought, he is still angry and just doesn't want to wake her and have a conversation right now. She walks back into the shop, no work lights have been turned on, which means he is probably still up in his room. She is hesitant to go up there, but really has no other place to go and feels like she is being squeezed into a corner, the same way she felt before falling asleep last night.

When she enters his room he is on his phone probably talking to his boss from the way the conversation is going. She starts to back out of the room so that he can have his phone privacy- but when he sees her he waves for her to come in while still maintaining his conversation on the phone. He is laughing at something that had been said on the other end of the phone conversation, making Katie's mood a little lighter, as she is thinking that laughter is signaling that things may be fine now.

When Loren finishes his conversation he says "good morning" and seems observant toward her and asks her where she'd spent the night. Kate tells him of her falling asleep in her jeep, but not of the dismal crying spells, as she doesn't want this present positive attitude to go sour.

Loren then asks her nonchalantly if she is ready to be a film star. She looks at him hesitantly and pauses before saying, "Yes". Not that she really wants this role, but she wants to help him and to hurt the bad people he works for.

Loren walks over to her and starts fondling her roughly without tenderness or affection and pushes body contact with her in a very coarse and detached way. Then he pushes her down so that her face is next to his groin, then he unzips his pants. Katie is feeling a little dizzied by the quickness and force of his movements, she wants to say, "Hey wait a minute" but doesn't. What she does is just what he wants, and what he wants is her being sexually dominated by him in a hard and powerful way. Katie reaches in his clothing and touched his penis, but he is in a rush and takes her hand away and pulls it out himself and then takes her head and forces it down on him. He pushes hard down into her mouth and throat, at first choking her and making her have a gag reflex. He then he holds her head tight to him as he continues to thrust back and forth until he comes in her mouth. After she wipes her mouth and starts standing up he gives her a loud stinging spank on the butt with his hand and looks directly at her saying, "Bitch, you are my bitch", but the words are not said with a teasing-warm tone but a hard tone, and then he adds, "and no one else's."

Kate is floored by how he is treating her, she feels even more con-fused and hurt- he had never been this rough with so much crude meaning, usually when they had harder sex there was also an under-tone of warmer sensuality and affection from him towards her, but not this time. It felt more like a rape than anything else to her, but it wasn't rape because she had consented to him, in her mind anyway.

The following morning Loren takes Kate with him to pick up Rex at a dog kennel in Ladue, where they find Rex so happy to see them a leash isn't needed to lead him to Loren's truck. Within an hour of picking up Rex they start the drive back to the cabin, with Loren insisting that she needs to be there instead of the warehouse.

Kate really doesn't want to go because Loren's actions are becoming increasingly erratic and she is having more doubts that she is any safer with him than trying to fend against the boss and his henchmen on her own. Her insecurity has been heightened by her belief that Loren is regularly snorting meth again. After thinking things through, even in her confused state of mind she realizes she remains trapped, more or less, with no choice but to leave for the cabin with Loren.

As they drive not a word is spoken and Kate's thoughts drift as she stares at the road ahead. Her thoughts are of how Loren has turned her life upside down. He is intense and cold toward her most of the time and she feels when he shows her concern and compassion- it is just a game he is playing with her to keep her guessing or to keep her confused, although she admits to herself that she already has more than her share of confusion in her life. Since just before she performed sex on him last night nothing further has been mentioned about her doing films. Right now she feels it was a mistake to even mention such a thing to him and, at least for the moment, she doesn't intend to mention anything about making films again. Now what is she to do with the sexy garments she purchased in Chicago, she wants to throw them away as soon as they get to the cabin. Distrust is also a problem. For some reason she feels Loren distrusts her, he watches her every move and doesn't give her much time to herself before he is checking her exact location. Katie is beginning to be as scared of Loren as she is with his boss Frank, but especially she is most scared of this Jack Colbert who tried to run her over on the street.

Kate is thinking of some way to leave and not be found by anyone, but that is hard to do without cash. She is starting to think that Loren is changing so dramatically that he is turning on her.

Could she live without him? To be honest with herself- he has been in and out of her life for such a long period of time she finds it impossible to be without him at least on occasions. He is her fix and she is addicted to him and his unfocused way of treating her. He gives her love and pain, he gives her softness & hardness, he gives her most things in life that take her from black to white and from lines to circles. This is all true and explains why Kate's love is forever for Loren regardless of the balance of positive and negative forces that are present within him at any point in time. However, Kate fails to see the other side, where are embodied the opposite and contrary forces within her which have an inexplicable although intermittent hold on Loren.

They arrive at the cabin early in the afternoon; Kate announces as soon as she gets out of Loren's truck that she is going for a run. Loren gives her a hard look but says nothing. Kate hurriedly carries her suitcase into the cabin and changes into running clothes, then comes off the porch with a bolt of speed and turns right unto the road exactly like she had done the last time she ran here. When she is by herself she feels free and, as she continues to run, worries start clearing from her head; this is so good for her, to run- to be away from everything that seems to be creating so much negatively in her life right now. The next thing she becomes aware of is she has company running right beside her. It is Rex! Loren must have let him out so he could run with her. Rex is not a problem for Katie, she actually feels more relaxed and a little safer with him running by her side. After they run quite a long distance, more than normal, she stops for a few minutes to rest. Once she feels refreshed she starts the return trek to the cabin but at a slower pace than before. After a few minutes she and Rex come to a comfortable area where she takes the time to sit down on a large boulder on the side of the tree-lined road. Rex checks out the immediate area then plops down by her feet and pants contentedly. She takes her time being by herself, taking in every simple and beautiful detail of nature around her, and enjoying every minute of it.

Katie and Rex eventually return to the cabin with Katie feeling very rejuvenated. Loren is on his cell phone and she can hear him talking. He must be just inside the door because she can clearly hear everything he saying.

While sitting on the porch steps, Katie hears Loren's words, "You mean the police report now reads that Susie's death is accidental? That's good Frank; it kind of gets everyone off the spot, huh! I figured that it would work out in the end, thank God you have friends in the PD." There is silence as Loren listens, then Loren again speaks saying, "Look she's returning soon, I need to get off the phone". With that he must have hung up as there is only silence.

Katie stands up but remains outside. She seems frozen in place as she tries to decipher what she just heard and whispers to herself, "Loren and his associates are responsible for the death of someone named Susie"? Then the realization hits her like a lightning bolt that the "Susie" that Loren was talking about is the same Susie she has been reading about in the newspaper articles.

Loren walks out on the porch and stepped back a little when seeing Kate & Rex standing there. He says" Did you just get back?"

She replies, "Yes", in a casual way, which she hopes reflects no evidence of her knowledge or concern about what she had just overheard.

He then asks, "What took you so long anyway?" "Nothing in particular, just a long run", Kate replies nonchalantly, not to reveal her real feelings and concerns. Kate wants to spit in his face, but knows better, as she is still at his mercy.

However, it is now clear to her that she must immediately begin putting together a plan of escape, whether she has money or not. To develop an escape plan that will work, she knows she will need time alone, away from Loren, to think and rethink details of the plan plus contingency plans. Also, because of everything going on with Loren, including his increasing addiction to meth and involvement in the murder of the woman named Susie, Kate simply has lost any desire to be anywhere near him. In practical terms, she realizes that there are probably only two ways to be away from Loren while being at the cabin-- she can either stay in the cabin bedroom that looks like a "whorehouse designed by a tasteless idiot", which is the most accurate description she can think of for the room, or go outside, which she greatly prefers. After a few minutes she announces to Loren that she going to take Rex on a walk around the cabin area. Loren just looks at her and doesn't say anything. In the direction Kate walks she comes to the edge of a steep rocky slope. For several minutes she walks along the edge of the ridge before coming to a place where it looks possible to make a descent of 200 to 300 ft. She decides to try it and starts down taking small steps to try to keep her balance as the loose rocks on the steep decline makes the footing treacherous. At one spot she starts losing control of the pace of her descent but is able to remain upright by holding on to tree branches during the final slide to the bottom. Kate's descent down the rocky slope ends with her standing at the bottom with a big smile on her face. "That was really fun", she says out loud with a smile. After a few minutes of rest she is ready to start her climb back up the rocky slope, which is a hard physical challenge but she makes it fine. Rex is waiting for her at the top and she gives him a triumphal hug. These kinds of physical workouts always give Kate's moral a big boost and she is feeling great. She takes a quick look up through the trees and can see the afternoon sun and then she spots a small path going off in a southerly direction. "I think we have time for another short hike Rex, let's see where this path goes." Then they are off.

After their walk, Kate and Rex arrive back at the cabin just as the sun is setting. Loren is waiting for them on the porch, he is anxious and jittery and very upset that she went for such a long walk. "What is so precious about these walks, anyway?" Why can't you just be happy to be here, relax a little, huh?"

Kate just looks at him and says with sarcasm "It sure doesn't look like you're relaxed Loren, what's the matter with you? You seem to be the way you were a couple years ago when you were hooked on meth pretty bad." Katie knows she is taking a chance saying what she just told him, but she is sick and tired of his drug addictions and how it makes him act. They hurt not only him, but everyone who loves him, including her especially, and she is very sick of the whole thing and wants out as fast as she can get out. She frankly doesn't give a shit anymore!

Loren looks at her with a hard stare and says, "Go in the cabin-now."

Kate isn't budging, she firmly stands on the stoop of the porch, "Loren, I'm not that foolish- why would I go in there with you, especially with how you have been treating me. You seem to be very negative about me for some reason and I do not trust you one bit at this moment, no Loren, I'm going to sleep out here in your truck if I can, and if not, then on the porch. I don't want to be anywhere near you right now!"

Loren looks stunned in reaction to what she just said to him and he knows that when Kate makes statements like this she means it. He is too jittery to fight or argue with her and he knows this type of argument can lead to violence, which he hates, so he silently assents to let her stay outside. He then goes back into the cabin leaving the door ajar, just in case she wants to come inside from the cold fall air.

Katie sleeps in Loren's truck until just before dawn when the night air is the coldest. She has no blankets to keep her warm so she hesitantly and quietly goes into the cabin, where she finds the sofa is empty- so she gladly takes up residence on it and falls asleep immediately, under a warm throw, satisfied that Loren is asleep in the bedroom.

Rex slips out of the bedroom where Loren is sleeping and touches his cold nose to Kate's face. She pets him on the head a couple of times, and he then lies down on the floor beside the sofa and finishes his sleep with her.

It is late morning before Loren wakes her- he is being nicer to her than he had been the night before, but Katie has seen his rapid mood swings so many times before it doesn't mean much to her that his mood in the morning is the opposite of what it was when he went to bed. She also realizes, since overhearing Loren's side of yesterday's phone conversation about the woman named Susie, what he thinks of her life doesn't mean much to him either. She feels if Loren collaborates or is partially responsible for the death of anyone, he possibly could kill again or help his business associates kill again. But Kate is being recip-rocally pleasant to Loren this morning as a way to keep her distance without making it too noticeable. Also, it is now clear in her mind that nothing is going to keep her from escaping- she is certain of it.

18

PORN STAR

That afternoon Jack Colbert arrives at the cabin unexpect-edly, driving yet another new full-size pickup truck and the back is fully loaded and covered with a black tarp. He acts sheep-ishly around Kate but Loren doesn't seem particularly concerned about Kate's feelings in regard to the vehicular assault attempted by Colbert against Kate just last week. No one mentions the incident, it is as if it never happened and the new truck is not mentioned either--at least in front of Katie.

Loren and Jack spend most of the early afternoon talking outside behind Jack's truck, drinking a few beers and acting as if they are good friends. Kate spends her time split between steaming about the friend-liness Loren is showing towards Colbert and devising a plan for her to get back to St. Louis to get her jeep-- and she thinks she has come up with an idea which just might work.

Loren proceeds to drink heavier than usual, along with Jack up on the porch of the cabin until it is close to dusk when they start unloading some of the material and equipment from the back of Jack's truck and into Loren's truck to deliver these ingredients, lacquer thinner, some plastic bags containing cold medicines and a couple tanks of anhydrous ammonia to the factory."

Kate then watches them unload a couple of black plastic garbage bags of what she heard Jack call movie props. Kate is pretty sure she knows what the props are for.

After an afternoon ingesting meth along with quite a few beers, Loren is really feeling wired by now, and tells her, "Jack is going to spend the night here, and since you told me you want to be filmed and because I'm feeling in the right mood tonight, I have a hunch that tonight might just be your lucky night."

Kate tries not to show it but she thinks Loren's idea couldn't be worse and she just wants out--but she is trapped and knows that running from these two lunatics might get her killed tonight. They know the territory and she doesn't. If Loren alone could catch her as easily as he did the other night, she realizes she doesn't have a chance against two of them. Her heart is racing! It appears that Loren is planning to film her with Jack as her sex partner, and just the thought makes her nauseated. After a few minutes, Loren walks toward the front of the cabin, which prompts Kate to start walking nonchalantly toward the back of the cabin as if going for a walk.

Her movement catches his eye and Loren walks briskly over to her and looks straight into her eyes, his face only inches from hers and says in a firm -low voice, "Kate the last thing I would do if I were you would be to try to run. This time the outcome would be a lot more unpleasant than the other day, do you understand?" Kate looks at him then lowers her eyes and says, Yes, I understand". She realizes that she looks and sounds like she is being submissive to Loren's threat. However, even while her eyes are downcast she is silently committing to herself that her submission will only be for a short duration. Kate decides right then to play their game and she is sure, if she keeps her head she can win. She stays outside a little longer to try to prepare herself mentally before the night really begins.

Just at that moment Loren steps out to the porch looking for her as she is on the way inside. She notices that the beer seems to have mellowed-out some of Loren's meth-induced hyperactivity. He is noticeably slower moving, is slurring his words a little, and his voice is now lower and more gentle. "Kate, when are you coming in?"

Kate replies, "I'm on my way now, but can we talk for a second out here alone?"

Loren steps down off the porch and approaches her silently waiting for her to speak,

"Loren, why have you changed so much in the last few days?" Without saying so, Kate's question has a lot to do with the revelation that Loren had involvement with Susie's murder.

Loren replies, "Kate, I've always told you my business comes first over everything else, and then he hesitates before saying, "and that includes you."

Kate can feel her eyes swell with tears. To stop the tears before he notices, she quickly puts her head down while shutting her eyes tightly, then looking back at him she says without any emotion, "Let's go inside." Then she thinks to herself, "and get this over with as fast as I can", knowing that sex with someone she doesn't want to be with is on the agenda.

They walk into the cabin together, Jack Colbert is nowhere to be seen and then Katie hears noises coming from the bedroom. Loren offers Kate a cold beer- she takes the bottle and puts it to her mouth taking a long drink. It is cold and feels soothing to her, but she reminds herself to drink slowly as she needs to keep her wits about her.

Kate starts walking around the living area sort of pacing, which reflects her nervousness as to her fear of what may happen to her tonight. Her eyes are also anxiously darting around and then she fixes them on what looks to be the keys to her jeep hung on a key hook attached to the side of a kitchen cupboard.

Rex watches her move around, and Kate is sure that he can feel her anxiety.

Loren walks up to her and puts his arm around her and she tenses a little, which is barely perceptible to him. Strangely, she thinks of his arm as an offering of peace in a sense, although Kate distrusts him more right now than at any time since she has known him.

Jack walks out of the bedroom- his red hair hanging over his eyes and sweat on his forehead he nods to Loren and Loren acknowledges him with his eyes, as Kate is taking all of this in, all of her instincts are telling her to flee- now.

They all sit down on the sofa, but she immediately stands back up and moves over to the kitchen table to sit by herself. Rex follows her and sits down at her feet. Rex seems to sense that something is wrong and it is almost as if he is showing his allegiance to Katie by sitting at her side.

Jack is a slob in Katie's eyes-- his red hair is longish and wild looking, his complexion is a splotchy red especially tonight after getting drunk, and his eyes are small and cold. Also, it is obvious that he doesn't like her one bit as she knows too much about Loren's activities, including Jack's involvement with Loren.

She has also been wondering what other businesses Loren and Jack have been doing together to have gotten them so close. The very thought is so upsetting to her she reactively stands up and tries to go back outside but Loren's voice stops her.

"Kate, drink up, O.K.? I think you need to drink that beer just to loosen up, you're pretty tense." At that she hears Jack snicker, which sends her temper off the chart!

Kate turns to face him and says "You are just a sorry sack of shit" her voice becoming low and hard with anger, "You son of bitch, you tried to kill me the other day and now you sit here and snicker at me like an old woman –you're a major creep Jack, and I can see exactly why you cannot even attract pigs because they have more class than you could ever have." Then turning toward Loren, "you don't have the balls to tell this mother fucker to back off, you're nothing but a pair of real losers." Kate starts for the door fuming inside, but Loren heads her off by blocking the doorway. Rex jumps up and runs over and stands by Katie- he is confused, then Jack gets up off the sofa and walks over toward them, which causes Rex to start growling.

Kate, looking Jack straight in the face, says loudly, "You lousy mother fucker you!" Then Jack grabs her arm and twists it causing pain to shoot up into her shoulder.

Loren intervenes and tells Jack to ease off so he then releases her arm. Kate turns to Loren with a mixed look of fear and anger on her face, which causes Loren to lower his eyes so he doesn't have to look into hers. Jack brings a needle out of a nap sack, then mixes a powder and water mixture that he puts in the bowl of a spoon and, with a lighter held below the bowl of the spoon, he melts the contents in the spoon, after which he carefully pulls the liquid into the syringe. Then he looks at her and Loren, who is holding her, and then Jack injects her with the needle pushing the liquid out of the syringe into the flesh of her arm. All she remembers is the needle coming out of her flesh and then she fell, which seemed like floating, to the ground.

She can hear voices as she tries to adjust her blurred vision, she feels hands on her moving her or carrying her, then it seems, many hands on her as she senses she is being undressed. Numbness has overtaken her and she cannot sense exactly what is happening at any given moment, an aura of the surreal has taken over her mind and nothing matters at all. She believes it is Loren's voice that she is hearing, but it sounds distorted- like his voice is in very slow motion. She can feel her body being turned and her buttocks being raised up into a half crawl position with her elbows bent and another voice purring at her, "that's it baby show us". Then tightness starts to envelope her physical body, she can feel pressure points on her neck and breasts and lower thighs.

The voices seem to be getting clearer- she can hear Loren say in slow motion - "That's good now Kate, just hold that pose for me, sweet Kate- what a wonderful pose, let us see everything. "

She is becoming very intensely pleasured by something and the intensity level is growing, she feels something large between her thighs and ecstatic thrusts, then deeper thrusts, and she feels very wet, then she feels a hand on her mouth and it is soon full of hardness. At first she gags from the fullness but adjusts quickly to the pleasure enveloping her.

Another voice is saying "God, she's good... She has the right movements... Wish I was part of the action... Hold it Loren, that's a perfect clip... Now bring her up into a partial sitting position... Let her breasts show the marks from the rope, boy they are turning a little blue- that's perfect."

Kate feels only pleasure; she is semi-conscious but only of sensual pleasure and the hands that never leave her body. She remembers being hoisted up and her hands bound and body stretched up head to toe, her feet barely touching the floor and someone's hands pleasuring her by touching all the pressure points on her body. A prick in her arm makes her lose consciousness for a few seconds, thereafter she remembers almost nothing- but being touched, caressed and prodded.

Kate wakes at dawn the next morning- she is barely able to lift her head off the bed, her head is throbbing with pain, her body aches almost everywhere and her legs are trembling uncontrollably. She is worn out and remembers only vague parts of what happened to her. Her arms are stretched and she can't move them and she can feel tension in her neck and breasts and inner thighs. She lays there trying to gain more consciousness but still can't lift her body. It takes her a little while to realize that she is tied to the bed, which brings her back to reality almost immediately. The curtains are closed making the room dark except for little bits of light peeking through a couple of small openings. While she gazes around the room trying to adjust her eyes to the darkness she sees some ropes dangling from the ceiling, which seem vaguely familiar to her but she doesn't remember why. She starts to wiggle her arms and hands to try to loosen the cords that have her restrained. After a while she seems to be having some success as there is now a small amount of slack in the binding.

Then she hears Loren's voice in the other room, which is followed by her sickening recollection of Jack being at the cabin with them. She remains completely still to try to pick-up their conversation. However, the conversation is almost inaudible and the words too indistinct for her to comprehend, either because her hearing has been impaired or they are talking in low tones so not to be heard. After a few minutes she renews her efforts to slacken the cords which are binding her but, within just seconds, she hears footsteps close to the other side of the door and then the handle turns. Kate immediately closes her eyes as if sleeping, but she can sense a figure peeking in at her inside the doorway.

The door closes and she feels relief as it shuts. She knows she needs to get herself composed enough to think clearly, then she needs to get out of here!

The voices of Loren and Jack are now audible. She hears Loren say, "She's still out, and I think that she will be that way for a while. I need to get these supplies over to the factory- they've run out of the ammonia and can't make more meth until they get it. I'm paying them by the hour so this is wasted money on my part. If you want to see the how this business operates this is probably your only chance, Jack. Kate will still be here when we return." Loren finishes talking, and his invitation to Jack is just a ploy to get Jack to go with him. Things had turned out to be more difficult last night with Kate than he had expected. Loren made sure that he was the only one sexually involved with her as he had Jack operating the photo shoot.

However, Jack had wanted to be part of the action too, but Loren had refused. Also, under no circumstances did Loren want Jack to be here with Kate alone in her current weakened condition. He'd seen the results of the bazaar ways that Jack has treated women, and Loren will especially never forget the brutal condition he found Susie before she had died. He wishes that he had never involved himself with this son of a bitch, but is now in a position that he can't split from Jack right now especially with what had occurred in Chicago and the missing drugs.

"I'm leaving in a few minutes Jack, make up your mind if you want in or not", Loren says in a matter of fact tone.

Kate is listening and praying that Jack will leave with Loren as she realizes that if she is to be safe and have any chance of escape, it is imperative that he go.

Jack hesitates then says to Loren, "You're probably right, I'll get some things out of the truck and meet you outside." Jack turns his eyes to the bedroom door then, with a look of disappointment, he turns away and heads outside to his truck.

Kate, still feigning sleep, can sense her door opening one more time as Loren silently looks in on her. He shuts the door as quietly as he had opened it but, after looking at her laying tied to the bed, he is overwhelmed with gut wrenching guilt for what he has gotten her into. Loren leaves Rex inside the cabin with her, then drives off with Jack in his truck to deliver the supplies.

19

RUNNING HARD

Katie listens intently to the sounds coming from the direction of Loren's truck as he prepares to leave and, hopefully, with Jack with him. She hears the diesel truck being started and then being driven away once the engine is warm. As the sound of the truck fades in the distance, Kate intensifies her efforts to loosen the cords holding her captive. It takes her just a few minutes to loosen the bindings just enough so that she can get her hand into the slightly-loosened knot on her wrist, then with persistence she maneuvers her fingers, at first fumbling, then getting them partially into the knot, then she pulls with all the strength she can exert with her slim fingers—then it loosens and quickly unties. Once one arm is free the second arm is easy to free, then she quickly unwraps the rest of the remaining cords from her body. She is very sore and she checks herself out and finds bruises, mainly on her breasts and legs, which will heal within a short amount of time.

She quickly finds her clothing and dresses, then she opens the door to the living area and almost trips over Rex, who is standing right in front of the door to welcome her wagging his tail. She immediately steps to the cupboard to see if her jeep keys are still on the hook. She is in luck! She quickly lifts them from the hook and puts them in her jeans pocket, then she looks out the front door before going outside, just to ensure she is actually alone, which she discovers she is with only Jack's truck remaining in the drive-way.

Kate bounds down the porch stairs to see if the truck is locked, it is, but she looks through truck windows to see what may be inside. There is nothing visible on the seats or the dashboard, but as she is about to walk away she sees something so startling it almost knocks her off her feet! On the floor, just peeking from under the driver's seat, Kate sees a set of shiny new truck keys. Her heart starts pounding as Jack's truck may be the missing piece in her plan that can get her to her jeep in St Louis, which can then get her to a hiding place. Her heart is also pounding in fear as she knows she will be hunted and her time may be very limited as Loren and Jack could return at any time and could even spot her on the road leaving the area. However, she knows she can't just remain here and trying to hike away has already failed once—she knows she has to go for it. She jumps up into the back of the truck and tries to open the back sliding windows of the cab but they are also locked. She opens a tool chest sitting in the bed of the truck and takes out a hammer that she uses to bash the back window so hard the glass shatters into thousands of pieces, inside and outside the truck, including the shards that hit her. She then reaches in and unlocks the window that she has broken and slides the window open leaving a small entry into his vehicle.

Kate stops and thinks for a moment, then she quickly walks back into the cabin to go through drawers and cupboards in the hope of finding some dollar bills or at least some change. In the living area she finds a couple of one dollar bills that had been rolled to snort dope on the messy table, which she picks up.

Then she enters the dreaded bedroom to go through Loren's dirty clothes-where she finds seven more dollars and some change, which she quickly put in her pocket.

Rex silently watches her the whole time she is in the cabin, following her even between rooms. As Kate is leaving, she bends down quickly and kisses him on his forehead saying to him, "I love you Rex," then quietly adds, "Wish me luck."

She shuts the door so that he remains in the cabin. She returns to the back of Jack's truck then lifts herself into the truck bed then proceeds to stuff herself through the small back window of the cab. Going head first she puts her head and shoulders through the opening and then wiggles the rest of herself down onto seat in the cab. She could feel the sharp edges of broken glass as it scraped along her body as she fed herself through the opening. Kate grabs the keys off the floor under the driver's seat and holds her breath hoping that one of them is the ignition key for this truck, once again luck is with her, After turning the ignition on and adjusting the seat so her foot will reach the gas pedal, Kate puts the truck in reverse spinning the tires on the loose gravel on the driveway and then she makes a right turn onto the road. She has only a very vague idea of where she is and how to get to St Louis, but she knows she can't remain at the cabin any longer. Her heart is still racing and she is constantly watching for traffic as she is driving down the gravel road at excessive speed- praying that Loren will not pass her, or otherwise see her, on her way out of the area...

Loren is driving in a southwesterly direction going toward the factory located farther into the hill country. He is tired of listening to Jack brag of his accomplishments and the variety of problems he has with women, such as they nag too much, or they spend too much money, or they don't like rough sex or they have already dumped him.

Jack even mentions his disappointment that Loren hadn't shared the camera the night before nor had he shared Kate. He said something like, "after all we are partners, so to speak, with possibilities of future partnerships in other businesses".

Loren eventually blocks out Jack's words as his voice just becomes background noise droning on, as Loren's thoughts drift to thinking about Kate and the night before and what he had done with Kate, "She is a natural, she doesn't know it, but she is, and the big problem is that I should never fall in love with someone like her because, in a business like mine, you eventually have to share her. Usually women who are free-spirited like Katie don't mind that, sex is open to them- 'skin is in'- that sort of thing, but Kate is kind of conservative and would never consent to just anyone being called in to fuck her." Loren then shakes his head while thinking to himself "and I really don't want anyone else fucking her either, especially someone like Jack."

Loren is driving up a winding gravel road with his destination now less than a mile away, as he rounds the last dangerous curve and, while trying to avoid the ruts in the road, he finds himself now thinking about possible ways he can get rid of Jack. He wouldn't have brought him up here to see his business if Kate wasn't alone at the cabin, but he also has no intention of letting Jack be part of this business, he just needed Jack not anywhere Kate with no one else around.

He pulls up by a stone house that is in need of repair, there's an old wooden barn out back that is half caved in, the grass is mowed only occasionally and is in desperate need of it again, but probably won't get mowed again until next spring, as winter is coming on soon.

Loren is greeted immediately by a man who walks out on the front porch of the house, dressed in flannel shirt and work jeans, he steps off the porch smiling then says to Loren, "Glad that you got here, we've needed these ingredients for a couple days and there is some meth in the garage that's ready for the streets."

Loren introduces Jack saying, "Pete this is Jack', which is all he says before walking into the house, with Pete and Jack following close behind. Loren is not going to elaborate on Jack whatsoever and as soon as he can he plans on getting Pete aside and telling him not to give Jack information on anything.

The factory is set-up in the old kitchen area sprawling out to the enclosed back porch, and all of the windows on the porch are covered with plywood so no one can see in. It all looks and smells like a lab, with ammonia tanks connected to various lines leading to other vessels, and there are nauseous smells that stink up the lab area and even drift outside the house into the yard.

Jack has to walk outdoors to get away from the odor, which suits Loren just fine, because it gives him an opportunity to talk to Pete alone. Loren employs 3 men who work at this factory, although Pete is the only one who lives on the premises. Pete is very close to Loren- probably Loren's best real friend- and their bond, which has been long in the making, is such that no one can come between them or anyway that's how Loren feels.

Clay and Scott are the other two employees, and they make good money plus they receive a sizable supply of their own meth for personal use, which is a compelling incentive for them to keep their mouths shut about their employment.

Pete immediately starts hooking up the ammonia tanks while listening to Loren relating his issues with Jack about Kate and the fact that Jack is becoming more unhinged and violent at times.

Pete responds by saying simply, "Shit Loren" Leave the guy up here, you know how some people just get lost and are never found again."

Loren knows that Pete would help him with someone like Jack, and is seriously taking his offer into consideration-especially if things keep going the way they are with Kate. First, Jack trying to run her over and then his actions toward her again last night in the bedroom and also the death of Susie, which was so unnecessary and brutal, and all done by Jack.

But there is one detail of information that Loren needs to get out of Jack before moving against him and that might take some doing, at least a couple of days, possibly. Loren needs to maneuver Jack's confidence in him to a higher level.

Katie is on the second gravel road after turning off of the first gravel road a few miles back and she sees that she is approaching an intersecting paved road. As there is nothing else to try, she looks toward the sun to try to get her bearings, which doesn't help much but she senses that another right turn onto the paved road is the correct direction. She makes the right turn then starts looking for a place to stop to try to figure things out. She needs to find an inconspicuous place to park the truck away from the road because she has no idea which direction that Loren and Jack will be traveling when they return to the cabin—but there is a major risk it could be this road and if Loren sees Jack's truck, Katie's escape is over. After a few miles of narrow winding paved road, she comes to a roadside park and pulls over to see if there is a map in Jack's truck.

As she is pulling over to the side, a black truck drives by, which causes her to instantly duck her head in panic. It wasn't until it passed that Kate realizes it was a Ford not Loren's Dodge Ram truck. This incident makes her even more jittery- she is shaking so badly while looking for a map that she suffers more cuts to her hands on the shards of glass from the broken window which are scattered all over the interior of the truck.

She finds a brand new map that Jack placed in the middle compartment. When she unfolds the map she notices that a certain area has been circled which is close to Riverbend and she realizes immediately that the circled location is almost certainly where the cabin is located. Kate is fairly good at reading maps so she just needs to get back on the road to see the road number on the next road marker, to give her the coordinates for getting back to St Louis. Suddenly, time, precious time, has come to the forefront of her thinking. She knows that to get her jeep and to escape from St. Louis and Loren, she must get back to Loren's warehouse before he does.

Katie knows that the minute Loren and Jack get back to the cabin they will know that she has Jack's truck and they will come looking for her like there's no tomorrow. After leaving the roadside park, in less than a mile she comes to another narrow paved road and turns left. She soon comes to a road sign reading "K" -then she locates "K" on the map just about 20 miles north of Riverbend. Then using the sun for her bearings she takes some small roads in a generally northerly direction toward Highway 68. Soon she will run into Hwy.68, if she has interpreted the map correctly, and then Hwy.68 will take her to Inter- State 44 which will take her directly into St. Louis. Kate has a long hard drive ahead of her, however, her escape from the forces that threaten her may come down simply to fate in two parts: number one- Loren wouldn't hurry back to the cabin from the factory because of an unforeseen delay, and number two-he wouldn't call his hoodlum associates in St, Louis to keep a lookout for her because he would want to catch her himself.

When Kate arrives at Hwy. 68 she makes a left onto it and almost floors the gas pedal, as she takes curves at high rates of speed and sometimes passes 2 or 3 vehicles at a time.

She is not concerned that the police would pull her over and, in some ways, her wishes that they would. Kate is starting to develop confidence in herself again.

The first part of Highway 68 is a long sequence of hills and curves, which she is driving well in excess of posted speeds because she is terrified that Loren will catch up to her somewhere on the highway to St Louis or at his warehouse. Because of her good driving skills, Kate firmly believes right now that her safety and wellbeing is better served by her driving outrageously fast than by driving safely within the speed limit.

Pete needs some help with the details of a new written formula that Loren put together for him.

"These new ingredients" Loren tells Pete "make the meth less grainy and more even like a good cocaine high would give you."

Together they mix the powder ingredients after measuring each with pain-staking accuracy knowing that they may still have to tweak the mix a little bit more to get the dry ingredients within Loren's exacting specs - this is a time-consuming process but critically important in producing the right mix. After Loren and Pete are satisfied with the new meth mixture, Loren asks Scott and Jack for help in loading the meth into packages and then places the packages into pails with a layer of apples on top, to disguise the contents, then lids are securely placed on the pails. As the loading process for each pail is completed and prepared for transport, Scott and Jack will place that pail into the bed of Loren's truck, then cover everything with a tarp.

After observing Scott and Jack do their work for a while, Loren steps back inside to see how the 'new recipe' is coming along and to check with Pete if there is anything else for them to talk about. Pete says, "We've got it covered". Loren then checks his watch as he is starting to worry that Kate will be recovering from the drugs soon and he wants to get back to the cabin before that happens. So he says good-bye to Pete and gives Jack a wave toward his fully-loaded truck.

Jack isn't too happy about an early departure because he wants to have a look around at the entire meth operation since there is a chance that Loren and he might form another partnership for this business.

However, Loren is glad that he doesn't have time to oblige Jack whatsoever, as he really doesn't want Jack to know anything about his business. Driving back to the cabin with a large quantity of drugs could send them both to prison for many years if they are pulled over by a law enforcement officer, which means obeying all traffic regulations-including speed limits- for the full duration of the return trip to the cabin, whether Loren is feeling time pressure related to Katie or not.

Jack's mouth is going non-stop all the way back to the cabin, mostly about women who he has had sex with, wants to have sex with or who he will never have sex with again, which makes Loren dislike him even more. Loren pretends to listen and to be amused because he needs Jack a little while longer.

The second half of Rte. 68 going North is a breeze to drive, with fewer hills and curves, although the traffic has picked up somewhat but that doesn't stop Kate from passing everything in front of her. Once on Interstate 44, Kate is soon driving in excess of 100 miles per hour, "this truck of Jack's is really loaded" Kate says to herself "especially the engine." She wonders how he really made his money. She thinks to herself, "he must do real dirty work; otherwise he would be broke based just on his crude demeanor and low intelligence.

Loren and Jack both start sweating when a state trooper, who is on a side road at a stop sign, waits for Loren's truck to go past then turns on to the road and follows Loren for a few miles before making a left turn onto another road.

Jack, who almost had a nervous breakdown when the cop pulled out behind them, began sweating so profusely while they were being followed that Loren is certain that if the trooper had just stopped them- he would have searched his truck just because of Jack's obvious hyper-anxiety. When they arrive at the cabin and pull into the driveway- immediately Jack screams, "Son of a bitch, where's my truck?!" Loren turns white, he already knows what happened, but says nothing to Jack. He just jumps out of the truck, runs into the cabin, throws open the door to the bedroom, and then says, in a whisper, "Katie".

When he steps back outside Jack is still standing where his truck was parked and his mouth gaping open with nothing coming out. After a long pause, Jack mumbles, "Where's my truck, who would steal it, I had the keys?"

"He is so damned stupid that he still hasn't figured out that Kate has not only escaped but has also stolen his truck", Loren thinks to himself while shaking his head. Loren sees the remnants of shattered safety glass on the ground knowing it is from one of the windows in Jack's truck. Loren asks Jack, "You took your keys with you?"

"Hell yes", Jack says almost screaming.

"Did you have another set of keys in say in the truck or in the pocket of spare pants that you brought along?" Loren asks.

Jack thinks for a few seconds on this one, "Ah, yeah, sure, I had a second set locked in the truck- that's where I always keep the second set."

Loren just nods and walks away a distance in the effort to control his true emotions as he is thinking to himself, "I would like to just go over there put that sob out of his misery".

Jack then walks inside the cabin and almost immediately reappears screaming, "The motherfucking bitch took my truck didn't she?"

Loren says in a very deep and intense tone, "Her name is Kate. Don't ever call her that again, do you hear me?" He is looking at Jack with such anger and disgust in his eyes that Jack has to turn his face away from him, then he just quietly walks back into the cabin.

At least Rex is happy Loren had returned to him as he gives him a lick on the hand.

Loren is now stuck with just three options for dealing with Kate's escape, all of which are problematic for Loren. He can either unload the drugs and leave them here so he can drive at high speeds giving him a better chance of catching Kate, or take the drugs back with him to St Louis which is the best security option for the drugs but will take an extra hour of driving time to stay within the speed limits, or just call his business associates in St. Louis and let them take care of Kate. The third option sure seems the easiest but also the ugliest. 'Shit," Loren says out loud. Loren then holds his head in anguish as he makes a painful decision and whispers, "I have to call St. Louis and let Frank take care of her".

After Kate's escape, in Loren's mind she is now as good as dead. No matter how Loren looks at it, Kate's life will be snuffed out, eventually through him if he regains control of her, or through Frank who won't wait. Also, if Loren did find her and got caught once again trying to help her distance herself from the gangsters, who Loren calls business associates, he would likely end up dead too.

Kate wasn't cut out for this kind of life and Loren can no longer justify his attempts to save her. "Shit," he says aloud again, as the weight of the guilt he feels is immense and not relieved at all by his thought that "his work is his top priority".

He clicks on his cell phone and clicks in Frank's number, then Loren says into the phone, "Ah, yeah, something's come up-- Kate, you know my friend-- well, she is in Jack Colbert's truck and I'm sure she is headed back to my warehouse in St Louis, then there is silence as words are spoken in response on the other end. Then Loren says hesitantly in reply, "do what you have to do."

20

THE CHASE

Loren calls for Rex and tells Jack to get the truck ready, as they are delivering the meth to St. Louis tonight. "Let's get going", Loren shouts "Kate's way ahead of us already," keeping Jack in the dark about what he discussed in his phone call to Frank. They head out the driveway onto the gravel road, Loren already knows it will be late night by the time they get to St. Louis, as he will not be exceeding the speed limit with the cargo he has onboard. He is silent the entire trip and blocks out all of Jack's conversation as he had done during the trip from the factory. Loren wishes it was Jack who was being hunted down, and not Katie. Also, he is now regretting that he'd made that call to Frank, and is saying a little prayer that Kate will be able to somehow avoid what will be waiting for her at the warehouse.

Kate hits the rush hour traffic going northeast on Interstate 44 once she is in the St. Louis area. Traffic is always heavy on I-44 going into the city at this time of day. All three lanes are bumper to bumper and many times the traffic just moves at a crawl.

An accident slows her down at least for another 20 minutes while the wreckers towed the damaged vehicles away and the usual slowdown caused by gawkers makes the traffic even worse. Kate figures that it will be just dark when she arrives at the warehouse.

Her gas gauge is nearing the zero mark and she is very unsure if she can even make it to the warehouse without stopping for gas. She estimates she has another 20 or 30 miles to go. She was still driving in the passing lane trying to make speedy headway but even the passing lane traffic is running at only about 45 miles per hour. Her nerves are still on edge and the small scratches on her hands and arms from the broken glass cause her pain occasionally depending on how she moves her arms. She is starting to think more about what she will find at the warehouse. Katie hopes that Loren is a long way behind her and hasn't even encountered all the St Louis traffic problems yet, but her greatest fear is that Loren possibly called Frank after he discovered that she had taken Jack's truck and that Frank, and not Loren, will be waiting for her at the warehouse. She really doesn't think Loren would do that to her mostly because no matter how he treats her at times, she believes deep in her heart and soul that he really cares for her.

She is only a few miles from her exit on Jefferson Street, when the truck starts jerking a little bit, indicating she has completely run out of gas! The traffic is very heavy and she is still in the passing lane. Kate pulls over on the far left side of the curb, turning on her warning signals; she get out of the truck with just a cement barrier between her and the oncoming traffic and starts running down the left side curb of the highway as fast as she can, knowing that crossing the road would be suicide under the current traffic conditions.

"Hopefully a cop will spot her and help her." she thinks to herself as she runs. After close to a mile she sees an exit she recognizes called Vandeventer. "Only one more mile," she says under her breath while running even harder. Kate has to cross the highway some way to get to the exit ramp so she starts looking for breaks in the string of vehicles before she can start crossing one lane at a time, running diagonally she first crosses the passing lane then runs down the center line as honking cars pass her on both sides until she can cross the center lane, panting and thinking, "one more lane to go". Suddenly an SUV swerves almost hitting another vehicle to avoid running over her, then her chance comes at last because of several vehicles turning off onto the Vandeventer exit giving her the last big break to cross the slow lane. Kate then runs up the exit ramp alongside the cars with drivers staring at her in disbelief.

She knows where she is going, she remembers the bus stop that has a bus route that stops near the warehouse, but by now it is completely dark which is disorienting. She is out of breath and is panting hard.

Her sides ache from the over-exertion and she is trying not to double over from the pain.

After slightly catching her breath, she runs another ¼ mile from the exit ramp toward a bus stop. The people waiting at the bus stop can see Kate approaching and can only continue to stare at her as she pulls up at the bus stop and tries to catch her breath again. A kind black woman asks her if she needs help, Katie wants to cry but did not dare, and she just thanks the woman for inquiring. Then Kate sits next to the woman on the bench and they visit a little and Kate tells her a lie about the scratches and dried blood.

Kate catches the second bus on Grand Blvd. that will stop at the corner near Loren's warehouse. The traffic is much thinner now; most commuters were already at their destinations. She gets off the bus with a handful of other people and starts walking the block to the warehouse., As she is crossing the vacant lot that is adjacent to Loren's fenced back yard, she hears voices coming from that vicinity, which makes her instinctively stop still in a crouching position to remain unnoticed while she tries to evaluate what is going on in the alley behind Loren's fenced yard. She can tell from the voices that there are at least two people there, but because of the leafy vines growing profusely on the chain link fence nothing can be seen clearly but it appears there is a vehicle parked in the alley.

Then Katie hears a car door open softly, illuminating an interior light in the vehicle, which reveals that it is parked directly in front of Loren's gate. Kate instantly realizes then that Loren has called Frank about her escape and Frank is here to fix the problem. Her immediate reaction is fear and her heart beat is already racing, but she also has feelings of sadness from Loren's betrayal. It is difficult for her to believe and accept that Loren would do this to her. She closes her eyes for a moment to regain her composure then starts moving slowly and quietly away from the alley with the darkness and vine-covered fence allowing her to move without being noticed. She quietly walks along the side of the brick building that is next to Loren's warehouse, looking in all directions every few steps. When she reached the corner of the front of the brick warehouse, she cautiously peaks around it to see if anyone is in the front area- it is clear- so she quickly and quietly walks past the front of the brick warehouse and the adjacent building watching in all directions every few steps until she then quickly walks around the corner of that building into the untrimmed tree line that stretches from the back of the brick warehouse to the back of its adjoining fenced storage yard.

This is the only time that Kate had felt blessed that there are hoards of junk located next door to Loren's place. She quietly winds her way around junk and trees, slowly making her way to the back fence where she finds a large hole in the back fence and, when she steps through it, there is only a dumpster between her and the car parked outside of Loren's yard in the alley. She waits there behind the dumpster trying to listen and while doing so observes that the vehicle outline is that of a SUV. She then focuses in on the voices but they are muffled so she thinks they are probably inside the vehicle.

Katie is feeling exposed standing next to the dumpster so she carefully puts herself through the hole in the fence back into the storage yard full of junk. Then she tiptoes along the fence line separating the two storage yards being careful not to step on debris that would give her away. She is now facing Rex's metal shelter just on the other side of the fence- at one time it was old car hood that had been leaned against the fence to give him protection from the elements when he needs it while he is outside on his chain.

Kate sits down in the grass where she is totally hidden by Rex's shelter as her camouflage. She didn't realize it until now but she is exhausted and thirsty even more than hungry. The last time she had seen either food or water was yesterday. As she is sitting silently by the fence she wants to see exactly who is in the vehicle, but her mind which has already done the calculations, knows that Frank and his friend are the occupants.

Then the car door opens and she hears a male voice grunt as he gets out of the vehicle, soon she hears Frank's voice, he is talking on his cell phone saying, "Yeah, it's eight o'clock and she's not here yet, are you sure she's coming back to the warehouse?" Then silence again as Frank listens before he adds, "her jeep is still parked in your yard," then more silence before Frank says, "You got us into this mess, if she doesn't show in the next half hour we're out of here and you are going to have to find her yourself, I'm tired of this shit, and babysitting for some bimbo who is trying to run! And, when you find her Loren, you have the privilege of doing what needs to be done, and now I'm sure you realize that this problem has to go away permanently." Frank is gruff, short and to the point. Then Kate hears the car door open and then close meaning that Frank is now sitting back in his vehicle.

"It is so deathly quiet out here," Kate thinks to herself. As she is so exhausted she has to fight off sleep but still she dozes off, knowing that Loren is probably going to have to kill her, or have her killed.

She wakes suddenly when she hears Frank's vehicle start up and drive slowly down the alley. Kate gets up and tries to view the SUV driving away but the view is blocked by the vines, and all she can make out are the tail lights twinkling through the vines for a few seconds until they disappear as the vehicle turns onto the street.

Kate now has her opportunity to get her jeep and escape, but the opportunity may last only for a few minutes. She gets up immediately and goes over to a walnut tree that is growing next to the fence, she grabs a branch about 6 feet up and starts walking her feet up the trunk, she is weak from not eating but she still has enough strength to last a couple more hours, she hopes. At first she fails in her attempts to get her arms up high enough in the branches to elevate herself into the tree, but then manages to do it after a few attempts with her mind simply willing her weakened body beyond its physical limits. She is now half standing crouched in the tree, almost the same height as the top of the 8 ft. fence. She gets a good grip onto a branch with one hand and grabs for the fence with the other catching her hand on the barbed wire top, sharp pain shoots through her hand and arm but she doesn't let go, she then extends one foot up high enough to touch the top of the chain link fence, then using her other leg she pushes herself while letting go of the tree with that hand and holding unto the barbed wire with both hands, quickly bringing her leg over to Loren's side of the fence she simultaneously hoists the rest of her body over the barbed wire barrier. She hangs on for a few seconds before letting go and falling into Loren's storage yard, landing very close to Rex's metal shelter. Kate quickly gets to her feet, her one ankle hurts a little from the fall, but she keeps moving as she is groping around in the dark looking for something to use to either break or cut the padlock on the gate, so she can get her jeep out of the yard. She finds nothing in the storage yard that will work then, as she is almost in tears, Katie remembers that she has a key to the front door of the warehouse that Loren had given her that she had forgotten about and Loren must have forgotten about it too. As she is reaching in her jeans pocket for the key, her smile again turns to tears as she realizes that she will have to re-climb the fence to get to the front door and she is just too weak, exhausted and disoriented to do it again. Even though she is now sobbing in despair, she is determined not to give up. Then as she is looking at the set of keys in her hand, she remembers that she has a tool kit in her jeep and it may contain a saw or other tool that can cut a padlock. She quickly unlocks the jeep then grabs the small tool kit from her jeep and finds a small rough-edged saw and immediately starts trying to saw the padlock. The saw is small and not very sharp but, with a lot of effort, it is slowly cutting the padlock.

Knowing that Loren could possibly be here soon and find her still locked inside, some dark humor enters her mind. "What a laugh they will have thinking about me locking myself inside the storage yard and being unable to escape- as they're cutting my throat". Katie is distraught and crying but continues to cut the padlock--slowly.

Kate has cut about half way through the padlock when she hears Loren's diesel truck pull around the corner to park in the alley. Kate immediately runs to the side of the warehouse building next to a pile of scaffolding with high weeds surrounding it. She is sure she won't be seen unless someone walks right to where she is hiding, then she thinks of Rex, "Oh my God, Rex will unintentionally find me!"

She then jumps up and runs to the driver's side of her jeep, quickly gets in and ducks down. Her only chance now is to drive out very quickly as soon as Loren opens the gate to come inside the yard. She can hear the diesel engine in the alley now, but she dares only look up far enough to vaguely see that he is parking outside the fence next to the side of the gate.

Loren is relieved when he sees Kate's jeep still in his yard. This is the second time tonight he has felt relief, the first being when Frank called him and said she hadn't shown up at the warehouse, meaning that Frank hadn't gotten his hands on her. Loren realized on the long slow haul back to St. Louis what a grave mistake he had made calling Frank while he was feeling desperation back at the cabin this afternoon. Also, he knows that Kate is a victim and that he truly wants to do everything possible to get her out of this alive.

He shut the engine off on his truck, and a few seconds later she hears him arguing most probably with Jack, then she hears the gate start to be rolled back, it was at this moment that she put her keys in the ignition, while keeping her head bent below the height of the dash so she can't be seen, then she waits to hear the gate come to a halt which will signal that it is open as far as it will go. As she waits to hear the gate stop, it is an excruciating few seconds which seem like an eternity. Suddenly the gate is silent and Kate instantly flies into action by almost simultaneously turning the ignition key, springing to a sitting position, throwing the jeep into gear and hitting the accelerator—causing the jeep to virtually fly forward through the gate with tires spinning and almost running over Rex and Jack. All three of them were caught off guard by Kate's sudden and furious exit through the gate opening. However, they regain their bearings fairly quickly and she hears one of them hit the back of her jeep with something hard as she is making the left turn past the gate.

Kate drives her jeep as fast as she can through the alley making another left, then a right which put her onto the street. After stopping at a red light she looks in her rear view mirror to see if Loren is following her. At first she doesn't see him but just as the light is turning from red to green, she sees him pull out from the alley onto the street only one block behind her.

Katie is very scared, which is causing her to make mistakes. Instead of making a right turn at the intersection as she intended, she went straight with Loren right on her tail. As she is driving down Lafayette, Loren pulls up on her left side and moves over into her lane running her off the road and then her jeep rams hood-first into a large tree. She jumps out of her vehicle and starts' running down the sidewalk then crosses over to Lafayette Park; she enters the park at a full run scared half to death, praying they won't catch her.

Katie knows that neither Loren nor Jack can outrun her, which helps her maintain her hope of escape. She takes the diagonal path through the park hoping to exit at the opposite gate, but on getting very close to the gate she sees Loren's truck cruising slowly down the road near where she wants to exit. At that moment Loren's truck drives under a street light and Kate sees that there is just one person in the truck, which means that whichever one is not driving is in the park searching for her as she had seen two men in Loren's truck when they ran her off the street a few minutes ago. Katie makes a dash to the right getting off the path and into the grass and tree covered areas, she stops behind a large tree then slowly scans the area surrounding her to see if she could see a silhouette of a man, particularly among the trees or along the fence line. Seeing nothing but trees casting shadows over large areas, she moves more slowly now hiding behind trees occasionally as she goes, she can sense she is nearing the pond and remembers the rocky stream with the nearby bridge. Kate moves cautiously toward that area- staying as far away from the pond as she can because she could be spotted easily in such an open area. Then making her way down the slope she moves behind more trees until she reaches the stream and then follows it to the rocky area underneath the bridge.

The stillness is so intense; she hears every sound-- the running stream, an occasional hoot of an owl and just eerie noises of the night. She squats down with her back against the interior of the bridge wall, which gives her a good vantage point to see anyone coming from either direction. Also, she is thinking that a person walking by would be unlikely to see her because her spot it is so dark under the bridge.

Katie remains crouched for what seems like a long time when she hears leaves being shuffled by feet. "Someone is real close," Kate thinks to herself with her heart beating rapidly. She can then hear the person shuffling across the bridge, she has no idea who it is-it could be Jack, a vagrant or someone on drugs-it is just impossible to tell. She remembers Loren telling her the parks aren't safe at night in St. Louis.

Kate is dead silent and shaking from both fear and the chill in the air. She then sees a figure walking down the slope towards the interior of the bridge on the other side of the stream. The person hesitates before continuing down the slope, all she can see is a silhouette of a man. The man coughs scaring her even more, she is in a crouch position so that she can easily get up and run if needed.

The man in silhouette is still shuffling his feet, slightly tripping over the rocks as he enters under the bridge; and it is not until he is directly across from her that she gets up and bolts up the slope right into the arms of Jack, who grabs her tightly by her arm.

Kate is hitting and kicking him with all the strength she has, which doesn't stop Jack from dragging her farther away from the bridge as she is screaming. He then pushes her down to the ground hitting her face and upper body as she goes down, her screams can be heard throughout the park this quiet night, but Jack's wild anger toward her seems to keep him from even hearing her screams as he continues to hit and kick her while she is on the ground.

Katie has put her arms around her head in self-defense, and her screams are becoming more muffled. She can feel blood from her mouth and nose pouring out and it hurts her to breath. Kate is fading in and out, but trying her best to remain conscious. The last thing she hears is Loren's voice in a muffled but furious rage shouting, "You son of a bitch", and the last thing that Katie feels is a heavy weight falling on top of her.

When Loren had sideswiped Katie's jeep earlier, he did so in a sincere attempt to get her to come back to the warehouse for her safety, not to hurt her, but to convince her he really wants to help her get out of the mess he has gotten her into. He knows she distrusts him immensely, and with very good reason. But he also knew if she tried to run off in her jeep there was a significant risk that look-outs would catch her before she reached the outskirts of East St. Louis.

Loren knew he had a lot of explaining and making up to do-if she was going to believe him, and when he opened the storage yard gate and her jeep shot out of it, she obviously took both Jack and himself by surprise. He took major risks driving that truck in a wild chase to catch her while it was fully loaded with meth in the back, then sideswiping her vehicle knowing she wouldn't stop for him any other way except stopping her the way he did.

When she started running, Jack became enraged and jumped out of Loren's truck to chase her down in the park. Loren knew that Katie could outrun Jack and thought that he would find her before Jack would by driving around the perimeter of the park. When too much time passed, Loren could sense that things had gone wrong, so taking a huge risk, he parked his drug-loaded truck, then carrying a tire iron in his hand because of the danger that always lurks in this park late at night, he went into the park looking for her or Jack, and it wasn't until he heard her screams that he determined her location, then he ran at full speed toward her voice.

When he saw Jack standing over her kicking at her head, he knew he had to stop this psychopath and without hesitation brought the tire iron full force into the back of Jack's head, killing him instantly.

21

WITHIN AN INCH OF DEATH

Loren sees Kate's hand move evidencing she is still alive, but her body lacks any other movement and her breathing is shallow. After just a few seconds, he recognizes he must get her medical attention immediately if she is to survive the depraved beating she has just undergone. Jack's body is motionless and laying partially on top of Katie, effectively pinning her to the ground. Using his foot, Loren pushes Jack's body as hard as he can and is able to move it enough to get to Katie. He then gets her elevated sufficiently so that he can heave her over his shoulder. To the extent he can, with Katie over his shoulder, he glances in several directions hoping he doesn't see anyone who may have witnessed what had just taken place. He doesn't see anyone, which lowers his tension level a little. He wants to get Katie immediate medical attention but he is having anxiety about taking her to a hospital emergency room or clinic because such facilities often feel required to report injuries, like those suffered by Kate, to law enforce officials. He is thinking that the safest plan for Kate and himself is to get her to his warehouse then try to find a doctor who can treat her injuries—with discretion. Frank may possibly be watching Kate and Loren right now, so getting the police involved in any way involving a hospital emergency room or clinic, will get the boss' attention and would end in disaster for both of them.

Loren continues the long trek through the park back to his truck with Kate on his shoulder and the tire iron in his other hand. He is still shaking from the anger, fear and shock from seeing Jack's vicious blows to Kate's head and body while she cried out, as well as Loren's physical response which culminated in him delivering a death blow to Jack's head. As he continues to walk, his shock seems to be diminishing somewhat as he reverts back toward normalcy. He continues to look around as he perseveres toward his truck, which is difficult as Kate is lying lifelessly over Loren's shoulder unable to assist his movement in any way. . As Loren walks he sees no one, but also realizes that he and Kate may have been seen by people who were in the park tonight but who are unlikely to be the sort of folks who would call the police.

The dead weight of Katie on his shoulder is severely sapping his strength but he dares not stop, as he needs to get her to his warehouse for safety then get her medical assistance ASAP. Loren's worry for Kate is also increasing because he hasn't felt her move since he lifted her up on his shoulder.

Finally, he reaches the gate of the park closest to where his truck is parked. He scans the streets for passing vehicles then, when none are approaching, he hurriedly walks to his vehicle, where he leans Kate the best way he can against the side of the truck. After fumbling in his pockets for his keys for a moment, he finds them and quickly unlocks the truck and opens the passenger door. He lifts Kate as high as he can then pushes her in the passenger side and then lets himself in the driver's side. While driving to his warehouse, Loren is watching every second for possible trouble and also watching her for any movement of life beyond her faint breathing.

As they arrive at the warehouse, the backyard gate is still open exactly as they had left it. He drives his truck into the yard, parks it, quickly locks the gate and carries Katie inside and upstairs to his room.

After meeting them at the door, Rex follows them upstairs then stands back watching as Loren lays her on his unmade bed. Katie's lacerated face is covered with dried blood and her body is badly bruised and swollen, which reminds him of Susie's appearance the day he found her battered and lifeless body.

Kate's breathing is very faint and irregular and she seems to be getting more feverish. Loren sees a red woolen blanket at the foot of the bed and he unfolds and spreads it over Kate in case she goes in to further shock. He then reaches for an old directory in his desk, where he puts bits of information and scrapes of note paper containing names and contact information of interesting people he meets or who might be a potential customer. He turns to a scrap of paper which contains the name, "Dr. John Cummins on E. Grand Blvd". Loren pauses for a moment while thinking to himself, "this is a long shot but if Katie doesn't get help she will be dead within hours". He has only met Dr. John Cummins once but the story of this man has remained with Loren. Loren's memory drifts, "several years ago Dr. John established a successful medical practice in St Louis and had developed a reputation for being a kind and friendly person and a competent medical doctor. Then one day he was accused, many thought wrongfully accused, of committing a malpractice offence related to a child of a wealthy and politically-connected couple. In the end, there was a legal proceeding and John received an unjust ruling, which resulted in him having a tarnished reputation and losing his license to practice medicine, a profession he had always loved. Then in the aftermath of these events he developed a severe drinking problem in an attempt to ease his pain." Loren just shakes his head at this sad remembrance of Dr. John, then he dials the phone number on the scrap of paper in his hand. Someone picks up the phone and Loren hears a sleepy voice saying "Hello, this is John."

Loren greets him by saying, "John, this is Loren Goodwin over on Jefferson, I'm the guy who changed your flat tire on the side of Highway 55 about a year ago.".... "Yeah, that's me. Listen, John, when we were talking that day while I fixed your tire, you told me that if I ever needed a return favor just to call you—I'm afraid this is the night and I need your help badly. My woman has been hurt and she urgently needs medical assistance."

John pauses then asks, "Can you bring her to my place?"

Loren replies, "No, "I can't come to your place- I need you to come here. I have a living area above my warehouse- and bring your medical bag and please hurry. I'll be down stairs waiting for you to ring,"

Then John asks, "I'm assuming you need me as soon as possible?"

Loren replies, "ASAP."

John responds, "Give me a half hour, I have to get dressed and put my medical gear in the car."

Loren gives John directions then ends the conversation with, "Thanks very much, John, I'll see you in a half hour."

Loren goes back over to Katie's side to try to give her some comfort while waiting for John's arrival. She is still just faintly breathing and every 10 minutes or so she moans and her mouth opens like she is trying to say something, but no words come from her mouth. Loren gently rubs her arms and her shoulders, hoping that the gentle touch and stimulation might help her in some way.

In about 40 minutes, which seemed like hours to Loren, the shrill doorbell rings, which ignites Rex, who immediately starts barking loudly while running down the stairs ahead of Loren. At the door Loren roughly pushes Rex aside to let the doctor in.

Loren opens the door and greets John with, "Thank you for coming, particularly being so late. As John steps through the door, with a small smile he says, "It is good to see you again Loren. I still think about how you got me out of bind with that flat tire on 55. Now, where is the patient?" While holding on to Rex, Loren waves for John to follow him upstairs. He doesn't take the time to explain why John is needed because of the urgency of Katie's condition.

The moment that John sees Katie he moves to her side and begins taking her pulse immediately then opening each of her eyes to find that she is semi-comatose. Then John gently removes the blanket and loosens her clothing, and then begins trying to gently determine if her neck is fractured. As he examines her further he tells Loren that he is almost sure at least one of her ribs has been fractured, but an x-ray is needed to confirm it. Then John tells Loren to get some warm water and a cloth so he can clean the dried blood off her face and neck to further investigate her lacerations.

Doctor John doesn't talk and just works on Katie, but with his silence is the knowledge that she needs treatment in a hospital due to the seriousness of her injuries. He gently raises her head after realizing her neck is not injured. With her head slightly elevated, he can feel egg-sized lumps swelling in three different locations on the back of head, then saying, "How this woman is alive right now is beyond me!" John's statement is made with sternness in his voice which partially reflects condemnation and partially is just an inquiry as to what had happened to Kate to cause such serious injuries.

Loren moves closer to John to say, "Remember when you told me about how you lost your medical license and asked me never to repeat it? Now I'm asking this of you John, first, please save her and secondly, what I'm going to say to you can never leave this room," then Loren starts telling John the complete story of this evening while John tends to Kate and her various injuries.

Before long, John interrupts Loren to ask him to go out to his car to get a large brown leather bag out of the back seat. When Loren returns with the leather bag, he helps John set-up a make shift intravenous stand, which is actually a modified coat tree. Then John takes out a plastic bag of clear liquid and hangs it on the pole and inserts a needle to run the IV into Kate's hand.

After John makes sure that the IV is working OK, he asks Loren to, "Please finish telling me about tonight" and Loren proceeds once more. John stays the night sitting by Kate's side in the living area above Loren's warehouse.

Loren wakes up at one point in the night and, when he looks over at John, he sees a tear in his eye as he tends to Kate's injuries. For the first time in a long time Loren realizes that there are still some decent human beings in this world. Loren has been dealing with so many ruthless people for so long, that compassionate people almost seem not to existent to him any more- except for Katie.

The morning is early and it's still dark outside when both Loren and John, who neither had really slept, hear sirens not too far in the distance. Although sirens are commonly heard near his warehouse, Loren instinctively believes that the sirens are related to the discovery of the body of Jack Colbert. Whether this is really the case has yet to be seen but, after several hours, Loren has no feeling of guilt at all for killing the man, although he really didn't mean to do it. However, seeing Jack violently beating Katie to near death sent Loren into a defensive rage that, at last, has ended a long series of demented and violent attacks committed by Colbert against innocent women.

Loren sits in silence as he hears more sirens all within a few blocks of his warehouse and all the sirens seemingly coming from the same location.

John asks for a cup of coffee and Loren apologizes for not having any already made, then gets up quickly and puts on a fresh pot.

While drinking coffee together John insists that Loren get Kate at least to an emergency room, where she can get needed x-rays for head, chest and abdomen areas.

Katie is starting to come around somewhat, but they can tell that the painkillers that John has given her did not kill all of her pain.

Because Loren trusts John, he now tells him about his boss and that a trip by Kate to any emergency room, while in her condition, could attract police attention. For her own safety, she needs to be hidden for quite a while. She would be safer yet if no one outside of this building knows that she is still alive.

John intently listens and then hesitantly says to Loren he has to leave, but says he will be returning after he runs a couple errands that are of utmost importance. He then tells Loren what to do to keep Kate comfortable while he is gone. The sun is just starting to rise as John is leaving and he gives Loren assurance once again that he will be returning within a couple hours.

Loren's cell phone rings. He looks at the caller ID but doesn't answer and let's he caller's message go to his voice mail. It is after the call that a plan starts to emerge for Loren, which just may work, if it's put together properly, but it won't be easy. He checked on Katie- she was sleeping and her breathing is more regular and natural now, a definite improvement over how she was breathing earlier.

Loren leaves her just long enough to go out to his truck and hurriedly unloads the pails of drugs into his warehouse, hiding them under a large work table below the bottom shelf, where the pails can't be seen unless someone gets in a kneeling position. He then looks at his truck which has scrapes of green paint on the side fender and door from having sideswiped Katie's jeep in last night's chase. Loren is also assuming that Kate's jeep has been towed away by now, but a potential problem is that it was located across the street from the park near where Loren left Jack's body. Loren needs to get things set-up before he calls Frank for help.

John returned sooner than he expected and he has good news for Loren. He made contact with a veterinarian friend by the name of Paul who is willing to secretly x-ray Kate. "The vet is located out in St. Charles about 25 miles NW of the city. If we can get her out there, Paul will x-ray her and give her the medical attention that I cannot give her as I don't have the necessary equipment." John tells Loren.

Loren agrees wholeheartedly, then apologizes in advance for having to ask for the next needed favor. "John, I need to get Kate off my premises immediately and for a considerable length of time. The vet saving her life will be of no value if she isn't moved now because the people that don't want her around will be showing up here very shortly. I'm sorry to have to involve you but you are my only hope, I need your help more than you can imagine. I cannot leave here for long periods of time for the next day or two, and by then it will be too late for her if she isn't moved now. The only way to keep her alive, and even myself at this point, is for these people to believe that she is already dead. I don't know if I can pull this off, but I've got to give it my best shot. If you can, if you will, please get her to this veterinarian and then find a place where she can be hid until she's well enough to leave. I can't help much with money right now but I'll give you all I have, but in the near future- if everything works out according to my plan- I will have plenty of money to pay for all her expenses and reimburse you for all your time and effort." Loren's lengthy request and explanation ends and seems to have struck a chord with Doctor John.

John already knows from his and Loren's previous conversations of the danger involved for anyone getting in the way of Loren's boss, including himself. But John feels he really has nothing to live for and this gives him a reason to live- to be relevant and useful once again. Until today his drinking has been the only way he could cope with what life had dealt him these last few years.

22

SECRECY

Doctor John lost his license to practice medicine for malpractice in the death of a child that could have been preventable, but lack of knowledge in thoroughly researching the child's life at home resulted in the child's untimely death.

The parents of this child being very affluent and having much prestige did not only sue John and win but they also knew the right political groups and had his license evoked permanently when in reality the parents were able to cover up their severe abuse of the child and putting the blame on John's negligence.

Without letting Loren know the reason he had to leave for the important errands earlier, was to call his veterinarian friend in St. Charles, Missouri to see if he could help with the injuries that Kate has suffered, and also explained how dangerous the situation could become for anyone involved.

John says without hesitancy to Loren, "I knew you might ask me for more assistance considering everything that you are up against, and of course I'll do everything I can to help both Kate and you. Help me make preparations for getting her into my car right away plus getting everything packed that will be needed in St Charles. I'll put everything from the back seat into the trunk, so we can put Kate in the back. Please go up and get my medical bag and supplies, I'll need them too, afterwards we will get Kate into the back seat, and I'll be out of here pronto, o.k.?"

Loren just nods in agreement then hurries upstairs to get John's medical supplies while John goes out to his car to make room for Katie to lay down in the back seat for the trip to St. Charles.

It takes some effort for both Loren and John to carefully carry her down the long steep stairway, but putting her in the back seat of John's large older Cadillac is much easier than thought because of its large capacity.

Loren comments to John while loading Kate, "They sure don't make cars like they used to, do they John," making small conversation as a way of trying to deal with the pressure they are both feeling.

Then Loren walks around the Cadillac to John, looking up and down the streets to make sure they aren't being watched and gratefully shakes John's hand and expresses his sincere thanks for everything John is doing for him and for Kate.

John looks at Loren with concern in his eyes and saying "Keep your spirits up, there's one thing that I've learned over the years, if you're doing the right thing, and what we are doing is definitely right, then only good things can come afterwards."

Loren says," That's not what happened to you though John."

With John replying back without hesitation, "Yes it is, or I wouldn't have been here to help Katie and you." John then slides into the driver's seat, waves at Loren and heads for the expressway to take Kate and himself to St. Charles, Mo.

Loren had not mentioned anything to John, but he immediately jumps into his truck and follows John all the way to the city limit just to make sure that John isn't being tailed by anyone. Then he returns to his warehouse to follow-up with Frank regarding the voice mail message that Frank had left him this morning.

Loren clicks in Frank's phone number, and Frank answers immediately and demands, "Where the hell have you been, Loren?"

Loren replies, "I had some business to do early this morning, which I didn't want to do, and I believe you know exactly what I'm talking about, Frank."

Frank replies, "Is she gone?"

"Yes", Loren responds with sadness in his voice. "It was the hardest thing I've ever had to do."

"Get over it Loren, there are plenty of other broads all over the place. We need to talk today. Meet me at Leo's Place for lunch at 1:00 sharp," Frank says roughly, then hangs up.

Loren looks at his wrist watch. It is 11:30 in the morning, which doesn't give him much time to come up with a realistic story about Kate's demise. The meeting location, Leo's Place, is an Italian cafeteria-style restaurant, which is located in a warehouse- of an old business district of St. Louis. The hired help at the restaurant doesn't turnover much, the clientele never seems to change much either and the tables and chairs are just typical cafeteria style furniture. The first time that Loren had eaten here before he was involved with the mob, it was evident to him that they catered to certain people, and it wasn't white collar workers who go in there for an inexpensive, good tasting fast lunch. It was always a certain type of men who dress casual, who are unobtrusive and don't bring attention to themselves.

Loren pulls into Leo's at 12:57 and by the time he parks and walks in- it will be exactly 1:00. The way that Loren figures it-- Frank will think of him being less guilty if he is not early.

Frank and Joe are waiting at a table to the side of the room where less traffic passes through, both have frowns on their faces and both watch Loren like hawks when he sees them and walks toward their table. Loren is frowning too, he purposely wants to look slightly inconvenienced, but keep an air of confidence which makes him look not guilty.

Frank starts talking first, "So what happened last night?"

Loren responds in a low voice, "Katie and Jack are dead, that's what happened. It's done, both had to go, but I wasn't able to get the info from Jack that I needed to before he died."

"What information did Jack have?" asked Frank.

"I had just received info that Jack supposedly knew something about the disappearance of the load in Chicago, his mouth slipped-up at the cabin and it made me pretty sure then that the rumor was correct, but he and Kate took off in his truck before I could try to find anything else out", Loren said.

Frank replies, "We had been watching Jack ourselves. He's been acting a little funny lately and we can't afford not to find the stuff, there's too much money involved, and why the hell would Jack leave with that broad?" Frank looks disgusted when asking the question.

Loren looks at him like a man who's broken hearted, then says, "They had a thing, I didn't know it until I found them in the bedroom, and for Kate it wasn't just sex she seemed to like about him. I must have showed anger or something because the next thing I know they just took off in his truck. When I got back to St. Louis it was after they did, because I was driving cautiously with a load. Her jeep was just pulling out of the back storage yard when I arrived, I chased them down and ran her jeep off the road, then, like a fool, I chased them into the park. Because of what I did to Kate, Jack came at me in defense of her and I just hit him once, not trying to kill him, but I did. I have a problem if the police investigate her jeep, my prints are all over it and if they visit me because of those prints they will see my truck with her jeep paint on it, that's why I removed her body from the park, for my self-preservation."

Frank asks, "Where did you put her?"

Loren's voice is sorrowful when he hesitantly replies, "Frank, I really cared for that woman. This was the hardest thing I've ever had to do, she is not anywhere close to St. Louis, but buried deep in an area she dearly loved, her body will never be found. Because of how I feel- only I need to know where she is buried, it's nobody else's business. I was on my way back from there when you called early this morning and frankly didn't want to speak to no one at the time. I guarantee you though no one will ever find her. Loren then folds his arms and puts his head down, as if in mourning.

Frank changes the subject, asking "What do you estimate the street value to be for the load you brought up last night?"

Loren answers, "About half a million, give or take a few thousand."

"Well", replies Frank, "We need to get it out on the streets here in St. Louis, I know that it won't come up missing in this area and I've got to start making up for what happened in Chicago. I'll send a truck over tonight after dark, say around 7 to 7:30 to pick it up, and don't worry about her jeep, I'll talk to someone at headquarters and have it squelched, and we'll get auto-body to fix your truck tomorrow- pronto. Keep your ears open to whom Jack was paling around with before his demise." With a friendly tone, Frank adds, "Don't worry Loren, I've told you before there's lots of other broads out there, and they won't give you as much trouble as this Kate did." Frank started stuffing his mouth with an Italian sausage sandwich with peppers and onions oozing out from the roll onto his hands.

Still showing sorrow, Loren excuses himself from joining Frank and Joe for lunch then leaves the restaurant. He thinks what he told them probably they believed to some extent, but none of these guys ever trust anyone totally, including himself. Loren knows he will have to watch his step very carefully for quite a while.

After arriving at their destination in St Charles and her receiving medical attention from John's friend, Paul, Katie is starting to feel better within a few hours. X-rays show that she doesn't have a fractured rib, but her bruising is immense and the most serious injury she suffered, her brain concussion, is being monitored closely. For her head and body to heal, she is going to need a lot of bed rest. This is going to be a very difficult for Kate, because she is normally so active and on the go, she is not one to lie in bed; although after all she has been through and the sharp pains she feels from her slightest movements, she's thinking that just laying around will be fairly easy for her today, anyways.

Paul has set Kate up to recover from her injuries at his own home. He is a widower in his mid-60s, is an honorable person who shows strong loyalty to friends and is a rogue on occasion, having taken the road less traveled from time to time- so to speak. In his career he has primarily specialized in doctoring race horses, and he developed a hate for the mob because of their ruthless and unscrupulous tactics used in either making a horse run faster, or crippling a horse and then putting it down for insurance purposes. Paul loves all animals but has a special love for horses and applies his veterinarian medicine knowledge and skills for the conservation, health and welfare of all animals and most particularly horses. He has never been employed by the mob, but he has seen the terrible consequences that can happen to magnificent animals when mobsters own race horses.

In regard to Kate, John had to tell Paul many details about her and how she ended up in the critical condition she was in when she arrived at Paul's door. Paul would have contacted the police if John hadn't told him what had happened to her and the people who were involved in her nearly fatal injuries. Thanks to John, Paul now realizes that it is imperative that the police not be called about Kate.

John and Paul have been friends since they were in the Marine's together as young men, with Paul just few years older than John. Their friendship over the years grew, they are both very intelligent, both earned advanced degrees in their educations, both remained single, and over the years they supported each other through good times and bad times. They both liked to go fishing a lot and to gamble once in a while. Today they are having coffee in Kate's bedroom sitting in chairs next to Kate's bed talking and trying to cheer her up, while Kate occasionally tries to sit up even though it is painful to her body to do so.

Both John and Paul have taken a liking to her because she is feisty and is not afraid to speak her mind- is a real woman with thoughtful and genuine values and beliefs- she has some problems- yes but she tries to openly and honestly deal with her problems, she does not have a mean bone in her body, and she is in touch with her inner feelings and is very comfortable with herself and is just very natural. Men with the character and backgrounds of Paul and John, find Kate appealing. They both talked and kidded her quite a bit to bring her spirits up and it seems to be working. While drinking their coffee the two of them gently kidded and joked with her about how they can't understand that she could get herself so stupidly entangled in the mess she finds herself in, knowing full well neither of them had ever been shining angels themselves.

23

BAD OMENS

John is planning to stay out at Paul's house in St. Charles to help look after Kate for a few days as Paul is still active in his veterinary business, built mostly on long-time clients who he affectionately refers to as "seasoned citizens". On the rare occasion that Paul even talks about retirement, many of his clients make a fuss and fervently ask him not to do it. In reality, he doesn't want to retire because he still genuinely enjoys the business of helping and protecting animals, plus the regular friendly interactions he has with his long-time clients.

The arrangement for Kate is working out well. When Paul is at his clinic, John looks after Kate and keeps her company while she's not napping. Neither of the men wants her to be at the house alone. First, because of her weakened condition and the recovery she is going through and secondly, now that she is healing, she is becoming more active and wanting to go on short walks around the house, which could put her security at risk. Thanks to Loren, they are now aware of the ruthless and violent group she is up against. Also, with the numerous meth labs in the state, there are many thugs assigned to protect the meth operations, who also become paid informants if they can spot someone like Kate, who the boss is trying to track down. Just this morning John and Paul again discussed the importance of at least one of them being with her at all times, with Paul adding, "thank God she doesn't have a car right now".

Loren often wonders how Kate is doing and remains relieved that she is not too close to the city and is receiving good care.

But still he misses her, and has strong feelings of guilt and pain about how badly he has treated her. It wasn't until he saw explicitly what Jack did to her that he fully realized just what he himself has been doing to Kate and, in both cases, relates to the people he now works for. He knows he is no better than Jack, and has just been blaming his behavior on his greed for hard cash and his addiction to meth. As Loren honestly looks at his life, he realizes he has nothing to show for it and sees that his moral standards have plummeted to the level of a human cockroach. He also now realizes that the one person in his life, Kate, who is compassionate, kind, generous and warmhearted, who he knows loves him and has such a good spirit, is probably going to die because of him and his errors. This hit him like a bomb when he saw Jack kicking her face that night in the park. At that moment Loren makes vow to himself that he is going to find a way to get away from Frank and his thugs, and he is going to make damn sure that Kate will be free to live a full life. His vow is from the heart, but his mind is telling him that the chances of his survival are slim to none.

He moves to his shop to work on the cupboards to pass the time until the load of meth is picked up tonight. As he works, he begins thinking of plans for a trip to the south to the meth factory in the southern part of the state. He hasn't used his phone for any calls of importance since John took Kate to St Charles as he fears that in some way his phone may be tapped, which is why he hasn't been able to find out anything about how Kate is doing. Also, at least for the near term, he knows that going to St. Charles would be suicide for both of them. Loren's paranoia is running high.

Loren receives a pick-up call at exactly 7:10 p.m. A voice tells him that men will be at the warehouse in 5 minutes, and Loren states that the back gate will be open and to back the vehicle in as close to the warehouse door as possible. There is a "click" and the phone call ends. In five minutes a brand new Silver SUV arrives at the back gate of the warehouse yard. There are two men in the vehicle who Loren remembers meeting once through Frank. They are very tough looking men who have prison records, with prison tattoos and weight training muscles to show for it. After backing the vehicle to the open door of the warehouse, the two men get out of the SUV and walk to the back of the vehicle without a greeting or even saying word. They walk into the warehouse to the pails of meth and within a few minutes all of the pails of meth are loaded into the vehicle. There are no goodbyes spoken as they get back into the SUV and drive out the gate, and Loren is glad the load of meth and two thugs was gone.

Loren is fairly tired and it is already late, but he is not sleepy so he decides to make a phone call to Frank to tell him he is planning to go south as soon as his truck is fixed. Frank knows what Loren means by that comment and likes the idea of him heading south, as that will expedite the delivery of the next load of meth and the cash flow from its sale.

Frank just says, "See you when you get back, I'll get a new broad for you while you're gone, and she'll be waiting". He laughs as he hangs up. Loren just shakes his head and thinks to himself, "Frank places value on a life like most people value a piece of garbage".

Loren has one more day to hang around St. Louis to wait for his truck, which needs the imperative body repair and painting. Once the truck is ready he will hit the road going south, as he needs some time to talk to Pete alone.

To some extent, Frank had been playing games with Loren. Jack was a decoy to find out how much Loren could be trusted. Loren had come into the group with a bang, effectively utilizing his knowledge in a very short period of time, and it made Frank nervous. Frank also likes to play these types of games because it gives him a power trip. His mind is only on the money and the power that comes with it. The value of life is basically worthless to him. Although, he has to answer to a few people over him, they have the same perception of money and power as he does. Had he thought more quickly he would have staked out Loren's warehouse from the time he heard that Jack's body was found in Lafayette Park. Loren hadn't answered his phone that morning, which should have triggered Frank's suspicion that something was up. He didn't know what it was, but he is sure going to find out now.

Frank's police contact told him that there was a large amount of blood found on the exact location of where Jack's body was found- but there was no bleeding from the wound that caused Jack's death. The official report indicates that the cause of his death was fatal trauma to the head. The report goes on to say that there was a significant amount of blood found under Jack's body, but it was not his and there was no other body at the scene of the crime.

Because of Frank's contact within the department, Kate's jeep was immediately pulled from the police compound lot and was disposed of at an auto-wrecking compound, probably located in East St. Louis. Frank's big question simply remains—"is the broad that owns that jeep dead or alive?" He needs both her and Loren dead, but he needs to keep Loren around long enough to determine if she is alive or not—because if she is alive—Loren will eventually lead his associates to her. In the meantime, Loren is making him money, hand over fist, and as Frank always says, "Never look a gift -horse in the mouth"-- especially one who can help bring in around ten million dollars a year.

Frank likes to have sex with women but otherwise he has no respect for them. In his mind they screw up everything and this particular one, Kate, really screwed things up worse than most. Frank mentions to his friend and bodyguard Joe while having a cup of coffee, "Even Susie wasn't as bad as this broad, and look where it got her. Jack was no specialty either, he got on my nerves from bragging constantly about absolutely nothing- but at least with Jack you could always tell if he was lying, but with Loren it is a totally different story. After seeing Loren's reaction about this woman's death at lunch today I just have no idea if he is telling the truth or not." Joe listens intently and grunts in agreement with Frank.

Although Frank won't say much, he secretly fears Loren because Loren can have strong powers of persuasion which, in Frank's mind, is in itself a good reason to get rid of Loren in the near future, whether he is a big money maker or not. "You just can't trust what he says and just maybe he wants to take my place," Frank thinks to himself.

Loren wants to talk to John late tonight to learn how Katie is doing. He has been haunted by the image of her badly battered body and her faint breathing as he helped put her in John's car to go to St Charles, but he has gotten some comfort from knowing that she is in the best of hands under the circumstances. He is afraid to use his cell phone and decides to use a pay phone at the gas station across the street. He puts Rex on his leash and they step out the front door of the warehouse to walk across the street to the convenience store gas station, but as

Loren is crossing the street he notices the same small beat-up blue cavalier sitting across the street that has been there since Loren came back from lunch quite a few hours ago. The blue vehicle is occupied by the same large man he had noticed in the car earlier. This seems very strange considering the time involved, which makes Loren feel that the guy in the blue car is a stake-out. So instead of using the pay phone, Loren ties Rex to the bike rack outside the store and walks in the gas station to buy a six pack of beer, and he strongly senses that he is being watched. When he comes out he unhooks Rex's leash from the rack and walks back to the warehouse, purposely waving at the large man in the old beat up blue car. "Fuck him", Loren thinks to himself, "Fuck him." Loren's angry and scared as to what he has just experienced and what signals that bigger trouble has just begun.

Loren goes into his warehouse with Rex, locks the door and proceeds to open a can of beer. He is disappointed knowing that he is stuck in the warehouse the entire night and won't be able to find out how Kate is doing. Sleeping is hard for him tonight as he is focusing more and more on how to bail out of this whole mixed-up scene alive.

He receives a phone call at 8:00 a.m. the next morning to be informed that his truck will be picked up right away, and that hopefully he will have it back by early evening, just depending on how badly the truck body is damaged. Loren is starting to sense that things are just going too easy, like possibly someone is greasing the skids just to catch him in a screw-up sooner rather than later.

Katie is up and walking around the next morning, almost falling at first, until she clears the dizziness from her head from standing up. Around 8:00 John peeks in her room to check on her and sees her standing by the window taking in the morning sun. When he sees her up, he steps in the room and they exchange greetings and talk about the pleasant sunshine and beautiful morning. She requests a cup of coffee but John refuses her request because the caffeine may interfere with the rest she needs for her ongoing good recovery from the severe brain concussion that she suffered.

Katie smiles and selects orange juice as an alternative drink and Paul joins John when he returns to her room with a glass of juice. They engage in pleasant small talk while Katie sips a large glass of chilled orange juice and John and Paul are both enjoying their cups of coffee during the conversation. What makes the morning even more pleasant is the realization by the three of them that, in an amazingly short period of time, Katie has made a near miraculous recovery from a sustained and brutal beating inflicted to her head and body by a crack-brained psychopath. She was literally at death's door as Loren carried her through the park away from the scene that night. Part of her miracle recovery has been the result of her inner strength and determination to live, but mostly the miracle has occurred because of these two men who gently, patiently and adoringly nursed her back to health.

Kate is unable to go outside today, although she wants to badly. She always become claustrophobic being inside any building for too long, especially if she knows she can't go out. There is a psychological basis for this feeling, John is sure of it. Possibly she's had past experiences that made her like this he later told Paul. That morning the three of them joked and laughed about different life experiences they had all encountered over the years, bringing the three of them even closer together.

Loren's truck is delivered back to him late afternoon the same day, the small dent, scratch and green paint abrasion from Kate's jeep has completely vanished in less than 8 hours, an unheard of speed for a body shop, which brought the realization to Loren that 'miracles are being performed' just for him so he can go on with his business. Also, he realizes that certain people will be watching him 24 hours a day.

He calls Frank saying, "I'm on my way south and I'll be back within a couple days. I'll call you when I get back in town." He keeps his voice cool and calm- knowing this is the best way at the moment to maintain the appearance that nothing is going on out of the ordinary. He continually checks his mirrors on the way out of the city, but he can't determine if he is being followed or not. If he is being followed, they are either really being stealth about it, or they were using different drivers and different vehicles at various exits along the way, which makes it impossible to detect.

Loren takes his time driving down to the cabin, stopping every few miles for coffee and pit stops just to be a son of a bitch- just in case he is being tailed. He doesn't arrive at the cabin until 1:00 a.m. and he falls asleep immediately on the sofa that Kate and he had shared just a few nights ago, with Rex on the floor by his feet.

The next morning Loren drives to the factory, where Pete welcomes him at the porch doorway of the stone house. They have a brief overview of operations, which is positive—as the lab is operating at full capacity and is making the best quality meth that they'd ever produced. Pete is quite pleased that his work is going so well.

Loren acknowledges the good job being done then asks him if Clay and Scott are able to take over for a while, as he wants go for a ride with Pete in the truck to talk to him alone.

Pete looking questioningly at Loren for a moment then says, "Sure, I can get away for a little while, but not for too long, they don't know how to mix the dry ingredients properly. I'll tell them to finish what they're doing then to take a break if they get to the point where I'm needed." Pete walks back into the house tell the others he'll be back soon plus the instruction to wait for him if needed.

They take off in Pete's old red truck instead of Loren's, at Loren's request, then they head toward a little village called Summersville just a little south of Pete's place.

Loren is nervous, as he is starting to lose trust in everyone. Pete is one of the few people that Loren is reasonably sure he can still trust, and isn't on the payroll of the club. Loren starts telling Pete what has happened, which includes the stolen load in Chicago, Jack trying to kill Katie- and him killing Jack, and almost everything he can think of just because he needs help to sort out the whole mess in his mind. He tells Pete that whatever happens to himself has been due to his own fault but Kate is innocent and needs some way to come out of this alive and well.

Pete listens, shows concern and even grimaces when Loren tells him about Katie being beaten nearly to death by Jack. Loren also tells Pete he knows he is being tailed and that he and Pete are possibly being watched right at this moment, even as they are speaking.

Pete reassures him that they aren't being tailed presently and adds, "For Christ's sake Loren, do you see any other vehicles on this small road right now besides ours?" You have got to loosen up and start thinking straight, then I'm sure you will find a way out of this." Pete then asks, "What will happen to our business? How will we run it, if you're having real bad trouble with our street sources?"

Loren pauses then speaks hesitantly, "Pete we're just going to have to quit for a while. It won't be safe to have this business here because the club knows where it's located; I think we should consider something as aggressive as burning out the contents of the house- if it comes to that. I know that you have been stashing away your share of the profits and you'll be fine for quite a while, better than me that's for sure, I've used up most of my finances."

Pete looks Loren like he is crazy because Pete really isn't ready to quit, especially at the high production levels they have achieved at the moment. Pete's only comment is gruff, saying, "This is bullshit Loren, you are becoming too paranoid, and mostly just over a woman, and I'm not willing to quit over her like you are." Pete then turns his head to look out the window and is just ignoring Loren now. He has made his feelings known and that is final as far as he is concerned.

Loren feels the tension come between he and Pete almost immediately and he realizes that he'd better come from a different angle with Pete quickly if he hopes to change his mind.

The 4th Dream

A woman is standing on a small rocky island that has only a single tree, she is surrounded by oceans of water, all at once a tiger comes out of nowhere and chases her, she has to climb the tree to survive the attack of the tiger, but once up in the tree she hears funny scratching noises coming from the tiger, his body is made of pinecones and as he is moving and jumping up and down as the pinecones rub against each other and make a scratching noise. The woman knowing the tiger is now harmless, jumps out of the tree and starts running and takes a leap landing on a large stone in the ocean where a seal is sunbathing, the woman jumps on the seal's back and he jumps off the rock into the ocean and as the seal is swimming up over the water and then down to submerge under the water, the woman is experiencing a good feeling of cool soothing wetness but also a nervous feeling of no control. As the seal keeps swimming and submerging up and down, up and down, up and down for a long distance, it's body becomes longer in size, his neck grows very long and so does his tail and his body is now transforming into a huge size, he is becoming a sea serpent. The woman feels safe because the sea serpent seems gentle to her. Soon the woman spots a much larger island, with lots of buildings and houses, the serpent swims directly to this island and the woman slips off his back.

The town on the island is dirty and the people, she senses, may be dangerous. As she walks down the streets she comes to a large square wooden house, she then enters this house. The house is dirty and bare of furniture; she sits quietly in the corner of a large room watching, as many rough looking men walk singly through a narrow hallway into another part of the house. Then she sees a short man with a beard or go-tee, he seems to be the boss, the leader- the men do what he tells them to do. The woman is so quiet that no one seems to notice her. She is then in a kitchen, there is a baby in a highchair, she needed to feed this baby, but there is no food, and she sees food way up in the highest cupboards next to the ceiling, standing on the counter trying to reach the food to feed the baby the short man with the go-tee sees her and immediately falls in love with her. Then a good looking, clean young man comes to her entering from another room and tells her that his boss wants for him to cut off her face and put another face on her.

Katie wakes-up, sits up immediately in the bed and is sweating profusely, then she blinks her eyes to make sure she is awake. This and the earlier dreams are eerie and unsettling to her and she knows now that every one of them has something to do with both Loren and herself, but she can't figure out their meaning, they just frighten her.

It is still very early in the morning about 4:00 a.m. and she doesn't want to alarm John or Paul about what she has seen in a dream, so she leaves the lights off in her room but still gets up out of bed slowly because of the soreness which she still feels throughout her whole body and her head has started aching now as the pain medicine is wearing off.

She is afraid for Loren, Paul told her earlier yesterday about what had happened to her in the park after she passed out while Jack was beating her. Paul told her everything, including the worry and apparent love that Loren has for her. That night Loren had clearly saved her life, while putting his own life in greater jeopardy.

However, Kate knows she can't trust Loren, as he has left her so many times in the past using many different excuses, but during this trip to St. Louis his actions have left her in death's way. She loves him more than anyone else in this world, but she knows if she makes it out of this alive to a place free and safe from the thugs is St Louis, she can never be with Loren again. But because of her love for him, she still fears for him and these strange dreams have not only intensified her fear for herself but also for Loren. She knows there is a message in the dreams for her and if she could only understand the message it could possibly save her life. Katie looks out her window, seeing only shadows of trees with the wind blowing through the bare branches giving off a low moaning noise. As her eyes adjust to the darkness outdoors, she sees a human figure and it startles her- a man standing just to the side of a tree! Even in the darkness she can make out the silhouette of a man fairly easily. She moves silently back from the window, scared that he may have seen her, then realizes that it would be next to impossible for him to see anything inside of this very dark room. Katie stands to the side of the window and peeks past the edge every two or three minutes. The man remains standing where he was when she first saw him, he must have been there for at least a half hour. Katie now knows that she is still being watched, which makes her again feel very scared and vulnerable. She isn't dreaming this; it is too cold outside for someone just to be standing out there less than 100 ft. from her window at four o'clock in the morning.

She realizes she has to tell John and Paul about this. For the first time-she is too afraid to try to escape from the St Louis thugs on her own, especially after what Jack has already done to her.

PART THREE

FOR THE LOVE OF LIFE

24

Pete can't believe how Loren seems to change so drastically. Pete is mumbles to himself, "I'm not a fool and I'll be damned if I'll give up a quarter mill a year because of his friendship or love affair with some woman. I can run this business myself now," totally diminishing the fact that it was Loren who let him in and taught him the business in the first place.

Frank laid the groundwork for undercutting Loren in a phone call to Pete about an hour before Loren arrived at the factory. In the first part of the phone conversation, Frank appealed to Pete's vanity by talking in a flattering way about Pete's progress since joining the business. Then he not so subtly conveys to Pete that he is unhappy with the way Loren is managing the business and he added the words, "The factory is just too good to have something harmful happen to it and the way Loren has been acting lately it looks like the business isn't going to be around too much longer." Pete hesitates to respond as he takes in the meaning of these words. Frank knows exactly how to manipulate people, especially people like Pete, who was raised in poverty in the hills of northern Arkansas and never expected to make much money, due to the limits of his ninth grade education, which changed when he was hired into the business by Loren.

After the pause in their phone conversation, Pete responded," Look Frank, if Loren wants out in the near future that's fine with me, I know everything there is to know to run the factory, let me take it over," which is exactly what Frank was hoping to hear Pete say.

Frank then informed Pete that Loren was already on his way to visit him- and, when he arrives he should act like their current phone conversation never happened. Then, after Loren Leaves for St Louis, he is to call him back to let him know what transpired in his conversation with Loren. Frank then says to Pete, "you will be paid for your time". As the phone conversation ends, Pete wholeheartedly conveys his agreement to everything as laid out by Frank.

While driving down the country road, Loren mentioned to Pete, in his truck, that he thought he was being tailed, Pete was just thinking to himself, "no one is tailing you, you're riding with the tail." Pete now believes that if he sticks with Frank he will go a long way.

Loren is feeling very uneasy and that he may have screwed up letting his friend Pete know so much detail of what had happened when the two of them had talked earlier. He felt a lot of tension between them, especially when he told Pete he might shut down the business, and he definitely detected a lack of interest by Pete when he told him, "we'll open a new factory in a year or so after things cool down, and the next business will be much bigger and better than this one is."

Pete just didn't seem to take the bait at all. No matter what Loren would say the tension between them seemed omnipresent with Pete being less talkative than normal and he is not a big talker to begin with, which makes Loren feel very apprehensive. Loren also wishes now that he hadn't communicated to Pete about the vet, whom Loren has never met, that is putting Kate somewhere in the St. Charles vicinity.

It wasn't until the next morning when Loren departs the factory for his drive toward the cabin, that his mind starts mulling the dynamics surrounding his visit to the factory and the disconcerting meetings he had with Pete. Nothing is adding up and everything just seems nonsensical until it hits him! Pete must have been contacted by Frank just before he arrived at the factory yesterday. Loren and Pete have been good friends with a great working relationship ever since Loren hired Pete. They know each other well, and it was obvious to Loren that Pete was acting totally out of character from how he normally acts. It was if Pete was just a detached stranger. Until today Pete had faithfully followed Loren's instructions precisely without serious questions and always greatly valued Loren's guidance. Unfortunately for Loren, it appears he has lost a good friend and an ally.

When Katie walks quietly into to the kitchen for breakfast this morning, she startles John who is cooking a breakfast of bacon and eggs for himself as well as for Kate and Paul. After exchanging morning greetings, John refocuses his attention to breakfast making, but Kate wants to alert John right away about what she saw during the night and is trying to choose her words carefully. "John, something happened real early this morning, and normally I wouldn't say anything to you about this because I would usually feel that I could take care of the problem myself, but there was a man standing in Paul's yard for a long time- kind of looking towards the house, like he was possibly watching it or something."

John quickly looks up from the stove, a bit startled, taking in Kate's words. He reacts in a calm manner but with some concern in his voice saying, "Kate, why didn't you wake either of us up?" She just shrugs while John continues, "You know that we are very capable of protecting you within the confines of this house. I know you didn't want to wake us- in order to save our sleep, but that didn't help you. This is now water under the bridge- but we have to be concerned and to quickly find out if this was just some odd guy out at night due to insomnia or if he has been sent here to harm you." Did you see what he looked like at all?" John asks, still watching her intently, but feeling quietly inside that they may be facing big trouble ahead.

Katie thinks for a moment, "it was dark, John- what I saw was a silhouette of a man, he was tall, I know that and slender- most probably Caucasian, because of the highlights I could see reflecting off his forehead, but other than that I saw nothing."

John finishes frying the eggs and the bacon is already on the platter, as he calls Paul in for breakfast. The three of them sit down with the blinds pulled shut in the breakfast nook and John tells Paul what Kate had just told him. As they eat breakfast, they talk over the incident that just occurred, which seems like a serious problem. No one has any idea who the person was outside the house, but they all agree that there wasn't any good reason for him to be out there.

It was decided that John would stay with her all day at the house, and no doors would be opened and no phones would be answered without screening through voice mail. Paul volunteers to try to discreetly find out from his local business contacts if someone has been nosing around asking questions about him. If Paul pulls this off right, no one he talks to will have any idea what the real reason is that has prompted his questions.

Paul eats his breakfast quickly and he's becoming more agitated the more he thinks about what he has heard this morning. When he gets up from the table he angrily says to John and Kate, "I'll be damned if any son-of-a bitch is going to case my house."

Paul leaves the house immediately after eating his breakfast- with his own plans on how to thwart the people who want to see Kate dead, starting first with the 24-hour convenience store gas station, up the street. He knows the guy pretty well who has the early shift and he is still on duty. Paul is going to start with him. He walks in the gas station briskly and starts talking so loudly that anyone who happened to be in the store would hear him talking, " George- did you happen to see some dumb son of a bitch, kind of tall and lanky in here real early this morning like between 3:00 and 5:00 a.m.?"

His question startled George who had never heard Doc talk so loudly or so coarsely like this to anyone before. "Well", George is trying to think, " well- possibly, some guy I never seen before came in around 4:45 to 5:00 for some coffee, he was my only customer at that time of the morning- said he was real cold and needed the coffee to warm himself up. Why? What would make you ask a question like that?"

Paul responds, "I woke up early this morning and happened to look out my bedroom window- here's this man standing next to a tree in my yard seemingly starring at my house, he didn't move for a long time, I was ready to get my gun and walk outside to see what the hell his problem was, but he left before I got the gun out, I thought maybe he planned on breaking in my house and burglarizing it." Paul pauses and looks at George for any reaction, and there was none, so he continues, "what did he look like anyway, young-old- bald-pony-tail- did he happen to mention his name? George, anything that you can tell me about him will help!" Paul is so fired up and hot under the collar that George seems fearful of the way that Doc is talking.

George thinks some more and says, " I didn't pay too much attention to him- but he was probably about 6'2" tall, pretty slim, Caucasian...um...let's see, he was wearing a thin brown jacket, no wonder he was cold, had a deep voice, and that's about all I remember, Doc."

Paul asks, "Would you recognize him if he ever walked in here again?"

George answers, "Yes". Paul replies, "Do me a favor- if you ever see him again, call me, I don't care what time of the day, morning or night it is –just call me, I'll shoot him on the spot, he is up to no good and we don't need people like him around here. Also, pass this on to other customers about this guy nosing around in the middle of the night. We might stop him dead in his tracks before he does some damage or hurts somebody."

George says, "Doc, for you I'll do it- I've never seen you act this way, so upset I mean, and I'm sure this guy must be a menace. I'll tell all my regulars that come in about what's happened, o.k."?

Paul, with a grateful look, says "thank you", then leaves to go to a couple of other local businesses to pass on the word about the "burglar", before leaving for his veterinary clinic.

That same day at the clinic Paul has a new customer come into the store, a man in his mid-thirties with a mixed-breed dog. The first thing he notices is that the dog seems confused as if he doesn't know his master, then after the dog settles down, the man mentions that he is new to the area and his dog needs vaccinations, as he had just picked the dog up at a shelter. Reflexively, Paul asks the man the name of the shelter where he got the dog, because all the shelters that he knows of vaccinate and neuter the animal before putting it up for adoption. Before the man answers his question, Paul starts examining the dog, which allows him to determine that it could possibly have been vaccinated, but this male dog has not been neutered. The man sees the skeptical look on Paul's face then he nervously walks out of the building with the dog. Immediately Paul senses that this man and his visit to Pauls' office today could have something to do with the man that Kate saw early this morning in the shadows outside the house. Paul is upset and furious that Kate's location has probably somehow gotten out, putting Kate, John and himself in great jeopardy. Paul immediately calls a couple of other vets in St. Charles to see if they have had a similar visitor at their offices today. As he had suspected, both of his vet colleagues confirm they have had a visit from a man with a dog of the same description- who asked questions more about the neighborhood, families and local activities, all of which have nothing to do with caring for an animal. Paul now realizes that the mob has been leaked information about Kate's location, but they don't seem to know which vet has Kate in his care.

After visiting Pete, Loren goes to Riverbend before heading back to the cabin. He hasn't eaten for a day and his stomach is starting to growl. He can't think of anything but food right now and he knows a good place to stop just down the road. Leaving Rex in the truck he parks at Chuck's Restaurant and Bar, goes inside to get a cheeseburger and fries to go. After he is given the meal in a paper sack, he pays then goes back to his truck and quickly eats his Cheeseburger and fries. The meal helps to relieve his hunger, but the food doesn't stop his anxiety nor the feeling that he is losing control over events which have been set into motion.

Loren's thoughts never seem to stray from Kate for very long and he has been wanting to find out about the status of her injuries ever since she was taken to St Charles by John for her recovery from the attack and for concealment from the mob. John doesn't have a cell phone, and Loren figures that he must not be at his own home but is staying somewhere near St. Charles helping his vet friend take care of Kate. Loren is also fairly sure that Pete is now collaborating with Frank, which is partially confirmed by the fact that none of Frank's thugs seem to be tailing Loren, meaning Frank may be watching and following up with Pete now more than with Loren. If that is the case then Loren surmises that it is clear at the moment to use a pay phone to call John and there is one directly across the road from Chuck's. He dials John's home number and leaves a message for John to "call him on his cell phone immediately upon receiving this message". He also tells John that he is still near his cabin and his place of business and might remain in the area another day or so and cautions John that, when he makes his return call to Loren's cell phone, not to give his location with Kate in St Charles or to mention any names. Finally, in his last comment in his voice message to John, Loren mentions that he thinks that "the boss may know that Kate is somewhere in St. Charles so be on the watch for strangers just hanging around as they may be dangerous".

After hanging up the pay phone, Loren then starts to call Pete on his cell phone to tell him that he needs to talk to him again, but right after pushing the last digit, Loren quickly hangs up- he has a better idea- a more personal meeting would be better!

The Riverbend Liquor Store is just down the road and in a couple of minutes Loren parks his truck in front of the store and walks inside to buy a case of cold Budweiser and a quart of Jack Daniels. He knows that Pete loves his "Jack". Loren puts the beverages behind the seat on the driver's side and heads his truck back toward the factory. It is late afternoon by now and as he drives he is thinking of how to successfully finish the earlier difficult conversation he had with Pete. For one thing, he wants to surprise Pete- not give him time to call Frank- in case that crosses his mind. Also, he is taking his time in getting there by driving slowly to ensure that Scott and Clay will have already left for home when Loren arrives--so he can have the evening with Pete alone. He then reaches behind the seat to touch the Jack Daniels to make sure it is snuggly hidden behind his seat. "That's for later", he thinks to himself. Still several minutes from the factory, Loren stops the truck long enough to take a couple snorts of meth. He hadn't done any since he was at the cabin with Kate and Jack, but he is jittery and can't think straight at the moment and needs the meth to clear his head. He hates his addiction, but right now is not the time to go clean.

John is getting his voice messages from his home via Paul's phone and when he hears Loren's voice he gives his full attention and listens carefully to the full message. At first Paul hesitates to call him on his cell- then when he does call he is disappointed that Loren doesn't answer. He does leave Loren a voice message and is careful in what he says by not mentioning any names or locations. He also says everything is fine; he'll call periodically with updates and hopes he will continue to stay in touch.

Katie stands nearby listening to John leave his message for Loren, which makes her miss Loren and fear for his life. Although her heart is sincerely with him- she is also genuinely afraid of him.

John can feel her apprehension when he hangs up the phone and he instinctively holds her for a little while to give her comfort. As he holds her, John is feeling his own emotional connection with Kate and perhaps even starting to fall in love with her. In John's life journey, whenever he has experienced love he has also experienced pain and he is thinking he is not ready for that kind of pain right now.

After a few moments, they hear Paul's garage door open causing John and Kate to end their embrace and finish setting the table together. When they see Paul enter the house through the kitchen, his solemn demeanor signals to them that something is up.

Loren arrived at the factory at about 5:15. It was almost dark and the first thing he notices is that Scott's truck isn't anywhere around. Scott always brings Clay to work with him because Clay lost his driver's license years ago for getting caught drinking while driving too many times and probably isn't planning to hold another license.

Pete receives Loren with a very surprised look on his face and does not extend the happy greeting he had given as he had their last visit. Pete stands on the porch with a quizzical look on his face wondering what the hell Loren was up to.

Loren gets out of his truck carrying the case of beer then, while holding it up, Loren says, "a peace offering, Pete, I think we need to talk again, I think I made a mistake. "Pete relaxes a little and takes the can of beer that Loren offers to him. They sit out on the porch watching the red and orange colors in the sky right after the sunset, which gives Loren the opportunity to take his time and carefully think out his words before speaking. "Pete, I don't want to close the factory- there is too much money made here", he then looks at Pete and knows he hit home by his reaction, then continues, "I have a problem though- this is man to man- I know you are my friend, I love this woman and she is not supposed to live because of what she has witnessed, my careless mistakes caused the problem not hers, is this a fair thing Pete?" Pete just looks at Loren as if he doesn't really care, which causes Loren change his direction, saying, "But I also realize that she knows too much and that something has to be done about it, but is killing her really the only answer?"

Pete listens without much input, but he opens his second can of beer and is starting to loosen up a little. Loren is thinking to himself that he will soon have control of the narrative again. However, he knows he has to keep Pete in his sight at all times just in case he decides he should call Frank for directions in responding to Loren's conversation.

Loren also opens his second can of beer to try to keep the atmosphere casual and relaxed with Pete, although Loren is planning to space out his drinking, starting with this beer.

Pete starts talking more freely, with his conversation generally orientated to the factory, the financial aspects of the business and how he loves his job. Loren listens –more just listening to words than understanding the words being spoken by Pete. He is just passing the time needed until he can eliminate Pete who is no longer an ally but a problem. Loren has seen Frank manipulate people in order to get things done, no matter who it hurts. Loren is not proud of it, but he has learned his lessons well from the boss in developing the dubious skill of manipulation and that this is exactly what he is now doing to Pete.

John, Paul and Kate are packing a few belongings for Kate as she urgently needs to leave St. Charles. Paul won't even consider Kate staying some place near the St. Charles area as the mobsters are somehow already closing in on her in St Charles after almost killing her in St Louis. Considering the type of thugs who want her dead, Paul is afraid they will be breaking into his house within hours if she not moved to a safe place tonight.

Paul looks at Katie and says, "I believe they are checking out every vet in the area right now, trying to figure out where you are Katie. I have a small house on the river that has belonged to my family for many years; it's been pretty well kept a secret because it's always been my haven to get away. I want for you and John to go down there and stay a while, until these bastards give up trying to locate you."

John agrees, although he's not sure if he wants to be alone with Kate for any extended amount of time because of the feelings he is starting to develop for her, although it is urgent that they move now so John will have to put his feelings of the heart to the side for the moment.

John left first in his own car driving on Highway 70 West making sure he isn't being followed, then shortly after that Paul and Kate leave in Paul's car with Kate way down on the back floor until they know it is clear for her to sit up. Paul is a little nervous, but believes that these thugs don't suspect him of hiding Kate any more than any other vet in the area. From what he learned around town today, the chance of him being followed tonight is low, but give a couple more days at tops and they'd have figured out exactly where she was staying.

It takes only about one and a half hours to get to the cabin on the Cedar River, just East of Columbia, Mo. John is already there waiting for them, he has visited Paul's cabin many times, especially since losing his license to practice medicine. John has often thought that this cabin and his booze are probably the main reasons he is still living. Just being here seems to give him a sense of wellbeing and a glimpse of how peaceful life can be a times. He leaves the porch lights turned off until he sees Paul pull into the driveway, then he immediately turns them on so he and Kate can see their way up the path to the cabin. At night darkness somewhat enshrouds the cabin due to the moon being almost totally blocked out by the thick forest that surrounds it.

25

UP IN SMOKE

By 9:00 p.m. Loren has Pete right where he wants him, they have finished off more than half the beer Loren brought with him, with Pete having more than his share. Just as Pete is reaching for another beer, Loren stops him with the words, "Pete, I just remembered I have a bottle of Jack in the truck, let's have a shot?"

Pete looks at Loren in surprise but is grinning while saying, "Well, why didn't you bring it out earlier?"

Loren responses, "I just forgot I even had it, it was given to me as a gift last month for a favor I did and I just totally forgot it was even in the truck until now. I'll get it. You get us a couple glasses, O.K.?" Then Loren goes to his truck to get the bottle of Jack Daniels, while Pete walks unsteadily inside to get the glasses. While at the truck, Loren grabs a small vile of liquid G and puts it in his pocket.

Pete walks back out on the porch with the drinking glasses in hand and a grin on his face. Loren pauses for a moment to look at his erstwhile friend, feeling pity for him as they had made money together, but Pete has entered a treacherous business and it is self-preservation that Loren is thinking about now.

Loren pours about two shots in each glass, then they toast, "To the business", followed by both men quickly downing the shots, with Loren almost immediately pouring more liquor in each glass. Then they both raise their glasses and the Jack again disappears down their throats. Loren asks Pete if he has anything to snack on, who silently responds by nodding his head then walks very unsteadily back inside to get some potato chips. While Pete is inside Loren fills the glasses again, only this time he adds the liquid drug to John's drink from the vile he had in his pocket

Pete returns with the chips, then slurring his words, he says, "I'm glad you've come around Loren, I appreciate that you're going to miss this Kate but like Frank says, broads are a dime a dozen". Loren takes a few chips out of the bag and starts munching, while not reacting to Pete's drunken confirmation that Frank has given the order for Katie to be killed. Loren thinks to himself, "I just need for Pete to drink his Jack.

Loren lifts his glass for another toast just saying, "To the business" again, then both of them down their drinks. Less than a minute later Pete is lying on the floor of the porch. Loren has to hurry now. He quickly drags Pete inside the house and pulls him back into the factory area leaving him on the floor. He then takes three of the cans of lacquer thinner that they use for making Meth and pours it onto the counters and floor, then carefully ignites the area closest to the door as Loren runs outside. He gets in his truck and drives it out on the gravel road that passes by the house, driving it only a short distance to a spot where he can push the truck into a deep ravine. He gets Rex safely out of the truck then pushes it and watches it descend until it disappears in the trees far below. He then runs up the hill as quickly as he can with Rex on his leash leading in front. When he gets to the front of the house he can see the back of the house is fully ablaze.

Loren moves quickly to Pete's truck, where he finds the keys in the ignition just like Pete always left them, Loren and Rex jump into Pete's truck then Loren backs out of the driveway and turns right onto the gravel road to get to the highway. He knows it will be a while before anyone sees the fire as it is far out in the country on a desolate road and, by that time, the fire will have spread well beyond the house, particularly considering all of the dry leaves and timber in the area surrounding the farmstead. Loren has no time to waste- he needs to be back in St Louis by early in the morning, with a different vehicle because he knows his truck has been tagged by the mob.

Kate can't sleep tonight as she is sensing that something is terribly wrong, not in regard to herself as she feels safe, but she senses something is wrong involving Loren. Since she can't sleep, she quietly lets herself out of the cabin and takes a seat on the front porch overlooking the river. As she sits down she takes a deep breath—it is so pleasant and tranquil here--only the gentle flow of the river and an occasional chirping insect or far-away owl breaks the silence of the night. As she looks into the night, her mind is on Loren but her feelings are starting to change for Loren in some ways. He has never treated her with the kindness and respect that John and Paul show her. These guys, John and Paul, are true friends -- and their generosity is overwhelming toward her and, even when just conversing, she is always included in the conversation something Loren seldom does. In daily living, everything is on his terms – and only his terms. She still definitely loves Loren but he has put her very life in danger and at one point it seemed that he was going to permanently get rid of her himself, whereas these two gentlemen--John and Paul--are willing to put their own lives at risk to help her even though she has only known them for a short time. For a while Katie sits just listening to the gentle river sounds as the water flows by. She thinks to herself, "no wonder John loves it here so much." Then her mind wanders back to the darkness that has intruded into her life. Katie--who had always experienced happiness, now can't smile anymore and who always had peace of mind, now lives in constant fear--all because she loves a man who is involved with a group of very corrupt and violent people. She continues to sit for a long time thinking of Loren, no longer hearing the tranquil sounds of the night—just dead silence....

Loren is driving Pete's truck to its limits. He is almost to the Interstate now and almost all of the other vehicles on the road thus far have been semi- trucks, the road is virtually open.

Once he is heading into St. Louis he knows that what he has to do next is dangerous as hell and is possibly going to get himself killed. He is very alert and jittery as he has been doing more meth on the way. His first stop has to be his warehouse, where he plans to keep Pete's truck behind the back fence in the alley to keep his presence from being known, although probably no one in St. Louis has any idea what Pete's truck looks like. When he gets to his street he drives by his place slowly to make sure that no one is watching his warehouse.

The street is empty except for a couple of hookers who are a couple of blocks from the warehouse. Loren pulls the truck up next to the gate of his backyard, where he leaves Rex in the truck and lets himself in after unlocking the gate. Once inside he unlocks the back door to the warehouse and goes inside without using any lights. It is so dark that Loren has to switch on one low beam flashlight to find the cans of accelerant that he needs. He takes the first cans and sets them out by his back gate then he goes back inside to find an empty glass bottle and put a little motor oil in it then adding gasoline to almost fill the bottle. Lastly he sticks a rag into the opening then he sets the bottle outside his back door before he quickly takes two full gas cans upstairs and empties the gasoline around both his room and the large warehouse room on the second floor. Then goes back downstairs and does the same thing downstairs. As he leaves the back door, just like at Pete's- he ignites the liquid. Loren quickly grabs the bottle of accelerant and gas cans by the back gate and put them in his truck then hurriedly padlocked the back gate, which will make it more difficult for fire trucks to enter his building from the back. He needs for this fire to last a while.

He is gone from that area within a minute and has driven a few blocks away before he hears the first sirens in the distance. Loren's mind is really racing. Between the meth and the booze, he feels like he can conquer all and his next stop was Frank's house. Loren is fed up- he is thinking that he won't be living much longer and is going to take some people out with him, regrettably maybe even Kate, thinking that, "if he dies, she will die too, without his protection".

Driving toward The Hill area and down in the alley just a half block from Frank's house, Loren gets out of the truck leaving Rex again inside. Then he gets some of the cans out of the back of the truck and quietly steps through the neighbor's back yard next to his boss's residence. Then Loren leaves those cans near Frank's property line and returns to his truck to get the last two cans of accelerant and the bottle bomb, taking special care not to drop the bottle.

It is still very dark outside and quiet except for a dog barking down the street. Loren has the area to himself and luckily Frank hates animals thus making it easy for Loren to be right next the Frank's large wood-trimmed home without having to deal with barking dogs.

Loren proceeds to empty gasoline on the side of the house at the back then quickly moves to the other side and then the front porch. Starting with the front he quickly ignites the porch and the flames follow the path of liquid around to the back, then he picks up the bottle he left on the back sidewalk and forcefully throws it through the back window shattering the glass and landing it into the kitchen area before hearing it explode upon impact. Loren sprints through the neighbor's yard again, getting into the Pete's unlocked truck and speeds off. In a couple of minutes he hears sirens only a few blocks away this time. Loren has a delirious high, he has completely lost grasp of all normal thought, and he wants to find Kate now.

It is 6:00 a.m. and Katie is making coffee as quietly as she can in the kitchen, trying not to wake either of the men. She pours a cup and takes it back out to the porch overlooking the river, where she sat most of the night wrapped in a blanket. While sipping her coffee, she hears the birds starting to chirp and who seem so happy with life, which brings tears to her eyes. Also, she can very clearly hear the water moving in the river, which sounds so gentle yet strong and free. She wishes at this moment that she was the water flowing down that river. Her tears continue to flow from her eyes and so so softly trickle down her cheeks. She fears for her future and she knows that as long as she remains with Loren her life will probably never be completely fulfilled and happy. She has to break away from him after this is over- if it can ever be over.

Katie hears movement inside the cabin, it's Paul. Shortly, he steps out on the porch dressed and with a cup of coffee in his hand. He tells Kate that he will have to be leaving soon as he has clients due at the vet clinic at 10:00 a.m. Paul sits down in the old wooden rocker on the porch and begins gently pointing out species of birds to Kate, who is sitting with her back to him and Paul pretending not to know she has been crying.

He asks her if she wants a refill on the coffee and Katie says "yes", wiping her fingers across face trying to hide her tears. Paul gets up to take both cups inside and quickly returns balancing a full cup of coffee in each hand. He gives Kate's cup to her and then sits back in the rocker. All Paul says is, "Katie, I think the world of you, you are a good friend, if there is ever anything you'd like to talk to me about please do, you seem confused, and possibly just discussing it with a friend may help you."

In all her years, no man had ever said these words to Kate, not ever.

Soon they hear John walking around in the kitchen and he too joins them on the porch. "Good morning! Thank God for coffee, I think that it's the only staple we have at the moment so I'll be going to town this morning to get some supplies", John says with a voice full of cheer and energy.

He and Paul talk about fishing for a little while until Paul announces he has to get going back to St. Charles. He leaves his cell phone with John because there is no phone at the cabin.

As Paul is backing out while Kate and John are waving from the front porch, Paul shouts, "I'll be back up in a of couple days, we'll go fishing this weekend- Kate you're welcome to join us."

John and Kate return to the back porch to sit down and enjoy the river and all of the natural surroundings and wildlife. John tells Kate that he loves this place and it is like a second home to him, much better than his house in St. Louis, actually.

John hesitantly says to Kate, "I think I should call Loren, and tell him we've moved you, do you think he'll be up this early?"

Katie senses John's hesitancy when he asked her that question, and thinks that maybe he is tired of her being around and is hoping Loren can soon take her away somewhere. Kate responds, "He is usually up by now, sometimes even earlier, he doesn't sleep well so he's awake more than he sleeps. Sure, I think he's up."

John gets up and goes into the cabin to get the phone and returns to the porch to make the call. Loren answers right away, as if he was expecting a call, "Hello".

John replying, "Hi Loren, this is John, I just wanted to let you know we've moved Katie to a different location."

Loren asks, "Where is she?"

John says, "I thought you didn't want locations given over the phone?"

Loren replies, "Everything's fine now, I'm actually just outside of St Charles right now, trying to figure out how to locate you. I left a message on your home phone about a half hour ago, did you get it?"

"No", John responds, "this is the first time since yesterday that I've even been near a phone". Also, John is thinking that something about Loren's voice is sounding strange and asks, "Is everything ok?"

Loren answers, "Yes, everything is going towards the plan, so far we're in the clear. Is Kate with you right now?"

"Yes", John says with some resignation in the tone of his voice, "here, I'll let you talk to her."

Kate takes the phone from John, and John can see a slight hesitation in her eyes as she first speaks to Loren, Kate saying, "Hi, are you o.k.?"

Loren answers her with, "Yes, I'm fine, but I'll be better though when you're with me." Loren's voice seems very alert, in fact a little too alert and quick, as she recalls how he talks when he is on the meth, and right now his voice has that quick, jittery quality.

"Here talk to John, o.k.", as Katie quickly hands the phone back to John.

John then proceeds to give the exact directions to the cabin as Katie just sits and listens and is not feeling very comfortable about what is transpiring. Something feels very wrong to her, but she thinks, "It must just be her mind overreacting again", as Loren always tells her. Consequently, she says nothing to John about how Loren's inability to think clearly seems evident to her on the phone.

26

PANDEMONIUM

It is almost 9:00 a.m. when John finishes his conversation with Loren, he feels empty after the phone call. He turns to Katie who has been listening the whole time and softly says to her, "Kate, I'm going to town to get some supplies, a man can't survive on coffee alone. I know that you'll be leaving with Loren shortly, but I'm staying down here for a few days, Paul's coming back like he'd mentioned. Maybe you should wait here just in case Loren arrives before I return and, if that should happen, he sounded like he is in a hurry but I hope you both will wait for me to return. I'd like to inform him just how bad your concussion is and about the rest you still need for quite a while yet." John's true feelings were well hidden when he spoke to Kate about her meeting up with Loren. He really doesn't want Katie to leave with Loren, but he has been assuming that Katie loves Loren so much that she wouldn't consider parting from him.

As John is leaving for town he lets Kate know that it will take him a good while to buy the supplies and get them back to the cabin because of the distance and windy roads to the nearest grocery store. He is also taking Paul's cell phone with him just in case Loren calls to get more help with directions to the cabin, although the directions John provided to Loren earlier by phone were very detailed. Katie, who had just made her first trip to the cabin yesterday, wouldn't have the foggiest idea how to give directions to the cabin to Loren or anyone else.

Loren is in a wild hurry and is now focused solely on getting Kate back. His frenzied mind is reeling as he has snorted another hit of meth making him feel like Superman. He hasn't developed a plan, but he is thinking once she is back with him he will determine what he is going to do next. There is one thing that Loren has learned over the years about Kate and that is, if he totally focuses on her for a period of time, he knows he is able to control virtually every move that she makes. He has also been able to control Dale, Jack, Pete, and maybe Frank. So in Loren's mind, his shared destiny with Kate will be determined by what happened last night at the burning home on The Hill-- if Frank survived, that's it--the game's over. Loren has the accelerator floored on Pete's old truck, which is doing well over 90 miles an hour. He is thinking to himself, "I need to get Kate back now!"

Paul arrives at his veterinary clinic at 9:50 a.m. The traffic had been very congested, which caused his travel time to be longer than expected. During his commute he was listening to the radio in his car and heard a news story about the two acts of arson committed in St Louis very early that morning. It was reported that the police believe that the two arsons were committed by the same person. One of the fires occurred at a warehouse on Jefferson Street that was reported to be totally destroyed because of the large quantity of flammable materials that were inside the building. Authorities are presently trying to determine if there are any bodies at the scene on Jefferson Street but, because of the massive destruction and resulting debris, it is expected to take many hours to determine if there are fatalities, but no bodies have as yet been found at that location. The other fire, which occurred in the residential area on The Hill, had killed one woman from smoke inhalation, but her husband survived. The name of the deceased person is currently being withheld until all family members have been notified.

When Paul first heard the radio newscast in his car he immediately wanted to call John, but he had left his only cell phone with John at the cabin. He has a strong feeling that the burned warehouse is Loren's as he knows that Loren's warehouse is located on Jefferson. Plus he is aware that the underworld group that Loren is involved with could be very unhappy with him at the moment because of Kate's disappearance and Paul is thinking that it very easily could have been Loren's warehouse that was ignited as an act of retaliation against him.

When Paul arrives at his clinic, he immediately calls John at his own cell phone number. At the same moment John is placing a bag of oranges in his grocery cart just as the cell phone rings in his pocket. He fumbles around to reach the phone, once he pulls it from his pocket; he has to search for a few seconds to locate the button on the phone to answer it. On the fourth ring John answers, "Hello".

Paul skips any small talk and says, "Hey, I just heard a radio report about a warehouse being burnt down on Jefferson-- where did you say that Loren's warehouse is located?"

John tells him the street number and that it is on Jefferson Street. John then adds, "If its Loren's warehouse he doesn't know about a fire because I just talked to him about an hour ago--on his way to get Kate. I gave him explicit directions to the cabin and he seemed to be in a big hurry to see her."

Paul hesitates for a moment before speaking as thoughts swirl around in his mind, "Where does this Frank live- did Loren ever mention that to you?"

John answers, "No, but I'm thinking he might live in an area called The Hill- I've seen a couple of small news articles about him in the past." John is pushing his cart trying to pick up food items as he talks to Paul.

Paul immediately tells John about the burning of the house on The Hill being caused by arson and the police suspecting that the same person that started that fire also caused the warehouse fire.

John comes to a dead stop with his grocery cart as he remembers Loren telling him, "Everything is fine now". Then John blurts to Paul the words that Loren said.

Paul asks, "How long ago did you tell me that you talked to Loren?"

John replies," About an hour ago."

Both men can feel each other's apprehension building the longer the phone conversation continues.

John says, "You think it was Loren who committed the two acts of arson don't you, Paul?"

Paul says with a firm voice, "Yes, I have never met Loren but from the sounds of it and seeing Kate's condition when I first met her, whether he may have saved her life in the park or not, I think Katie's in very real danger."

John shouts, "Holy shit, I'm on my way back to the cabin now!" He leaves the grocery cart right in the middle of the isle, bolts from the store, and is back on the highway heading for the cabin in a matter of seconds. He checks his watch--it is now 10:20 a.m. It will take him at least a half hour to get back to the cabin, meaning Loren could easily get there before he does. He is hoping that Loren may take a wrong turn, but he is afraid the directions he gave him were too clear.

Loren now knows that Frank survived the fire as he heard the same radio newscast that Paul heard. He has gotten to the little gravel road leading to the cabin, but he is so distracted and bothered by the newscast that he misses the driveway, which is somewhat hidden by the tree-laden yard, and drives another mile or two before realizing his mistake and makes a U-turn to go back. There are no vehicles in the drive when he gets to the cabin and becomes angry because he is thinking that Kate left the cabin with John. Loren pulls in the drive with Pete's truck and, as he slows down, Rex starts getting anxious and wanting to get out to go hunt. Loren pushes Rex back to keep him in the truck and then walks around to the back area of the house, thinking no one is there.

Kate heard a truck pull in the drive and peeks out the window but immediately shuts the curtain as she doesn't recognize the red truck, which she assumes must belong to one of Frank's goons. Then she hears footsteps on dried leaves coming around to the river side of the house. She is quiet, hoping that this person doesn't try to enter because she just realizes that the door is unlocked to the back porch because she had been sitting out there watching the river earlier. She hears the doorknob slowly turn, she is standing frozen right in the middle of the room leading to the porch.

As the door slowly opens there is Loren standing there still holding onto the doorknob staring at her with an intense and half-crazed look on his face.

Kate backs up a little, as she is startled to see him. Loren walks quickly to her side then, while grabbing her arm says abruptly, "Quick, let's get out of here now."

Katie tries to pull herself away from his grip, saying, "We have to wait until John returns, Loren, please let go of me, you're hurting my arm."

Loren grasped her arm tighter saying, "What? Why do we have to wait for John? What's going on anyway? Are you fucking him too?"

Katie pulls her arm away hard, which releases his hold on her and she backs away farther, realizing her perception was right when she talked to him on the phone, he is sky-high on meth. The dazed look in his eyes verifies to her that he is pretty much stoned out of his mind.

"Loren," Kate says softly, "Remember, John helped us- me, he is a good friend and that's all", she says the words as soothingly as she can convey them to Loren trying to calm him from his agitated state.

Loren steps closer to her saying, "A good friend, huh, what kind of good friend?" Kate is becoming shaky in fear as Loren is now reminding her of how he was at the cabin the night that Jack was there-- intense, mean and sadistic. Katie replies, "Loren you are the only one that I've had sex with- honestly! John is a friend who saved my life," then adding, "just like you did."

Loren relaxes for a second, then says, "If he's such a good friend then he'll understand why we have to leave right now."

Katie's mind is churning to come up with ways to stay put at the cabin and to just run time off the clock. She is terrified by Loren when he is like this, and she remains very much in touch with the way her body feels in the aftermath of the beating and concussion that she had suffered. In her present condition Loren can probably even outrun her and she is still too weak to defend herself even for a short period. Kate replies to Loren, "I'll need some time to pack my bags".

Loren follows her into her bedroom, looking around nervously, then saying, "Hurry up, we need to get out of here now, I mean it Kate, now!" Not giving her any more time he grabbed her arms scattering the clothing in her hand and starts pulling her through the door.

John is driving flat-out speeding back toward the cabin. He is having strong feelings of regret, plus some guilt, for having not taken Katie with him to buy groceries. Also, he is realizing that there is much more to Loren than meets the eye. Loren is cunningly smart, hides his weaknesses well and is very proficient in the manipulation of people, which are all good qualities to have if you happen to be a criminal. John has had the car accelerator floored since he left the store but he is approaching the long stretch of gravel road where he will have to slowdown. His phone rings but he doesn't answer the call or even look at the phone as he is solely focused on driving to get back to help Kate. He has an ominous feeling about what is going on at the cabin....

Paul is watching his television between client's visits to see if there is any more news about the two arson incidents that occurred in St Louis last night. Around 10:40 a.m. a news bulletin flashes across the screen along with a photograph of Loren. The newscaster states that he is wanted for questioning in regard to the acts of arson that took place at two locations in the city the night before. The police department is looking for a man named Loren Goodson, who owns the warehouse that was burned on Jefferson Street and is believed to be involved with or have information about both arson incidents and should be considered armed and dangerous. Anyone having any information about the whereabouts of this man should contact the St Louis Police Department immediately. The newscaster also reports that at least one known death has resulted from the arson--a woman named Wanda Lazarro, who was a resident of The Hill area in St. Louis.

As the newscast ends, Paul almost falls over in shock and disbelief. He tries to call John, but John isn't answering the cell phone, so he left a short but explicit voice message telling John he is returning to the cabin immediately. As Paul is leaving the clinic he puts a sign on the door, which reads, "My apology that the clinic is temporarily closed because due to an emergency"

Loren has grasped a firm hold on Kate's hair and arm and is half walking her and half dragging her to the truck. As he opens the door to the truck, Rex leaps out and runs into a thicket area to hunt for squirrels and chase birds. Loren pushes Kate into the truck then whistles and calls for Rex, who is too pre-occupied to come to him. Loren is not in the mood to wait for Rex and just growls, "son of a bitch", then gets in the truck and backs out of the driveway almost plowing into the ditch on the other side of the road before hitting the brakes. He then stomps the accelerator and takes off down the gravel road the same way he came in.

John has just gotten to the gravel road; turning onto it as hard as he dares, then accelerates to the max toward the cabin down the narrow, tree-lined gravel road. After he drives a couple miles, an old red truck passes him going very fast from the opposite direction. He thinks he saw two people in the truck but they went by so fast he couldn't really tell. Anyway, John is thinking that seeing a red truck on this gravel road isn't important as he is on the lookout for Loren's black truck, and hoping that it is behind him and not already at the cabin.

Upon arriving at the cabin, John is relieved that Loren's truck is not there yet. He walks quickly to the cabin door calling for Kate, but there is no answer. Then he steps to the back porch to see if she is there and, instead of finding Kate, he is greeted by Rex! His mind is jolted by seeing Loren's dog, who John remembers from when he first went to Loren's warehouse to help Kate.

27

THE FINAL CHAPTER

John quickly steps inside going to Kate's bedroom and sees her clothes strewn across the bed and onto the floor, with a suitcase open on the bed in a way that gives the appearance she had to leave in a big hurry. John dejectedly sits down on the edge of her bed feeling physically sick with worry about Kate's abduction. It is also distressing to John that Loren left his dog at the cabin-- he must have been feeling very pressured or just mentally unhinged to do that. John clearly recalls how much love Loren seems to have for the dog. After contemplating for a few minutes what he should do to help Kate, John goes out to his car to get the cell phone to make a call to Paul. Upon dialing Paul's number, he immediately gets the voice mail service at the clinic. Then he notices a message waiting on the cell phone and is able to retrieve it the way Paul instructed him. John listens. Then his face turns pale when he hears the message Paul had left for him.

Loren is driving like a wild man, his eyes are glazed-over and red, he is dead quiet and his intense presence is very scary to Kate. She wants to jump from the truck, but doing so at this speed would likely kill her instantly. She sees John's car pass them on the gravel road and her heart leaps, but then she remembers that John won't recognize this red truck. As John's car disappears over the hill behind them, Katie re-focuses on trying to start a conversation with Loren, which might calm him.

She clears her throat and asks, "Loren, what did you mean when you were talking on the phone with John and said that everything is fine?"

Loren only continues starring at the road in front of him and says, "Exactly that Kate, everything is just peachy." His tone is anything but peachy- it is hard-edged and down- right scary. Katie doesn't remember ever seeing him this agitated and says, "Loren, please slow down, you're going to get us killed." He then looks at her with eyes so crazed they don't even look human- and says, "maybe that's just what I'm planning to do, bitch."

Kate moves as far away from him as she can get, leaning hard into the passenger door. She knows if she can't get out of this truck before getting on the Interstate she might never escape.

At about the same moment at the cabin, John is placing a call to the Missouri State Police, based in Columbia, to report what had happened to Kate and mentioning the news bulletin tying Loren to the arson attacks, including one fatality, in St Louis. He also tells the officer on the phone that he isn't sure of the type of vehicle Loren is driving.-but adds it is most probably Loren's own personal vehicle, a black pick-up truck.

The officer responds to John by saying, "Our best information indicates that he is driving an older red Ford pick-up, that they, the police had just received a bulletin of another arson & death in Southern Missouri where Loren's truck was found hidden in a deep raven and a body found in that arson, that the person found in the burnt out house owned an old red truck that was missing, then the officer said to John, that he should not try to approach this Loren Goodson, because he is dangerous and possibly armed. "John stammers for a moment--as he recalls the red truck speeding down the gravel road, then he tells the officer where he saw the red truck and his guess is that it is headed for Interstate 70- East or West, but what direction he didn't know.

The officer thanks John for the call and asks him to remain at the cabin as they are sending a trooper out right away to get more details about Kate.

Loren is not in good shape as he has been snorting a lot of meth, is sleep deprived and doesn't remember the last meal he ate. However, he is desperately trying to come up with ideas for saving his own skin. Then suddenly he is hit with the idea—if he turns Kate over to Frank, he might then have his own life spared. Then, on the other hand and after further thought, it was only last night that he killed Frank's wife and burned Frank's house down. "No, no, not goin' to work", he mumbles to himself. He is trying to think of multiple alternatives and ideas all at the same time, but his mind is unable to even focus on a single thought and is basically losing touch with reality. As he continues driving, every few seconds Kate subtly glances at Loren, who seems to be in a trance-like state as he drives.

There is no visible change in him, but he has arrived at a grave decision and internally hears the words, "we will die together". Within a few seconds, he pulls the truck over to the side of the gravel road just a couple of miles from the paved road that connects with Interstate 70. When the truck comes to a stop he puts it in park, then he looks at Kate with eyes that reveal a sadness and a sense of loss, as he tells her that they are going for a walk. Katie has sensed what is in Loren's mind and she's scared to tears. She is unsure if she should try to stay in the truck or take her chances outside the truck-- she senses that either way, he is going to kill her.

Loren says, "We're stopping to take a walk. Come on Kate let's get out--NOW KATE!" Loren says the last two words in a roar.

Kate stares at him- tears streaming from her eyes, "Loren why are you doing this to me? You know how I've always loved you, why are you doing this?" Katie is sobbing and trying to talk at the same time.

This sets him off, his anger is back big time! Loren screams at her, "Get the hell out of the truck bitch, I mean now, bitch!" Then Loren grabs her arm and roughly pulls her through the driver's side of the truck out onto the gravel road with Katie fighting and struggling against him all the way.

In the meantime, John can't wait for the police, he has to at least drive back to where the paved road junctions with Interstate 70, in the hope that the speeding red truck is somewhere along the road, perhaps in a ditch, against a tree or just stalled somewhere. He gets in his car and drives much faster this time on the gravel road with a loaded hunting gun by his side.

At this moment Paul is about halfway back to the cabin and is starting to realize that whatever happens to Kate will likely be done and over with by the time he gets there to try to help her. Paul has a very ominous feeling about the situation as he drives.

By now, Kate is being pushed by Loren into the trees on the side of the road, then she stumbles forward over some leafy branches, which causes Loren to quickly reach down to pull her back up—and holds onto her firmly as he knows that she could easily escape from him. He is feeling very weak as the meth is starting to wear off and he's weak from hunger and hasn't slept at all in the last 48 hours.

Katie looks up at him as he is pulling her up and she witnesses a weariness in his eyes. Loren's mind and body are literally collapsing in front of her. The intimidating man who was menacingly controlling every thought and move she was making a few minutes ago is now looking pathetically tired and lost. Her fear of him is receding and is being replaced by compassion and the longing for him to think clearly and to be free from the drugs that are making him like this.

Kate calmingly says to him, "It's alright- it's alright, Loren you'll be fine- honest." She continues quietly talking, as her voice seems to be soothing to him and coincides with him letting go of her arm. Next he blinks his eyes repeatedly--then shuts his eyes completely--as if he is trying to come out of a mental fog. Kate has no idea of what he's done in the last 24 hours. But what she does know, if she treats him gentle right this moment, there is a chance, just a chance she can get away from him sometime very soon.

After he clears his head somewhat, Loren stands up and walks back to the truck. Katie stands up also and watches him with fateful hesitantly, but when he looks back at her, she silently walks over to the passenger side of the truck and gets in. Loren starts driving toward Interstate 70 then after few minutes enters the freeway going east bound back toward St. Louis.

John, who had been driving uncharacteristically like wild man since he left the cabin, spots the truck just a half mile in front of him still on the paved road about 3 miles from I-70, John pushes the gas pedal farther to quickly catch the truck with the intent to somehow get Kate out of that truck. When he sees Loren's truck get on the ramp entering I-70 east bound, John phones the State Police and tells the officer on the phone the location of the red truck, then continues to try to catch them himself.

By now the police have an all-points bulletin out on Loren throughout the State of Missouri and several patrol cars are now starting to converge on the red truck coming from both directions.

Loren looks in his rear view mirror and sees a patrol car coming up fast with its lights flashing. Because he's tired he didn't realize they are after him and was anticipating that the cop would just go around him. As Loren is unresponsive to having the patrol car right on his tail with lights flashing and sirens screeching, the patrolman pulls his vehicle up beside of him in the passing lane then signals for him to pull over. Loren responds by putting the pedal to the mettle and pulls ahead of the patrol car.

As John is witnessing all that is going on, he responds by accelerating his car also. Soon there are three patrol cars and John (who is slightly behind), all speeding along I-70 trying to get Loren to stop. One of the patrol cars pulls in front of Loren then slows down once in front of him, which prompts Loren to take to the right shoulder at 90 miles an hour slightly bumping the cop's car and barely missing the guard rail, then he speeds on ahead.

Since they got on I-70, Kate has been sitting paralyzed with terror as several massive wrecks have barely been avoided during the high-speed chase. She is starting to realize that she may have trusted Loren one time too many. There are now six patrol cars following him with John tailing not far behind.

Paul, who is going west on Interstate 70, witnesses all the patrol cars pursuing the red truck, which makes him realize that his worst fear has happened, they are all too late. He had done all that he could to help his good friend, John, save Kate from a group of sleazy treacherous people who value money and power over the sanctity of an innocent human life. As Paul looks at the rush of mayhem and flashing lights moving past him on the other side of the freeway, all he can do is mutter a few prophetic words of regret, "I'm so sorry that we couldn't save you, Katie. I wish we could have done more."

Loren is very intensely focused on somehow coming up with an escape route that includes keeping this old red pick-up truck on the road for a couple of more hours, he is driving nearly 95 miles per hour on I-70 east bound and is surrounded by no fewer than six patrol cars from at least two counties.

Despite the noise of the straining truck engine and multiple sirens from the pursuing patrol cars, Kate pleads, "Loren why don't you stop for God's sake, what's the matter with you?" Loren looks at her with his eyes full of tears.

He responds calmly and quietly, yet audibly so that Kate can hear him as he says, "Katie, I've gone crazy these last few days, I just wanted to help you- not hurt you- I'm so sorry. If I stop now or whether I don't stop, it doesn't matter, we are both dead, either by the cops or by Frank. I'm sorry, Katie, so- so sorry."

All motor vehicles, including semi-trucks, are being exited from I-70 by patrol cars several miles ahead of them. In the immediate area around the red truck, the police have patrol cars in all lanes, including in front of Loren's truck. Nevertheless, the odd caravan continues on at 95 miles an hour.

Then Loren sees the Missouri River Bridge up ahead of them and as they approach the massive bridge at 95 miles per hour it appears to grow larger in size and length and manifests itself as the escape route Loren has been looking for. At this moment, he almost serenely realizes the end of his life journey--with all its pain, addiction, disappointment and an imperfect and self-centered love for Katie--is at an end like the final grains of sand slipping from an hour glass. As he drives onto the bridge, he floors the gas pedal with even more force. Upon reaching the mid-point of the bridge he veers hard to the right, which causes the front of the truck to elevate to the top of the guard rail ripping off the side of the truck. As the truck goes airborne, there is almost silence as it descends and Loren says loud enough for Kate to hear him, "I love you Katie," then there is a moment of silence, then a horrific impact as the truck smashes front-end first into the embankment of the Missouri River, killing them both instantly. Kate was about to respond to Loren's tender words before she died but there was not enough time. The words she was about to speak, "It might have been"--are the saddest words a lover can hear.